Dr Craig Cormick is an award-winning author and science commun-
icator. He is former President of the Australian Science Communicators
and former Chair of the ACT Writers Centre. He has published over
40 books of fiction and non-fiction and has twice been shortlisted
for an Aurealis Award. He has been a guest at several international
conventions, including leading panels at WorldCon, and. has been a
writer in residence in Malaysia and Antarctica. Check him out at www.
craigcormick.com.

Demoniacs

Book 1 of
The Revelationary War

by
Craig Cormick

IFWG Publishing International
Gold Coast

www.ifwgpublishing.com

This book is dedicated to all those who have lost their lives or freedoms as a result of wars on terror, on all sides.

"Neither love nor terror makes one blind: Indifference makes one blind."

– James Baldwin

Terror: *noun.*

    1. extreme fear.

Belief: *noun.*

    1. an acceptance that something exists or is true, especially one without proof.

    2. trust, faith, or confidence in (someone or something).

"We must not be enemies. Though passion may have strained, it must not break our bonds of affection. The mystic chords of memory will swell when again touched, as surely they will be, by the better angels of our nature."

– Abraham Lincoln

Part 1

Paradise Lost

1

EVIE HAD a bad feeling about the mission from the moment the two helicopters took off from the forward base in Afghanistan and headed towards Pakistani airspace. She called it her Spidey-sense, like that tingly awareness that Spider-man got when something seriously bad was going to go down. For her though, it felt like a shaking throughout her body. Like all her joints were coming undone.

"All okay?" the officer in charge shouted to her, over the roar of the rotors, as if he could see the change in her face.

She nodded and mouthed, "Fuck you very much," —knowing it would be lip-read as a thank you.

Evie spent a moment trying to clarify the feeling she had inside her, to see if she could discern any more detail to it. Any particular danger. There was something bad looming. But it was nothing she could put her finger on.

She shrugged.

These guys had trained too long for this mission and only had a narrow window of opportunity, and weren't going to change things due to any feeling of unease she might have. They all had a look of unease. Intel said the mark was preparing to move location again soon, and they'd been tracking the fucker for almost a decade already.

The officer in charge was sitting back in his seat now. But he never really took his eyes off her.

Evie glanced around at all the other guys in the chopper. Navy SEALs. She'd been on half a dozen missions with some of them, but knew they'd never really regarded her as one of the team. She was referred to simply as 'the asset', and was passed around the armed forces or between the FBI, CIA and Homeland Security, or whoever else needed her special talents the most. It made it hard to form any lasting professional relationship with anyone.

When they hit the ground, she knew there would be one SEAL deployed close in front of her, and another close behind, both to clear a path and take any bullets meant for her. She also suspected there might be a third SEAL, a little further back, whose job it was to shoot her if she ever looked like she might fall into hostile hands. Yeah, good luck with that, she thought. Military paranoia! You just had to work with it.

She looked around at the other men in the chopper, and most avoided her gaze. Couldn't blame them really. Particularly those who had worked with her before.

She'd sat through the most recent briefings and knew they'd be flying low to the ground to evade radar, and would be arriving at their target close to 01:00 hours local time. She settled back and closed her eyes. Felt the thwump, thwump, thwump of the chopper's rotors in her guts. Mixing with that shaking feeling inside her. A warning of something bad. She closed her eyes and took deep breaths to calm it.

Nothing to do but wait. If something was going to go wrong, and there were always so many things that could go wrong on a mission like this, the feeling would spike.

Thwump, thwump, thwump.

"Fifteen minutes," a deep voice in her earpiece said. She opened her eyes and snapped back awake. She looked at her watch. It was too dark to see it clearly. All lights were off now except for a soft glow from the pilots' instruments. The guys around her had their bulky infra-red goggles on, but they would be a hindrance to her, so she didn't carry any. The other men would be her eyes in the darkness.

She turned her head a little and looked out into the night sky. The second Blackhawk helicopter would be out there somewhere, just behind them, also weaving around the contours of the hills, the men and the one dog inside all tense and silent. That made her grin. They had a dog in that copter and these men had her. "Woof, woof," she muttered softly.

"Ten minutes," the voice said. Evie nodded. She knew the men around her would be checking their equipment now. Or counting. Or praying. Anything to fill that time until the five-minute call. Then time would seem to speed up and they would be over the target faster than five minutes could possibly pass. She wondered for a moment who the men about her might be praying to, if any were praying. They might well be from several denominations or faiths. Or none at all.

Evie checked her own equipment. Side arm and several torches. They were her main weapons for fighting in the darkness.

Then, there it was. "Five minutes." Almost a whisper. She felt her Spidey-sense starting to tingle again, but it was too late to do anything about it now. She began taking deep breaths and pushed her hands down hard onto her thighs to stop her legs from starting to tremble. You never got used to this bit, she knew. Never.

Men around her were shuffling now, bumping her as they got into positions. This mission had to run smoothly. They were invading a notionally-friendly nation's airspace without telling them and would be landing only a few miles away from a major military base.

Evie felt a hand on her shoulder. She looked up but couldn't see who the figure was in the darkness. "I'll lead you down," said the voice in her earpiece. It was the SEAL Brady, who would be the one taking the lead in front of her. Evie nodded. Even if there had been more light it would be near impossible to tell the men apart with their insect-like night goggles on and identification removed from their uniforms. In fact they weren't even technically SEALs during this mission, having been transferred to the CIA, so that this could not strictly be called a military invasion of Pakistan. Military paranoia!

Evie let herself be steered over to the door of the Blackhawk where she readied herself by the jump line. The helicopter swung around in a slow curve. She braced her legs.

Thwump, thwump, thwump.

"Go!" Men around her started dropping down to the ground. Evie was in the second wave and once she had leaned outside the copter there was enough dim nightlight to see it was hovering over the large courtyard of the target compound.

She slid down the drop rope quickly and released herself at the bottom. The men around her were already in position and she felt Brady take her hand and place it on his webbing at his back. "Hold tight," he said, and she felt another SEAL in turn move in close behind her.

As the helicopter moved away and the air stilled Evie could smell its moist heat. Her nostrils filled with the foreign taste of it all. Then they were running towards the house ahead of them. The men paused only long enough to shoot out the lock in the door and then were in the guesthouse of the compound. Evie heard shots ahead. Friendly shots, not the ugly bark of AK-47s they were likely to encounter. They'd probably found a guard half-asleep, with his hand on his dick rather than his gun.

The team moved through the guest house quickly, as they had in practice, and after breaching another door they were in the main building. Each of them had studied photos and maps of the compound buildings endlessly, but they did not know what it would really be like on the inside until they stood there. And the word that came to Evie's mind was 'family'. This wasn't a battle HQ, it was a home where men and women lived. There was a dining room and lounge room and a TV and toys on the floor. They had been briefed to expect children and to not harm them. If possible. Who knew at what age these little fuckers were taught to fire a gun?

Suddenly Evie's thoughts were interrupted by a babble of noise over her earpiece. One voice was saying there was resistance on the stairwell, which was followed by a series of loud gunshots. Then another voice was saying that the chopper was going down. A bright light had struck it. That was the second chopper that would have been hovering over the compound. Something had gone wrong. Had they encountered heavy fire? Had someone fired a missile at it?

Evie wanted to know, but the man behind pushed her forward and they were running again. "Fuck! Fuck! Fuck! Fuck!" Evie said with each step. The voices in her earpiece were a jumble of shouts and commands. The chopper pilot was saying he was going for a soft landing, and the men in the chopper were bracing for impact. Then she was on the stairs and being pushed up them. At the top of the stairwell was a man in a white robe lying in his own blood. She paused and thought, "What a waste." She could have prevented this man's death.

"Clear," a voice said and then she was being hurried up the stairwell again, past the second floor, where she could see some SEALs were clearing rooms. She could still hear the men on the helicopter in her earpiece, calling to each other as the helicopter hit the ground, endeavoring to get out safely. She wondered about the dog. Then she was being pushed forward again. Brady turned around and gave her the hand signal to be ready for anything.

They rounded the last turn on the stairs and saw a SEAL ahead of them, crouched by the top of the staircase. Then he fired a shot and was gone. They hurried up after him. There was an open door in front of them and the SEAL stood in the door. Not moving.

"Deploy the asset," she heard in her earpiece and Brady stepped out of the way. The man behind her took his hand off her back and the SEAL in the doorway stepped aside a little, but not lowering his gun. "Light," said Evie, giving the SEALs warning that she was going to switch on a light, and for them to guard their eyes. She flicked the switch on one of the fluorescent lights she carried and held it down low by her side. They were much more effective than single beam torches for her use.

She stepped up closer to the door and looked in. There were several people in the room. Two women, two children and a tall man in a light robe. There was no mistaking him. The one they had hunted so long. But he stood behind one of the women with a pistol in his hand, jabbering away at them in high-pitched babble.

Why hadn't the SEAL taken a shot at him? Evie wondered. They trained for shots like this. And then she saw why. There was a young child, maybe five or six, clinging to the woman's robes. Injuring moral-less bad-ass women was permissible, if you needed to take a kill shot, but injuring a small child was not. Evie stepped into the room, locking eyes with the tall, bearded man who now pointed the pistol directly at her.

The moment their eyes made contact, everything changed. Her Spidey-senses peaked so strongly that her legs nearly gave way beneath her. And the man's face didn't drop. Didn't go blank as it should have. Instead he seemed to rise taller in the room. Seemed to fill it with his dark, laughing face. He was something inhuman and his eyes ripped into Evie like a flame, scorching her, filling her with pain. Evie tried to regain control. Tried to do the control thing over him. But the man just laughed louder. Evie felt her eyes being seared, like staring into the sun. The man was changing. Growing taller. His face distorting into something fierce and savage.

Then she blinked. And in that moment, she broke eye contact and turned her gaze to the woman, taking control of her instead. The woman's face went blank at once. Then she moved quickly. She clawed for the man's hand with the pistol in it, and as he tried to pull it back from her, she used his arm's momentum to push it up under his chin. She squeezed his finger, and the shot went up through his head.

He fell to the ground with a heavy thud. Evie blinked again, to get a better look at him. He was just a man. An evil fucker assuredly, but just a man.

She heard Brady say, in his best Bruce Willis voice, "Yippie-ki-yay, motherfucker!" The other woman then started screaming and threw herself at the fallen body, and Brady was steering Evie out of the room. They left her on the landing to try and figure out what the fuck had just happened, while they went through the rooms, binding the women and children for the Pakistani army to find whenever they got their asses up here from the nearby base. They smashed computers apart to take the hard drives. Wrapped Osama's body in a portable body bag. And photographed everything.

They didn't need Evie getting in their way, so she walked back down to the second floor, rubbing at her eyes. Then she heard renewed shouts in her earpiece. "Here she comes again!" "Take cover!" "We're a man down!" The second squad were under attack. She looked around and saw a balcony ahead of her and hurried over to it. She stepped out onto the concrete area and saw it was facing the wrong direction. She hurried to the end of it and leaned out over the balustrade. She could see the chopper now, where it had ditched into the sand outside the compound wall. And she could see the SEALs gathered in a small group behind it defending themselves from attack. From where?

Then she saw her. A single woman, not dressed in combat gear. More like something out of a comic book, wearing a tight red outfit with what looked like knee-high dark boots. And a blossom of long blonde hair. She looked a lot like Storm from the X-men, Evie thought, dark skin and all. Just like Evie's. She could have been her sister. All these thoughts at the same moment, and then her Spidey-senses spiked again. It was like a wave of panic filled her body, and all her sinews and tendons had come undone.

She fought hard to keep standing. And not to pee herself. She gripped the balcony edge for support and saw the woman raise a hand and a blast of light and fire seemed to come out of it. It hit the chopper which seemed to distort and change shape, falling apart like it had exploded. How was that even possible?

She saw some of the SEALs raise their weapons and fire at the woman, but none of the bullets had any effect. Marvel Gal, or whoever she was, raised her hand to fire another of those lightning bolts at them and then suddenly paused. She turned her head until she was staring straight at Evie. As if she had felt her presence. Evie knew she was too far away to get an eye-lock, but she was not too far away from Marvel Gal's reach. She pointed her palm at Evie and sent a bolt of light and fire towards her. Evie ducked just in time and it distorted and blew out a large section of the concrete railing.

"What the ever-loving mother of fuck?" Evie said and reached for her pistol. Ridiculous, she thought. Her hand was shaking too much to even consider an accurate shot. Then, something she couldn't explain afterwards made her put it back and instead reach into her shirt pocket and pull out metal talisman. It was round, like a large coin, with arcane writing on it. She put it to her lips, kissed it for luck, and then stood up again. Marvel Gal was waiting for her and sent another lightning bolt in Evie's direction. Instead of ducking though, she held up the talisman and the bolt struck it. The bolt was chill, not hot, and she felt the force of it run up her arm and almost push her over. But she remained standing and felt the bolt bounce back at her attacker.

There was a flash and a shimmer and then nothing. Marvel Gal was gone. Not a dead body. Just nothing.

But the talisman in Evie's hand had cracked and broken into four pieces. "No way," she said. That wasn't supposed to even be possible.

She looked down to the SEAL troops who were cautiously advancing forward again now that their mysterious attacker was gone.

SEAL Brady suddenly appeared behind her. "What's the sit rep?" he said into his helmet mike. "Clear," came the reply from one of the SEALs on the ground. "We came under attack from a small squad with heavy weapons, but they've been neutralized." Like he had no memory of Marvel Gal zapping him.

"Roger that," said the SEAL, then said to Evie, "We'd better get the hell out of here before the Mexican army show up."

"Mexico?" she asked. And she suddenly knew he was right. They were not in Pakistan. They were in Mexico. They had flown over the border from Texas. They had raided the headquarters of one of the leaders of the Southern Right—an extremist group working to bring down the democratically-elected US government and make several right-wing states independent.

She had no idea how they'd been in Pakistan one moment raiding the headquarters of an Islamic terrorist and then raiding a southern extremist hideout in Mexico the next. Like she had no idea how she knew that the members of the other SEAL team would have no memory of being attacked by Marvel Gal, and would swear that they had been attacked by a small well-armed group of defenders.

She did not know what the hell was going on, but she sure as shit knew somebody who would know. The same somebody who had given her the talisman and made her swear to never go anywhere without it. And she would be having a very frank talk with him about all this very soon.

2

American Airlines flight 370 was late to take off and didn't clear the runway and lift into the air until well after midnight.

The passengers, mostly Chinese nationals returning to Beijing after a holiday or work trip, were tired and many didn't even wait for the plane to level off before tilting their seats back and wrapping themselves in a blanket. Many wore eyeshades.

The flight crew, spread throughout the plane and still buckled into their seats, wished perhaps they could do the same. Night flights were a two-edged sword. The passengers slept though most of the flight and didn't make endless demands of you, but you missed a night's sleep yourself.

The pilot and co-pilot, already primed with plenty of coffee, went through the post take-off protocols and then took the plane up to its cruising altitude of 35,000 feet, which it reached after twenty minutes.

At 1.01 am the pilot then radioed confirmation of their altitude to the flight control tower at Los Angeles International Airport. He then looked across at his co-pilot. The man was notably nodding in his seat. A slight dribble of saliva was coming out of the edge of his mouth. He'd be fast asleep any moment now. And not waking up again.

The pilot kept the course steady, keeping an eye on the flight path. The crew would be moving around the aircraft now, providing extra pillows and blankets or getting drinks and settling passengers down for the night. One might come and knock on the door and ask if he wanted more coffee or something, but he'd send her away.

At 1.19 am LA International Airport contacted him, informing him he was being handed over to Hawaiian air traffic controllers. "American Airlines three seven zero, contact Honolulu one two zero decimal nine. Good night."

"Good night. American Airlines three seven zero," he replied.

Then he reached up and turned off the radio with a deft click. After that he turned off the satellite communication link that tracking their flight progress. They were now well out over the Pacific Ocean.

Their next verbal check-in was not due until 1.37 am, and he knew that there would be a series of communications between LAX and Honolulu then, each trying to push the blame on the other for losing contact with the aircraft.

The pilot next put the plane into a large and gentle turn. No one on board would even feel it. He kept a close eye on the compass until he was on a south-westerly setting that would take him between Hawaiian and Mexican airspace. There was a strong possibility that military radar would be tracking him, he knew, but they were so poorly coordinated with civilian aviation authorities that they wouldn't share data until the morning at the earliest. Far too late.

He looked across at his co-pilot, Phil, who was now starting to gurgle and choke a little. His head had lolled forward, and he was having trouble breathing. He was a good man, he thought, young and a bit impetuous, but might have gone on to make a fine pilot. He considered reaching over and tilting his head back, but she had told him to ignore him. Like the 227 passengers and ten other crew, he was effectively dead already.

The pilot suddenly found his mind drifting to his wife and children and what impact his death might have on them, but then he remembered her warning and focused himself on the task before him. He looked at the instrument panel and compass bearing. He would make another turn to the west soon to avoid going into any tracked airspace. Then he'd correct that back to south-west. His family had been increasingly concerned about his erratic behavior over the last few days, as she had prepared him for this mission, ordering him to pay no heed to anything else.

And the mission was firmly embedded in his mind, like it was a program on the flight simulator that he practiced on at home. He knew that now he had made the final turn to the south-west, there was nothing to do but sit in the cockpit and wait. They would not run out of fuel for about seven more hours and would be out over the vast and deep Southern Ocean by then.

The passengers and crew would be wondering how much longer the flight would last, and maybe the cabin crew would look out the windows and wondering why the rising sun seemed to be on the wrong side. But he doubted they would figure it out.

"We will be too far out of contact," he said to Phil, as if it were normal cockpit banter. "And the cabin crew will be unlikely to do anything to cause any panic amongst the passengers. They themselves might not show any signs of distress until the engines start failing and the plane begins falling towards the icy waters."

He thought again about that long seven-hour wait, and considered taking the same pills that he had dropped into his co-pilot's coffee.

But she had forbidden it. She had told him this was a holy mission that he was undertaking, and that it was a part of the war for control of the world's future.

He would have liked to have at least been able to write a note to his family explaining his actions, but again she had told him it was necessary that it was to remain unknown.

"There will be all kinds of crazy conspiracy theories, you know," he said to his co-pilot. "I should like to know what some of them would be. Hijackers, most likely."

The man just gurgled again and some more spittle fell from his mouth. No, better not to go slobbering like that, he thought. He would stay awake at the controls.

Then he leaned across and tilted the man's head back so he was no longer choking. It would be good to have someone to talk to over the hours ahead. Even if he couldn't talk back. "Rest, my friend," the pilot said to the insensible man beside him. "We have a long flight ahead of us."

3

CLEVELAND had really seen better days. Really! Something had changed here as well.

Evie had already had to cover her surprise when she got back to Washington from the mission to find high fences and the national guard around all the major buildings. She almost got caught out by the 8pm curfew too, which everybody seemed to know about except her.

She had flown to Cleveland and gotten a hire car and driven into the city with a sense of heaviness. It wasn't so much that Evie hated Cleveland, but she had spent most of her teen years here yearning to get out, and now here she was coming back. Voluntarily.

Downtown was a complete ghost city, with bullet holes in the few windows that weren't boarded up. Though there were some pockets of prosperity hidden in the outer city. And at least it wasn't winter. Cleveland really sucked in winter!

At least, she thought, thankfully he didn't live in Detroit. That still made Cleveland seem well off, as the Motor City had never really recovered from the race riots and the following insurrection. The Government had sent in the police, and then the national guard and finally the military—even though that was in contravention of some decree or other about using the military on American soil. And it was just the first of many such insurrections. Cities and towns that had had enough of vain promises and even vainer politicians who promised to make the world good again. Promised to make the country great again.

Evie felt sympathy for them all. No matter which party was in power, the downtrodden seemed to get trodden on just a little more. And with the mutations in the pandemic, civil unrest, soaring unemployment and the nation divided into blue and red states and zones—it felt like Detroit was just the shape of things to come all over the country. All over the world if things kept getting out of hand.

Evidently.

These things were clear in Evie's memory, although she knew they had not been memories she'd ever had before.

And she had to know why.

The debrief she'd had with military intelligence was more informative for her than it was for them. Discovering how much the world she thought she knew was no longer the world she was living in. A world in which the USA was on the brink of civil war, and was under siege from home-grown terrorists from the far left and far right, each seemingly intent on tipping the country into chaos in their war against each other.

It had been bad—but never this bad.

She drove down one particular quiet neighborhood street, noting there were more weeds growing around the pavements than she could recall, and she stopped across from her father's house. It was one of those two-story wooden things that had once been smart and fashionable, but now required too much work to look its best. A bit like her father, she supposed.

She climbed out of the hire car and looked around cautiously for any street kids. There was a small gang of them up on the corner. "Hey," she called and beckoned them over.

They looked at her. Then at each other. Then back at her. Giving her that look people so often did, trying to fit her into the stereotypes. Coffee-colored skin. Short, neat hair. Neat clothes. Athletic build. Then, slowly, they came ambling over, as if burdened by the weight of their attitude. "Whatchu want?" one asked. And then the question that she expected, "You a blue or a red?"

Evie let them get closer and then fixed them all with her stare. Their faces dropped and they stood there blankly.

"You are going to look after my car here, see, make sure it's in as good a condition as it is now when I come back for it."

The boys didn't say anything. They didn't need to. Evie smiled and took a few steps towards her father's house. Then she turned back to the boys. "In fact," she said. "When I get back I want it to be in better condition than it is now. Go and get some buckets and rags and give it a good wash, okay?"

The boys nodded and then headed off in different directions to fetch everything needed to wash her car. She supposed none of them had ever washed a car in their lives, and might not do much of a job of it, but it would keep them busy.

She turned and went up the path to the house. The door was open and she could hear the sound of multiple televisions on inside. There were a few busted sets on the front porch. There would probably be others in the back yard too.

She knocked once and let herself in. She stepped down the small hall into the lounge room and stopped. She had walked in on something. Her dad was sitting in a lounge chair, wrapped in his robe, like the Dude from the *Big Lebowski,* and a tall guy stood on the other side of the room facing him. He looked like Keanu Reeves in *the Matrix,* dressed in that long leather coat and dark glasses, except this guy's face was as white as milk or snow or something with no color whatsoever in it. And there was something else about him. Like he was slightly out of focus. Like he shimmered just a little bit at the edges.

Both men had turned their heads towards her before she even stepped into the room. "Evie," her dad said, as if he had been expecting her. Of course, he had been. The other man said nothing. "Dad," Evie said and looked to the stranger. He, however, turned his head to Evie's father and said, "Consider it carefully." Then he was gone. Not like he stepped away or anything. He was just gone.

Evie shrugged. Her childhood had been filled with weird visitors like that. And other memories she'd run a long way to get far away from.

She glanced around the room. Her dad had really let it run down since she'd last been here, what, three years ago. Or was it four? There were five televisions on one side of the room, all on different channels showing news programs. The screens on two of them were distorted by static. They'd be out on the porch soon. Replaced by two new ones. Or two second-hand ones more likely.

It had been very frustrating growing up in a household where electronic devices only had a short lifespan. Her father had the power to really get into people's minds, like deep inside them, without even needing to be near to them, and to turn the world back from war or the brink of a nuclear arms race—but he couldn't stop a TV from going on the fritz in his presence. Thankfully she never let him near her smartphone. That would have been a killer for a teenager.

The rest of the room was a mess, like her dad. Evie's mother wouldn't have put up with it.

"Nice to see you," her dad said, in a genuinely pleased voice.

"Yeah," Evie said. She tried to say it the same tone, but it just didn't come out right.

"You seen this?" her dad asked and pointed at one of the TVs. Evie turned her head and tried to make out the picture. It was one of the soon-for-the-porch sets. It showed cars bogged down in traffic with something browny-green all over the road and the cars.

"It's raining frogs in Utah," her father said. Evie didn't reply. She'd seen a documentary about that kind of thing once, about how a tornado could pick frogs or fish up out of a lake and dump them on a nearby town. But this was like thousands and thousands of frogs, not just a dozen or so.

She watched the screen a while and then said, "That's weird."

Her father shook his head. "You know the Dylan song?" And he sang, in his beautiful deep voice. "A hard rain is gonna fa-a-all!" Evie felt the hair on the nape of her neck prickle. Like the first time hearing Enya—before hearing too much Enya. Like it always did when he sang. Evie said nothing. Dylan had been one of her mother's favorites. That was one of the reasons they had stayed in Cleveland. It didn't have much, but it had the Rock & Roll Hall of Fame. She went there every week as her time drew near, Evie's dad pushing her in the wheelchair. She loved music. Loved singing Dylan songs and turning his raspy tunes into something pure and angelic.

"They give you a medal for that Mexican thing?" her father asked.

"Or was it Pakistan?" Evie asked.

And her father looked surprised. Just for a moment. Something she didn't often see. "Oh," he said.

"What's happened?" she asked.

He just sat there in his chair. Once a giant of a man, now slumped there, robe half-open with his faded Sergeant Pepper's Lonely Hearts Club T-shirt peeping through, and slippers on his feet. Goddamned slippers! It was like seeing Thor wearing glasses and a hearing aid.

He shook his head. Tried to change the topic, "Time was," he said, "you'd have only gone on a mission like that if you could have brought him back in for interrogation."

"Time was," said Evie, "the mission I went out on was the same mission I came back from."

He puffed out his cheeks. "Time was things were so much simpler."

"Time was I didn't need to go on missions like that because you and the other Guardians were keeping us safe."

"Time was I had powers that could keep you safe," he said.

"You still have your powers," she said. "Don't give me that."

"Don't tell me what powers I have and don't have," he said tersely.

Both stopped and looked at the floor. Let the bad air flow out of the room. This was the same argument as the last time she was here.

Evie imagined a scene like this one being played out in lounge rooms all across the country. All across the world. Daughters railing at their fathers. But none would really ever be quite like this.

And she envied those other girls and women and their fights with their fathers over clothes and money and politics and choice of partner and career and every goddamned thing that filled their heads and hearts. And she sighed, the long and deep sigh of one who would never know a world like that.

The televisions chattered and mumbled. Evie looked around the room once more. She hadn't come here to fight. Not again. There was a photo of her mother and father together on the far wall of the room. It was just an enlarged phone shot, but it captured a moment a professional portrait might never have. They were dancing in the back yard one evening. The light was dim but their bodies glowed. Her mother's deep brown skin. Her father's golden. The matching smiles. Like when they sang together. That pure and perfect sound of happiness they made. She'd always loved that photo, and was glad that her father had not taken it down. She was angry enough at him when she found he'd taken all her mother's clothes and things out of their bedroom. But then she discovered he'd set them all up in a spare room. All her things. Like she might be coming back one day. She didn't know whether to feel angry or sad about that.

"Did you ever consider you might be suffering depression, dad?" Evie said. "You seem in a really bad place."

"Cleveland?"

"You know what I mean."

"Yes," he said and looked closely at his daughter. "I know exactly what you mean."

Evie was trying very hard not to mention her mother's name and tried not to sound like her when she said, "But look at you! You've become a slob!"

"That's the second time today I've heard that," he replied.

Evie sat down on an old chair. Heard it creak beneath her. She didn't know what else to say. Her father watched her and then said, "So go ahead and ask me what you came here to ask me."

"I already did."

"Ask me again."

Evie took a deep breath and said, "Something changed after the Mexican thing."

Her dad nodded his head slowly.

"Things haven't just started changing now. Things change all the time."

"But it's like I used to live in one world, and now I live in another. I wake up one day on a mission in Pakistan and suddenly I find I'm in Mexico. I have these memories of different pasts, like different dreams. What the hell is going on?"

"Dream girl!" he said. "Remember when you used to play being a superhero with dream powers?"

"Of course I remember," she said. "But it was never anything like this."

He nodded his head. "It's always been happening," he said. "It's the way of things. It's just that you were never able to remember."

"I don't understand," she said.

"Think of it like quantum physics," he said. "You know how every single decision you make creates optional paths or different versions of reality, and each of those realities can branch out into a million or more possibilities."

"And?" she asked.

"Well, imagine that all those pasts and all those futures are in motion, and everything is changing all the time. In one future World War One and World War Two happen. In another they don't. Or you wake up one day and Trump is president again, against all belief. But you wake up another day and he never was. Then you wake and find that superheroes really exist. Not Superman and Batman—real superheroes. But then you wake up another day and they only exist in comic books and movies. Every reality is happening but you can only know the one you're currently in. It's like the old TVs out on the porch. They no longer show a clear version of what you want to see—so you go and get a new one that shows a clearer view, and you forget the old one."

Evie just looked at him.

"Imagine at one time there were four heroes, called the Guardians," he said, "who used their superpowers to save the world. But in another strand of reality they don't exist. Or they exist, but don't have the same powers."

She had been prepared for weird, but hadn't been prepared for this.

"You still have powers," she said. "You must have. I still have powers. That hasn't changed."

Her father sank a little deeper into his chair. "No," he said. "That was a different past. I discovered I had no real powers when your mother got sick and I couldn't do anything to save her."

"But if what you say is true, and I have to tell you it's a pretty big IF, then how come I'm the only one who seems to remember the other realities?"

"Why do you think you're the only one?" he asked.

"You?"

"I've always been able to see them. The good and the bad and the wondrous and the catastrophic—all at once. And what do you think that does to a person?"

She felt her cheeks redden a little. Said, "Mom was the only one who ever really understood you."

"Amen to that," her dad said and reached down beside the chair and lifted up a bottle of beer, taking a large swig from it. She felt a deep pang of pain at the thought of how different her father would be if her mother was still alive—something she had told herself she was not going to feel today. But seeing her father come undone without her, it was impossible not to.

"So why me?" she asked. "And why now?"

Instead of answering he dragged himself up out of the chair and made his way over to stand in front of her. She stopped herself from pulling back as he took her head in his hands, one warm palm on either side of her face. She let him tilt her head this way and that just a little as he looked into her face. Then he said, "You had the scales blasted from your eyes."

"So being able to see all these versions of things, pasts and so on, is that something good or bad?"

"Unmitigated bad. Unambiguous bad. Paradise lost bad." He still held her. She was tempted to put a hand up and hold one of his. Instead she frowned. "Okay. But there's something else. I saw this man and this woman in the compound. Fighting us. They were stronger than me."

He nodded his head. Like he had been waiting for her to say this. "Who were they?" she asked.

"Let's call them the others." He dropped his hands. Stood there a moment and went across and picked up the TV that was most on the fritz. Evie watched him carefully. She'd seen this before. He carried it over to the front door and opened it with his foot.

"Here, catch," he called. And he threw it out onto the lawn.

Evie lifted her head to see a man in a local government uniform and thick dark glasses dodge the thrown TV. He raised a fist and shouted something about calling the police. She hadn't seen that before.

"Why did you do that?" she asked.

"I didn't like the look of him. Didn't trust him. Probably a spy reporting back on us right now."

"Yeah, to the police," said Evie.

"No," said her dad. "These others are the ones who want to wreak havoc on the world. The ones who seek to steer us down a path into more chaos. They can control the weak minded so easily."

Evie stared at him. If she had not seen what happened on the mission she would think him paranoid. And she found she was suddenly angry at him. "How could you have never told me any of this? Don't you think I had a right to know?"

"Knowledge brings danger."

"Why do they want chaos?"

"Because it's their nature. This world has only ever existed to them as a battleground for control."

"Your world too," said Evie.

"Yes, my world too," said her father, his face softening for the first time. "I chose this life." He gestured around with his arms, the robe flowing out around him like a slob Caesar. "I chose to be its defender." He smiled. "And look how that turned out."

"How do they do it?" Evie asked. "Change things so drastically?"

Her father pointed at one of the other TVs, showing a scene from some civil war somewhere. "A little push here. An intervention there. Sow fear and hate. It sends the planet a little in another direction. Sow more fear and hate and violence and it moves even further in a new direction. And the nudging can be little, but the consequences can be huge."

"But surely you can tip things back the other way?" asked Evie. "Push it back to a more stable reality?"

Her father just shook his head. Then he stepped closer to her again and said, "There are things you're going to need to know."

"Such as?"

"If the others know you can see them, they will come for you. They'll send demons."

"Demons? Seriously?' Is that a new reality too?"

"Demons exist in most realities," he said. "They always have."

Evie thought of all the books on demonology that her brother had, and was constantly reading, while she had been trying to live a normal life, learning to dance and date and be surrounded by the normal crises of acne and friends' social media posts.

"Maybe we protected you too long," her father said. "You're going to be in danger."

She felt anger rising in her again. "I can handle myself," she said, with more confidence than she felt.

"There are other things too."

She waited, wondering how much weirder things were going to get.

"Something I never told you. Something I kept from you. Something you do have a right to know." Then he walked to the far wall where that photo of him and Eve's mother stood. "Your mother's sickness. Her cancer. It was from being too close to me. From my powers." He turned and looked at her. "I killed your mother!"

Evie felt a blow to her chest like somebody had stepped up very close and hit her. "What?" she asked.

Her father said nothing. Then, "I caused her to die painfully of cancer." He paused. "Knowledge is danger."

"Did she know?" Evie asked softly. Almost a whisper. And she saw tears forming in his father's eyes. "I think everybody knew it except you," he said.

Evie nodded her head. Felt tears stabbing at her own eyes. "So, Adam?"

"That's why he's crazy angry with me."

"Goddam!" said Evie and stood up. If he had been closer she would have hit him on his broad chest with her fists.

"Amen to that," said her father and reached down for his beer bottle again. Stopped. Walked across to the door. "Don't move," he said.

"What is it?" she asked.

He tilted his head a little and Evie could see he was listening carefully. Then her Spidey senses started up and she heard it. Faint at first, but then more heavily. Like stones being thrown onto the roof of the house. Evie's dad waved an arm at her to keep down. A window exploded on one side of the door. Then another somewhere else in the house.

Evie saw a large hailstone on the floor, about the size of a baseball. Then another bounced in through the broken window. Her father kicked the door shut then threw the curtains closed, as if that had any hope of really stopping them. Evie could hear the hail increasing until it sounded like a heavy machine gun being fired at them. Then there was a massive bright light and a crack of thunder that shook the whole house. Evie could smell the burning energy of it as her Spidey-senses started screaming.

"Missed," said her father, peeping out between the curtains.

Then there was another bolt and crack of thunder. Then another. Evie felt the last one hit the house. Heard the crash and splintering of things upstairs.

"Ohmygod," said Evie, but her dad just stood there. Like he had expected the house to be hit by lightning and hail. Like he knew it was going to soon subside as suddenly as it had started.

"Please tell me that was just a crazy natural phenomenon," she said.

"Maybe, maybe not," he said. "I think there's some serious damage upstairs."

"Don't worry about it. I'll get it fixed."

The two of them stood in silence for some time and then her father pointed to another of the televisions. "You following this story about the missing airliner?"

Evie turned her head distractedly and said, "Yes. Sure."

"That's definitely them," her father said. "They're trying to sow the seeds of war between the loopy right and the loopy left, and that puts you in danger. More so now that you can see them for what they are."

"Some of those loopy right are my political bosses," Evie said.

He shrugged.

"So we have to fight them, right?" said Evie. "Put things back onto a less chaotic path. That's what you've spent your life doing, isn't it?"

"Life?" he asked. "I thought I was going to spend my life with your mother."

Evie said nothing for a while, then, "Tell me about that woman who attacked me."

Her father narrowed his eyes. "Uh-oh," he said.

"What?"

"I've seen that look before. If you're going to develop an infatuation for anyone, don't let it be her."

"What makes you think I have an infatuation for her?"

"What makes you think that you don't?"

Evie frowned. He knew her too well. It was true. She'd been thinking of Marvel Gal a lot since their encounter in Pakistan. Or Mexico. Playing it out over and over in her head. Drawn to her somehow.

"If a hard rain's going to fall," her father said again, "make sure you're under cover."

She stood there for some time and then asked what she had perhaps really come to ask all along. "So if bad things are coming, what about the Guardians? What about getting the band back together?"

But he shook his head. "Go and see your brother. Don't waste any time."

"That's all?" she asked. "Go and see my brother who hardly ever talks to me, like that's going to change something?"

"To everything there is a season, and a time to every purpose under heaven," he said.

"I know that one," she said. "Bob Dylan, right?"

He smiled. An old joke. She turned and left the house. Didn't even look back to see the damage done to it. Found the boys still working on her car. Seriously dented now by the hail. Though they seemed to have found cover. "That's enough for today," she said. She hopped in and then remembered she hadn't shown her father the shattered talisman. She considered going back inside for a moment, but then changed her mind. She put the car in gear and headed back out of Cleveland without looking back. Once again playing out in her mind the different ways things with her dad might have worked out better.

4

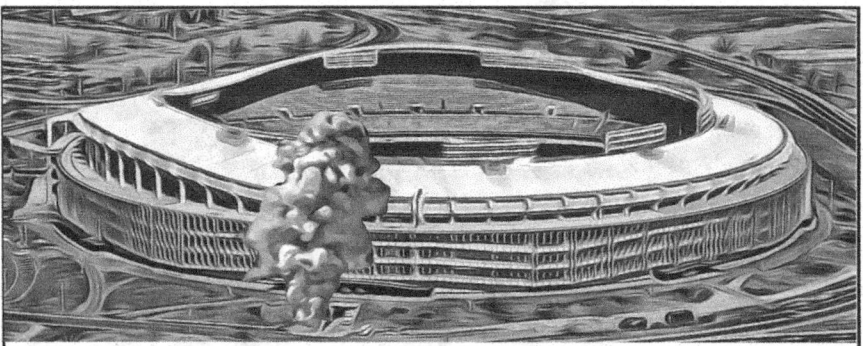

The first anyone in Washington knew of the coordinated attacks upon their city was an explosion outside Nationals Park Stadium, at 9.20pm. A baseball game was underway that evening between the Washington Nationals and their arch-rivals the Baltimore Orioles that had attracted a capacity crowd.

Twenty minutes into the game a man wearing a suicide belt attempted to enter the southern gate, but was stopped when a routine security check detected the explosive. Security forces drew their guns and told the man to raise his hands. Instead he detonated the explosives.

The bomber and a single passer-by were killed.

Immediately following the explosion, two other men detonated their suicide vests, also outside the stadium, having failed to gain entrance, and knowing security would be on high alert.

Security forces thought they had a lucky break. If even one of the men had gotten into the stadium, dozens might have been killed.

That feeling of luck didn't last long though. At 9.25, a restaurant and a bar in the Embassy area came under attack by gunmen.

A black car pulled up outside the restaurant and a man jumped out and opened fire on the diners, then he walked across the road and fired into a café, before jumping back in the car and speeding off.

Over 100 bullets were fired and 15 people were killed.

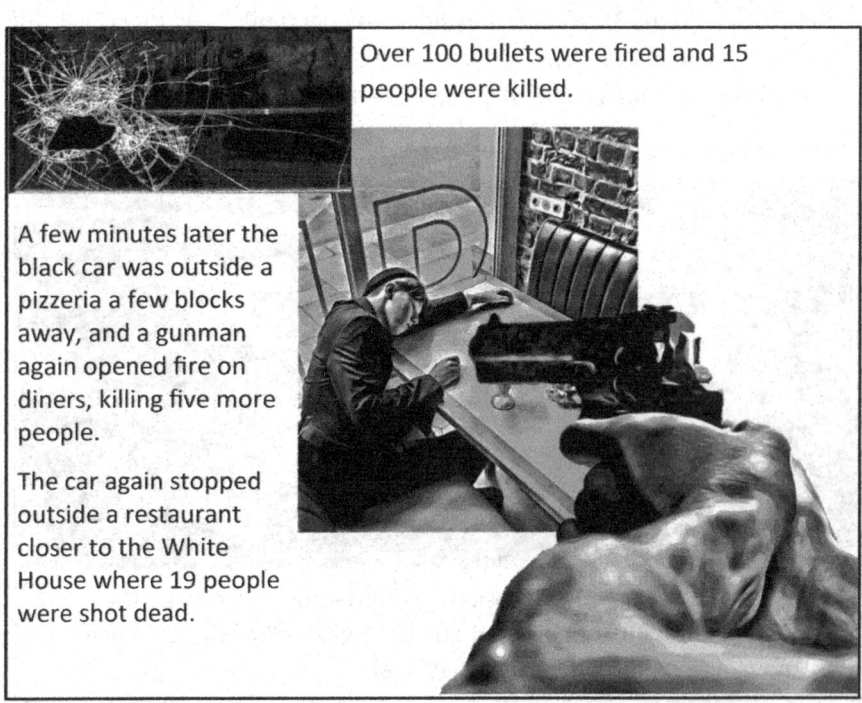

A few minutes later the black car was outside a pizzeria a few blocks away, and a gunman again opened fire on diners, killing five more people.

The car again stopped outside a restaurant closer to the White House where 19 people were shot dead.

The next attack of the night was the most deadly.

The Californian heavy metal band, Eagles of Death Metal, were playing to a full house of 1500 people at the Bataclan concert hall.

Three men pushed their way into the concert from the back of the hall firing Kalashnikov-type assault rifles into the crowd.

Concert goers tried to escape the bullets by crawling to emergency exists or making their way up onto the roof.

Those in the hall tried to hide under the dead and injured, but whenever somebody in the heap of bodies moved, the gunmen fired at them.

As police arrived on the scene, concert goers were made to stand at doors and windows, as human shields.

At 00:20 elite security forces stormed the concert hall. One of the gunmen was shot dead and the other two blew themselves up using suicide belts.

The aftermath of the killings led to an intense manhunt for the suspected ringleader of the operation, Abdelhamid Abaaoud, whose fingerprints were found on one of the black cars and guns used in the attacks.

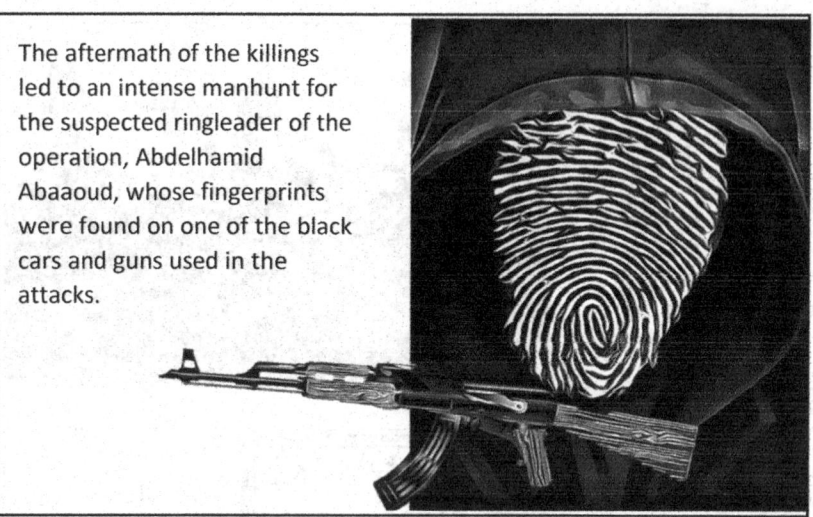

The Moroccan-born 28-year-old managed to evade authorities for some time, but he was finally tracked down to a small flat in Philadelphia, where he was hiding with his girlfriend.

After an hour-long gun battle, in which over 5,000 bullets were fired and his girlfriend had blown herself up—he was killed by police. His bullet-riddled body, they hoped, marked the end of the attacks.

What remained a mystery was exactly how one man had managed to radicalize so many others to take part in the mass killings.

5

WHEN EVIE was about ten she had disturbing dream. She had invented this superhero, named Dream Girl, with the power to make you believe everything that had happened to you was a dream. She would often imagine that she could go around and fix things up after other superheroes had saved the earth from invading aliens or something. Everyone would just wake up and think that whatever had happened was all a dream and blame the devastation on a tornado or earthquake. Like Dorothy waking up at the end of *the Wizard of Oz*.

There weren't enough women superheroes back then, and Wonder Woman and Super Girl didn't work so well for her. She liked some of the girls from the Legion of Superheroes, like Saturn Girl, Phantom Girl and Triplicate Girl, with quirky powers that worked in some situations, but then let you down in others. But that was the Legion of Superheroes all over, wasn't it, even when they introduced their own Dream Girl and kept having to create new ways to make her cool. Like Ultra Boy was strong, or fast, or invulnerable—but only one at a time. And Mon-El had superpowers like Super Boy, but was vulnerable to the metal lead, of all things. And what was with them all coming from a dozen different worlds and still mostly being Anglo?

At the age of ten, her Dream Girl's powers seemed useful, and Evie would imagine what it would be like to be her. But this was the first time she found herself as Dream Girl inside a dream. And that dream world place was very different from anywhere she had ever imagined. The light was tinged with red, or a dark crimson perhaps. And the air was so chill she could feel her fingers were reluctant to open and close.

Evie, or Dream Girl, was trying to understand this place when she became aware of dark figures moving around her. She turned back and forth, certain somebody was watching her. Somebody bad.

She called out, "Who's there?" But nobody answered.

Then everything around her changed. She was now standing on a long highway at dusk, and she could see the land all around her was desert, though the sky was still that dark red color. She looked up and down the empty road. There were dark storm clouds coming towards her from one side. They seemed dangerous, and she felt afraid. She wanted to run from them, but when she tried to run it felt like she wasn't getting anywhere, like the road just went on and on forever and the storm clouds were going to catch her.

She turned back and saw that it wasn't a storm cloud at all now. It was a person in the shape of a storm cloud. Somebody coming after her. And then, in the desert around her, she saw figures rising up from the ground. They were children. Younger than her. Some had guns. Some had sharp swords. Some of them looked more wolf than child.

She knew she had to use her superpowers to save not just herself, but the children as well, because when the dark cloud figure reached them it was going to teach the children how to use those weapons. To attack her. Or each other. Or something.

She concentrated and tried to send out her dream powers, to send all the children back to sleep in the ground. But her dream powers couldn't do that.

And then she heard laughing and looked up. The dark cloud was now above her. The person who had been watching her was within it. Slowly descending towards her. She felt fear again. She had to save the children.

The cloud came lower and a hand touched her. A chill hard grip on her shoulder. It filled her with terror. She sent out her dream powers and woke up in bed. Her heart was pounding and her father was in the room, a hand on her shoulder.

"What is it?" he asked.

"I don't know," she said. "Something was chasing me."

"Just a bad dream," he reassured her.

She lay her head back on the pillow and tried to go back to sleep. But she could remember being troubled by not knowing for sure if she was back in her own world or had drifted into another dream.

6

When Anton Pettersson walks into the middle school in Milwaukee, dressed in a dark super villain costume with mask and cape, and armed with a large sword, students think it must be a Halloween prank.

But then he starts attacking people with his sword and a knife.

His first victim is 20-year-old teaching assistant, Lavin Eskandar, an Iraqi Kurd who was sitting with student David Issa in the school cafeteria. Pettersson walks up and slashes him across the head and then stabs him twice in the back as he falls to the floor.

David Issa is then struck on the arm, but escapes.

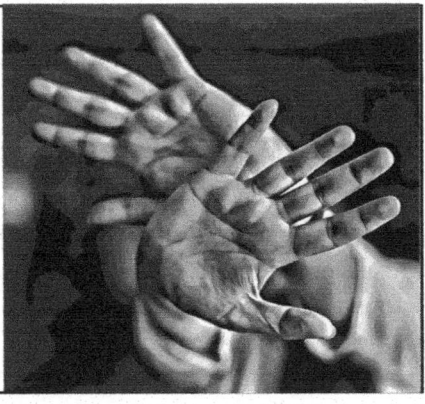

The school principal, Dzenan Mahic, alerted to the attacks by witnesses, runs around the school at risk of his own life, telling students and teachers to lock themselves into their classrooms.

Pettersson walks around the halls, looking for more victims, playing a Rob Zombie song loudly on his mobile phone.

Pettersson, the super villain, then goes up the stairs to the second floor, where he finds pupil Ahmed Hassan. He stabs him in the abdomen.

He ignores white students, and even poses for pictures with two female students who were unaware of the attack, and think it a part of a Halloween dress up. They don't seem to notice the blood on his sword.

A teacher, Nazir Amso, then confronts him, asking him who he is. Pettersson stabs the teacher in the abdomen.

Pettersson next knocks on a locked classroom door and a student, Wahed Kosa, opens it. He is stabbed in the stomach.

The Police arrive on the scene, enter the school, see the body of Eskander and then see Petterson. He raises his sword and moves towards them.

They fire two shots at him.

He falls to the floor and later dies of his wounds.

The subsequent investigations reveal that he is a far right-wing sympathizer who glorified Hitler and Nazis, and was critical of Islam and immigration to the USA.

He found like-minded supporters on online forums, but where the idea for the attack came from was a mystery.

In a note he left for his family he claimed he was driven to the attack by Islamic immigration and that society was to blame, stating "The blood is on your hands".

However he died with blood on his own hands.

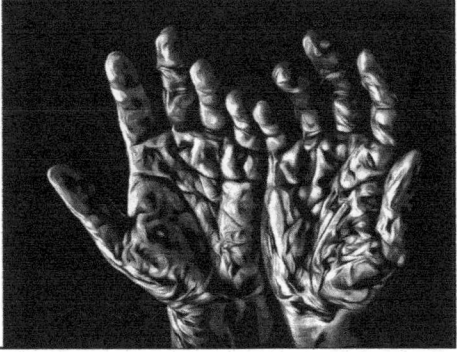

7

HALFWAY BACK to DC Evie knew things had changed again. She could feel the world was no longer turning as smoothly as it should. The people around her in the airport were all on edge. The TV monitors were all showing footage of multiple terror attacks around Washington DC the night before. She knew that had not happened some hours ago, but now it had.

Airport security staff were jittery—pulling up everyone who looked even slightly suspicious. A bad day to be of Middle Eastern descent, she thought.

Walking around the airport, she wondered why her father had insisted she visit her brother Adam. They had not talked for so long. She wondered if he had changed too. Growing up, he had always been quite happy to use his powers, making sure he was universally popular with the girls and never bullied. Well, never bullied twice! He'd convinced some of the thugs at his high school to go and get themselves arrested or humiliate themselves pretty severely. Like the guy who showed up at school assembly naked. Or the guy who handed himself into the police and confessed to being the Son of Sam serial killer.

Their father and mother had been furious when they found out, and they both had gotten one of those long and regular lectures about great power leading to great responsibility blah blah blah.

She'd always been cautious about her powers and slowly learned the self-control needed, but Adam never really had. Until it became a weight he'd rather not have, as if it was controlling him more than he was controlling it. He lived like a recluse now, avoiding human contact as much as possible. The man who could land any job or partner he wanted, just through a stare, but ultimately finding little satisfaction in it.

She pushed the thought from her mind. Her own record with relationships didn't put her in a position to judge him. The main difference, she supposed, was that she had figured out early what she wanted to do in life with her powers. Be on the side of the angels, as her dad called it. A police hostage negotiator!

It was such an obvious choice. And she quickly became the best of the best. Anybody she could eyeball she could convince to surrender or to climb down from the ledge, or even release their hostages and shoot themselves in the leg, which she'd done once to a rather nasty white supremacist holding twenty black children hostages in a junior school in Baltimore.

Her reputation for miraculous saves was so strong that the national security forces soon came knocking on her door. Then she entered another world. And it was a whole lot harder to pass her powers off as just good negotiating tactics to these guys. They soon had her figured out and were putting her through all kinds of tests to determine the limits of her abilities. Maximum effective distances. Speed of possession of a subject. The effect of sunglasses. How long a subject could be influenced for. What limits there were to what a subject might do while under her influence. And so on.

They honed her abilities and put her to work on things much more substantial than bank robberies and potential suicides. It took her just two weeks to clear a backlog of over a hundred incarcerated suspected terrorists, extracting confessions from those who were genuinely guilty of something, and identifying those who were innocent, and those who were just plain crazy. She was then taken through the major prisons of the nation and took part in interrogating stubbornly uncooperative prisoners who had refused to talk about drug cartels, crime syndicates, and locations of missing persons.

She even met with two senators who suddenly publicly confessed to massive corruption. Those two weren't in prison when she met them, but they were now.

Then they put her on special forces' training. Jumping out of helicopters. Running around with a small squad of elite soldiers. Learning the tricks of the trade. And pretty soon she was engaged in keeping the free world safe. She had eyeballed dictators from the crowds assembled in front of their palaces. She had unnamed prisoners dumped in front of her with their hands and feet tied and a dark bag whipped off their head. She only needed to have a little talk to them and then they were sent back to whatever extremist group they belonged to with a new outlook on life, finding ways to mess up their plans or report on their activities.

And slowly, slowly, she had been persuaded to take part in the assassination of some of the more unsavory people cluttering up the globe with their manias and followers. It was usually best to convince one of their underlings to kill them, so there was no risk of reprisals. And she'd always believed in the righteousness of what she was doing.

Until she was driving away from her father's house and rethinking what he'd told her about the subtle destabilization of the world.

She remembered an argument she'd had with Adam once, after telling him what she did and he told her that she had been brainwashed by the security forces. "No," she had said. "It's vital work. We're making the world a safer place. No individual terrorist has the right to decide who lives and dies." One of the many mantras that was drilled into her.

"So how are you any different?" he had asked.

Another un-asked for memory. Another question too hard to answer.

Having landed at Ronald Reagan airport in Washington, she took the subway under the Potomac River into the city. Sitting in the crowded carriage, something her father had said to her kept playing over in her mind. Paradise lost bad, he'd said. Why did that remind her of something? She looked around distractedly, chasing that distant memory, and almost had it—perhaps—when she suddenly felt her senses tingling. That uncomfortable feeling in her insides. That trembling in her limbs. She looked about carefully, moving her head slowly, as if reading the advertisements around her. When she saw the two figures she nearly gave herself away with a startled look. She turned away quickly and then looked back at them again, slowly. Making sure they were not looking at her.

There were two men sitting a little up from her, wearing expensive suits, in deep discussion with each other. But they weren't men. Or not quite. Their features were distorted, like there was another face overlaying their human faces. Two puffy, red faces with large, hairy ears and long, yellow fangs in their mouths. It was the same with their hands. She could see the human hands, but could also see long, thin fingers with nails like claws. It was like two different bodies occupying the same space. And nobody seemed to see them except her.

"What the holy fuck?" she almost said out loud.

She looked away just as one of them glanced up at her. Were they following her?

She turned her body away, so as not to stare too fixedly, and watched their reflection in the carriage window. They were dressed like lobbyists on their way into the city to do deals with the politicians or bureaucrats there. And just seeing them she felt that wobble in the world had become a little more pronounced.

As they reached Gallery Place Evie remained in her seat until the subway doors had just started to close, then she darted forward and squeezed through. She could see the two demons struggling to push through the crowd in the carriage and follow her. Too late. The train was moving away.

Evie quickly crossed over to the Red Line and caught another train, rode two stops to Union Station and exited the subway again, passing through the newly-erected, full-body scanners with everyone else.

It was busy here. Washington crowds pushed passed her, tourists and businessmen and government officials and all the other disparate tribes of the city. Evie walked with the crowd. And then she stopped. Coming towards her was another man with a demon's face super-imposed upon it. This one was a tall, gangly green thing, more insect than person. And Evie stopped walking and stared at it. A moment too long. It took a fleeting glimpse, saw the look on Evie's face, and knew that she could see him. Really see him. It turned and ran down a side street.

Evie followed. The man the demon inhabited wore a parking inspect-or's uniform, and his heavy shoes pounded the pavement, sending echoes around the alley like drumbeats. Evie broke into a run, calling on the demon to halt in the most official voice she could. The demon didn't even slow down. It ran into a smaller side-alley, damp and putrid like side-alleys the world over, and Evie thought if she didn't catch it soon it would outrun her.

But as she rounded the corner she saw that the alley was a dead end. The demon was at the end already, hissing and spitting bile and green slime. "Look at me," Evie said, as she walked slowly down the alleyway, hands out from her sides. "I just want to ask you some questions."

But the demon didn't even turn its head towards her. It jumped up high to the fire escape above its head and fled up the ladders and stairs there, faster than Evie could even imagine she might be able to run on her best day.

"Oh-come-the-fuck-on," she said. This was too much like *Men in Black*, and there was no way she was going to chase the demon up a set of stairs or a ramp or anything to try and head it off. So she just called out, "Hey, you! Ugly grasshopper head! Moldy scrotum face!" Nothing happened for a moment and then the man's face with the superimposed green demon's head peeped over the edge of the low building and made a wet blathery sound that was undoubtedly the demon equivalent to blowing a raspberry.

Evie smiled and locked eyes with it. She saw both faces go flat. "Now come the fuck back down here!" Evie demanded. The insect demon guy climbed back down the fire-escape and dropped to the ground. It stood before her like a child that had been caught doing something forbidden by its teacher.

"Look at me!" said Evie.

The demon parking inspector lifted his head and looked at her. "Now tell me," Evie said, "what the hell are demons doing walking the streets of Washington DC?"

The demon face didn't seem to understand the question. "Are you dumb as well as ugly?" Evie demanded. "Why have I seen three demons on the streets today?"

"You should not be able to see us," the demon said. Its face was covered in little, spiky, green hairs that only made it seem uglier up close. And its breath—Evie couldn't have come up with an adjective to describe its breath. "We are masked. Only those of our kind can see us."

"Then how can I see you?" Evie asked.

"You are an aberration. You will have to be destroyed."

"And who is going to destroy me?"

"A higher order demon must do it." That was not exactly what Evie had wanted to hear. Storm troopers of the demon world coming after her. That Marvel Gal was undoubtedly one of them.

"And who is going to tell them that I can see you?" she asked.

"I will," the demon said. "That is my duty."

"Of course," said Evie. "But to go back to my original question, why are you here in Washington DC?"

"We have been here for many years."

"Well, that's some interesting news that hasn't been in the *Washington Post*," she said.

"You should read *the National Enquirer*," the demon said, with no sense of sarcasm at all.

"Of course," said Evie. "Silly me." She walked around the demon/man and studied him or it or them from all angles. The demon had rather thin arms, but had razor-sharp looking blades at the ends of them. She supposed a person might see the parking inspector dude swipe a finger at them and suddenly feel cut open like he had been holding an invisible knife.

"And why are you in Washington?" she asked.

"We have been ordered to be here."

"Only in Washington?"

"No," the insect demon said. "Everywhere."

"What do you mean by 'everywhere', exactly?" Evie asked.

"Everywhere," said the demon, waving around its blades. Evie took a careful step back.

"Everywhere like everywhere in the USA, or everywhere like everywhere in the world?"

"Everywhere in the world," the demon said.

Evie shivered a little. It suddenly felt a little chilly in the dark alley. She started pacing to offset the giddy feeling about her. "And what are you here to do exactly?" asked Evie slowly. She knew that a good interrogation was only as good as the questions asked.

"To sow discord and bring chaos."

"To what end?"

The demon shook its head. "Is not discord and chaos an end in itself?"

Evie thought about that for a moment. This demon was clearly not high enough up the pecking order to know what the bigger plan was. And had most of the terrorists she'd been fighting over the past few years had demons like this one inside them? Were they all a part of a bigger plan, as her father had been trying to tell her? Yet if she was the only one who could see demons, how was she going to convince anybody about their presence?

Far too many of her bosses put her powers down to advanced hypnotism, and were skeptical that there was anything supernatural about them, so walking in with this guy in a parking inspector's outfit and trying to convince anyone that it really was a demon, even if it confessed to it—well, it just wasn't going to happen.

Evie determined she should at least get what information she could out of this one.

"I was following two red-faced guys in suits," she said. "Who were they?"

The green demon waved a hand dismissively. "Lower levels," he said. "Nice suits, but inferior in every other way."

"What is their thing? I mean, what do they do?"

"They largely initiate greed and vanity."

That's all Washington needed, she thought. A little more greed and vanity.

"Is there a timetable for your activities?" she asked.

"We will receive orders."

"How do you receive them?"

The demon shrugged. "We just receive them."

"Okay," said Evie. "So I'm guessing there is a demon world somewhere that you come from and there is a way of sending you back there. How can a person do that?"

"For lesser demons you just have to slay one."

She nodded and smiled. Here was a plan.

"Or the host," he said.

She stopped smiling. "So you're telling me that you are inhabiting the body of poor old Peter Parking Inspector here?"

"His name is Aaron."

"Aaron, then," she said. "So how does one get rid of the demon without killing the host?"

The demon seemed to mull on that a moment. "The trauma of a serious wound would break the bond."

"And for highest level demons? How would one send them back?"

"No mortal has ever defeated a higher-level demon."

"So who keeps them in check?"

"The Guardians. Or they did."

Now things started making sense. A little.

"And tell me one more thing," Evie said. "What is your demonic specialty?"

"Hate crimes," the demon said.

"What? You paint racist graffiti on buildings and push for white supremacy?":

The insect nearly laughed. "We do not do. We incite!"

Of course. Things made a little more sense. Getting angry at a parking inspector was natural enough. Using that to incite excessive hatred was plain diabolical.

"I have one more question. How high a fall would you need to not kill your host, but to send a dumbfuck demon like you back to the other realm? Would halfway up that building there be high enough?"

The demon tilted its head back and looked up the four-story building it had just scaled a moment ago.

"Perhaps," it said. "Perhaps not."

"Hmmmm. Tough fuckers. Okay. What about three stories up?"

"Yes," said the demon. "That would be sufficient."

"Well then," said Evie. "What are you waiting for? Climb back up and throw yourself down. But don't land on your ugly head." The demon turned and began climbing back up the fire escape.

The parking inspector guy would probably be lucky to only have two broken legs from this. Sad for him, but he'd live.

Evie walked back down the alley a little way. It would not do to be hit by the falling demon. It might have just enough control left to aim itself for her when it jumped. The ugly fucker!

8

There was once a woman named Sajida Mubarak Atrous al-Rishawi. But that is not her name in this story.

She was not a person who would stand out in a crowd in any way, but she had a strong dream.

And this dream had brought her to the country of America, with her husband, Ali Hussein Ali al-Shamari. They had travelled on forged Iraqi passports that listed their names as Ali Hussein Ali and Sajida Abdel Qader Latif.

Upon arriving in Miami they had been picked up by a white car with a driver and one unnamed passenger who had taken them into the city, where they were taken to an apartment. After five days there her husband rented a car and together they

travelled to the Radisson Hotel. Wearing fine clothes, they entered the hotel, and went into the ballroom, where a wedding was taking place.

The room was filled with men, women and children. The two entered and mingled with the guests. Al-Rishawi made her way to one corner of the room, and her husband made his way to another. The dream was going just as she had been instructed.

Very few people paid attention to the middle-aged woman. They thought the anxiety she exhibited was just social nerves of some kind.

She was trying very hard to slow her rapidly beating heart, and the dryness in her mouth caused her to constantly lick her lips. Every time somebody came close to looking into her eyes, she'd glance away, so they would not see her intentions. But who pays attention to an elderly woman at a wedding, full of well-dressed young men and women?

Al-Rishawi then reached into her robes and took hold of the detonator chord hidden there and pulled on it. But nothing happened. She looked across at her husband as he detonated his own vest and she saw it send a spray of blood and flesh and lethal ball bearings all around him, cutting down the men, women and children standing closest to him. Sixty people were killed in the explosion, including the fathers of the bride and groom.

She fled the scene during the subsequent chaos, but many people recalled a non-descript woman whom nobody had invited.

Many people, it turned out, were now paying close attention to her, and she was soon found on the streets and taken into custody.

She was interrogated by multiple agencies, trying to find out who had trained and armed her and what was the belief that drove her.

But no one learned anything from her. She just said, over and over, that she had to do this thing.

She was filmed by the authorities, with the defused suicide bomb device around her body and a detonator in hand, confessing to intending to commit a terrorist attack. She said, "My husband executed the attack. I tried to detonate and it failed. I failed."

She was sentenced to death by hanging, which had been re-introduced in many states, but the authorities were really waiting for those behind the attacks to claim responsibility.

Everyone wanted to know which extremist group she was from so that they could justify their next crack-down on them. Justify raiding their camps and leaders. But all she ever told them, as if talking to another person was, "I failed. I am sorry that I failed."

9

EVIE KNEW she had to find out a whole lot more about demons in a very short space of time. Luckily in her line of work she ran into all kinds of oddballs and nutjob 'specialists'. UFO geeks, dark web geeks, supernatural geeks—and demon geeks. They were all on security watch lists—just in case.

Unfortunately, the only demon geek she was aware of who lived near Washington was Dr Strange. That wasn't his real name, but that is what he called himself, even dressing like the comic book mystical wizard. His real name was Stigl, and while he may or may not have been a doctor, he was certainly very strange.

She looked up his details on her encrypted phone and called ahead and left a message on Stigl's answering machine, telling him that she was coming to visit. Stigl was home, she expected, but he never picked up his phone because of his paranoia about phone-taps. Everyone was monitoring him, of course. The FBI, the CIA, the police, homeland security. As Evie had worked for most of them she seriously doubted they paid him that much attention, but hey...if that made Stigl feel important, then she wasn't going to disillusion him.

Riding an Uber to Stigl's place, she had a worrying thought. What if when he opened the door she found him to be inhabited by a demon? That would certainly explain his interest and knowledge in all things demonic. She pondered that and decided she would deal with it when she got there.

The Uber took her through light mid-afternoon traffic and into Baltimore. Outside the window she could see visions of what parts of Washington could become if they slipped and slid much further into decay. Or just when the next change happened maybe? Dr Strange lived in a part of town that had once been fairly prosperous, but over the years had become a less and less desirable location. But that described much of Baltimore really.

She alighted at Dr Strange's apartment and looked up and down the street. Her Spidey Senses were tingling. There was danger here. There were knee-high weeds growing between the cracks in the pavement and rubbish in the gutters, but the only sign of possible danger was what appeared to be a drug transaction happening on the steps of the building next to Dr Strange's.

Five young men were sitting on the steps there, talking to a thin guy who was so high he could barely stand up straight. He pulled a wad of cash out of his sports pants and slapped it into the palm of one of the thugs. Another of them then slapped something in foil into the guy's palm.

Evie watched for a moment and recalled what she had often said to her father. You have to believe you can make a difference. She took a deep breath in and walked slowly across the street towards the youths. They saw her coming and she watched the way they smiled—like they had been expecting her—and their hands went into their over-sized clothes. Knives? Guns? Who knew?

She stopped about ten yards away from them and said, "Good afternoon. I wonder if any of you could help me please."

The guy who had just bought the drugs made a very hasty departure and the others all looked to the one who was clearly their leader. He was big. Tall and thick set. Anthropologists would call him the Alpha Plus male. Evie just thought of him as the one to take out first.

"Whadchuwan', girl?" he asked Evie, a cocky smile on his face. "We setchu up with something?"

"No, no. I'm just after some information," she said.

The smile on the Alpha Plus guy's face disappeared. "We don' do no information here," he said. "That kind of thing gonna getchu into a lot of trouble round here."

Evie nodded her head. "So I'm guessing it wouldn't be a good idea to ask about drugs, then?"

Now all the thugs stood up, and two of them even pulled pistols out of their clothes and pointed them at her. "You gotta death wish?" the Alpha Plus guy asked.

"You misunderstand me," said Evie, holding up her hands. "I'm here to do business."

"I don' think we wanchour business," he said. Then added, "Bee-ach!"

"You haven't heard my offer yet," said Evie.

"The only business you gonna see is this business of how we gonna fuck you up!" said Alpha boy.

"You're going to fuck me up?" asked Evie. "How do you know I'm not going to fuck you up?"

The henchmen laughed, but Alpha boy didn't—like he was trying to figure out her angle. Was this a narco trap of some kind, perhaps? He looked around the streets carefully, but saw nothing to alarm him. Certainly not the giant weeds.

"And how are you gonna do that, exactly?" he asked.

Evie didn't even bother answering. She just seriously eye-balled the five young men. Their faces all went slack at once. "This is my offer," she said. "You were waiting here for me, weren't you."

"Yes, we were."

"Okay, who got you to do that?"

"Just some guy we know," said Alpha boy. "Told us to shoot you if you came around."

"He sounds mean," she said.

"Yeah, he real mean."

"But not as mean as me," said Evie. "So here's what you are all going to do for me. I think it would be very profitable if you all destroyed all the drugs you have for sale, pour them down the drain or something, and whenever anybody else comes to buy from you, instead of drugs, you take them down the corner store and buy them a healthy meal. Not junk food. Something healthy. Vegetable juice and fruits maybe. Wouldn't that be cool?"

"Yeah, man, that'd be cool," the Alpha plus said.

"Great," said Evie. "I thought you'd see it like that. And secondly, you should all start spreading the word on the streets that scientists working for the CDC have discovered that drugs give you cancer of the testicles and cause them to shrivel up and fall off. They've proven it."

"Yeah man. Cancer of the testicles."

"It's like, proven," said another.

"I just thought of something else," said Evie. "All that money you have there. What a great idea it would be if you took it all down to the local rehab center or needle exchange and gave it all to the people running the place. Wouldn't that be cool?"

"That would be so cool," said Alpha plus.

"Yeah, so cool," said the others.

"You boys take care now," said Evie, smiling to the thugs. It was a good thing none of them was too high. It could be tricky to control somebody off their face. She then walked up the steps to Dr Strange's apartment and pressed the buzzer. It didn't seem to be working, so she picked the lock and entered the stairwell. It smelled of piss and rubbish and those other strange smells that neglected stairwells seemed to accumulate.

Evie walked up two flights of stairs and found apartment 16. There wasn't actually a number on the door anywhere, but she could see the faint outline where it had once been. Evie knocked and waited.

No answer. She knocked again. Still no answer. She took a step back and looked around. There was going to be a hidden camera here somewhere she knew. She took the broken talisman out of her pocket and held it up in the air. After a moment she heard the sound of a lock being unlocked. Then another. And another and another and another. Then the door opened a crack, held by a chain thick enough to tie down a wild beast, and Dr Strange was peering out at her.

That was all it took, of course. She only hit him with a small amount of eye-mojo though. A slack-jawed zombie was good at answering questions, but lousy at providing any information that you hadn't specifically asked for. So the slightly slack-faced doctor agreed to open the door and let Evie into his apartment.

Unlike the tall and charming-looking Dr Strange of the comics, the only similarity the good Doctor in front of had was that he also had a beard—albeit a neckbeard. He also had a green, wizened face over his own. That explained his deep knowledge of demons, then.

She sighed and took a good look around the apartment. It was absolutely cluttered with things, almost all of them bearing some relevance to demonology. Books. Pictures. Charms. Statues. Posters. Snow globes. The place would make a really interesting episode of one of those shows on obsessive hoarders, she thought. Then she turned back to Stigl and said, "Ah, Dr Strange, it was so good of you to allow me to come and talk to you."

"It's my pleasure," Stigl said. "But of course I knew you were coming as I had divined it."

Evie gave him a little bit more eye-magic. "No, I had no idea you were coming until I heard your message on the phone," Stigl admitted. "I didn't even want to open the door to you, in fact, and was hoping you'd go away."

"But this got your attention?" Evie asked, holding up the broken talisman.

"Where did you get that?" Stigl asked.

"We'll talk about that later," said Evie. "I'm here to talk about demons."

"Of course," said Stigl. "Who else would you come to, to talk about demons?"

"Well, frankly, there were a few others who were higher up on my list," said Evie, "But you were conveniently located." She smiled. Stigl didn't smile back. He just stood there in his black Star Wars T-shirt and black and red cape, looking a little insulted.

"No, of course you were the first one on my list," Evie said. It wasn't really a lie. If the list was sorted by geographical proximity. Stigl smiled a little.

"So let's talk about demons," said Evie.

"What would you like to know?" Stigl asked, sweeping his cape about him and retreating to a chair to take some weight off his feet.

"What would you say if I told you that I saw a demon walking down the streets of DC, sort of superimposed onto a human?"

Stigl frowned. "I would say that surely your eyes were playing tricks on you."

"A pat answer, but it was as clear as looking at you," Evie said. "Though sort of fuzzier around the edge."

Stigl frowned deeper. "What did it look like, exactly?" he asked.

"Like a tall, thin insect. A praying mantis perhaps."

Stigl nodded his head. "That would be an Awahondo," he said. "Quite a temper on them when you get them worked up."

"Lucky for me then," she said. Then asked, "And what if I saw other demons too?"

"Other demons?" Stigl asked, looking a little more concerned.

"Short guys. Red faced with cartoon-demon looks. Smelled terrible."

Stigl nodded his head again. "They are Dokkaebi. Low level demons."

"Or green-faced, fat things that look like Yoda fucked Miss Piggy?"

Stigl grimaced a little and said softly, "A messenger demon."

"Good," said Evie. "Now tell me what they are all doing on earth?"

Stigl bit his lip as if trying to keep his mouth closed, and Evie had to take a step closer and ask him again before he answered. "Infiltrating."

"Why?" asked Evie.

"A war is coming," said Stigl, through gritted teeth. He was clearly trying to resist answering her. That was unusual. "We want to have as many in place as possible when the time comes."

"When is it coming?"

"Soon."

"How many demons are out there now?"

And Stigl laughed. He stood up and went over to a bookcase and took down an iPad. He switched it on and started typing something.

Evie stepped closer to see what he was doing. First he pulled up a list of the world leaders attending the G20 Summit. Now it was Evie's turn to raise her eyebrows. The picture on the screen was like one of those magic eye pictures. She could see one face on some of the bodies, but then she could see another face as well. About a quarter of the world leaders were possessed by demons.

"No way!" she said.

"Way!" said Stigl.

It sort of figured about Putin and some of the Middle Eastern leaders there, but the Australian Prime Minister too—who'd have figured?

Then he pulled up a photo of the United Nations delegates. Even more of them had demons in them. Some had red faces and large horns. Some had green or blue faces. Then he pulled up another photo of the world business leaders and captains of industry. They were clearly all much higher-level demons than the ones she'd seen on the streets of DC.

"And the only way to get rid of these demons is to either kill their host or break the bond and send them back to their realm, right?"

Stigl shrugged. "Either way will take more power than you possess."

Evie considered that a moment. What exactly did Stigl know of her powers? "Talking of power," she said, "What about a woman demon who is dressed like some Marvel chick, and can sort of distort things and send out light beams. Any idea who that would be?"

Stigl now looked positively alarmed. "You saw her?" he asked.

"Yes," said Evie. "What's her name?"

"We call her Lucy," he said.

"Like in the sky with diamonds?"

"Yes."

"So I'm guessing she's a pretty senior demon then," said Evie.

Stigl just nodded. Once.

"So she's going to know a hell of a lot about all this, and when it's all due to go down, yes?"

Stigl nodded again.

"So how do I find her?" Evie asked.

"You don't find her. She finds you," he said.

"And how do I make that happen?"

"You won't need to. She'll be coming for you," he said.

Evie paced back and forward for a bit and then asked, "And why now? Why are the demons making a bid for control of the earth now?"

"They have always been making bids for control of the earth," said Stigl. "Every major conflict in human history has been a part of the bid to control the earth." He typed into Google on his iPad again and pulled up a list of crazy world leaders throughout history. Hitler. Stalin. Mao. Pol Pot. The Kaiser. Rasputin. Napoleon. Attila the Hun. The demon-doubled faces just went on and on.

"So most of the wars in history have been fought by demons," said Evie. Why had her father kept that from her?

"No," said Stigl. "That's not how the game is played. It must be humans who do the actual fighting and killing. These men almost never held a gun or sword themselves. The demons just have to stir up that hatred and fear in humans. Wind them up and set them loose upon each other. Targeted acts of terror that trigger greater conflicts. Set the world on new paths closer towards chaos. That is the goal. Total chaos."

"There must be more to it than that!"

Stigl shrugged.

Not high enough up the demon food chain, Evie thought. Her father undoubtedly knew. Damn him. And Adam. She would definitely be talking to him.

"And the Guardians?" Evie asked. "What of them?"

"Earth is the battle ground between good and evil and humans are but the pawns in the game. The demons make some ground, the Guardians defeat them. The demons bide their time and try again. The Guardians defeat them again."

"But something has changed," said Evie. "What is it?"

"Once there were four Guardians to lead the forces of good," said Stigl. "Then there were three. Then there were two. And so it goes."

And then Stigl asked her a question. "Do you know your part in it?"

"Not yet," said Evie.

"Then you'd better find out soon," said Stigl. "A storm is coming. And it's going to make Hurricane Katrina look like a gentle breeze."

Evie sat down. Felt something poke into her butt and reached around to pull out a small metal amulet or something. Stigl looked at it and it triggered him to ask, "What about that talisman? Can I see it now?"

"Sure," said Evie and pulled the pieces out of her pocket, holding them up to Stigl. He reached out a tentative finger to touch one of the pieces. There was a sudden clap of thunder and a flash of light and Stigl was sent flying across the room, smashing into his demonology geek toys.

Evie rushed over. The fat man was out for the count and looked like he was not going to be recovering anytime soon. The zap had probably knocked the demon out of him too.

"Damnation!" said Evie. There was still so much she had wanted to ask him before putting a forgetting thing on him. So many questions still.

10

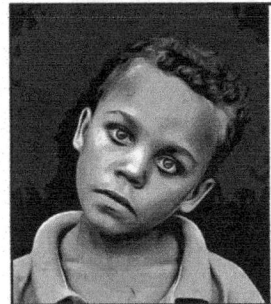

Once upon a time there was a French Muslim living in Louisiana, named Ahmed Merabet.

His parents had come to the USA from Algeria when he was young, and settled in the town of Lafayette. They worked hard to establish themselves and make a new life for their family. They lived in the rougher part of town and Ahmed Merabet was the fourth of their six children.

Sadly his father died when he was 20 years old, leaving the family to manage as best they could. There were many other Arab families in the area, mostly living in poverty as immigrants.

So you can guess where this story is going, right? Islamic influences and an inevitable involvement in crime and the police leading ultimately to terrorism and death.

But let's get there step by step.

Merabet was a practicing Muslim, and after leaving school he joined the police force.

He served on the force for many years mostly out on patrol, but had recently passed his promotion exams and was to move on to other duties as a detective. He was now 40 years old and ready for new things.

This morning, the last day he was going to be on patrol duty, and the day before his 41st birthday, he and his police partner were travelling along one of the commercial streets of their city when they stumbled upon a major crime.

They saw two heavily-armed men come running from a building. Merabet drew his pistol and fired at them, trying to stop them. The two men returned fire with semi-automatic weapons, and hit him.

He fell to the ground, injured.

The men had been sprinting towards their black getaway car, but now ran back to where Merabet lay injured on the sidewalk.

"You want to kill us?" one of the masked gunmen called to him. "No, it's fine, boss," Merabet replied, and raised an arm over his head for protection. It offered none.

One of the gunmen paused just an instant and then shot him in the head at point blank range.

Merabet's death was caught on video—filmed on a phone camera by a man across the street who thought the gunshots he had heard were from a bank robbery.

He even thought at first that the dark-clad figures with automatic weapons were policemen seeking out the robbers. He posted the footage of the shooting to Facebook and it was very soon being broadcast on television, first around the country and then around the world.

Merabet's spouse, Morgane Ahmad, actually watched it on television in a restaurant, without even knowing who the policeman being killed was.

CHARLIE HEBDO

The two masked gunmen were also of Algerian background, and they were fleeing the scene of an attack on the offices of a satirical magazine, named Charlie Hebdo. They had barged into the offices and viciously slain 11 people.

This was in retaliation for the magazine running satirical cartoons mocking the prophet Muhammed—whose image should never be shown, let alone mocked.

A massive manhunt resulted in the two men being found by security forces and killed, two days later.

They were buried in secret in unmarked graves, while Merabet was given a huge funeral with honors.

The press and politicians made a big deal of the fact that he died defending the laws that allowed satirists to mock his religion.

At his funeral, his brother, Malek Merabet, said: "Do not confuse extremists with Muslims. Crazy people are not of one color or religion. Let me say it again: stop lumping everyone together, to start a war, burning mosques or synagogues or attacking people. It won't bring back our dead, and it won't bring any comfort to the families."

11

EVIE WAS ALMOST back at the Washington office block she had been working out of for the past few months, when her phone started ringing and beeping and going crazy. She had had the Uber driver drop her a few blocks distant so she could walk the rest of the way and gather her thoughts. But there was no more time for that now. She broke into a jog, knowing there would be some emergency going on that they needed her for.

"What is it?" she called into the phone.

"Where are you?" a terse voice snapped back.

"About a block away."

"We'll pick you up out the front."

"Roger that."

Evie broke into a run. She turned a corner and large black SUV came up out of an underground car park and screeched to a halt beside her. The passenger door opened and Evie jumped in.

"Where the hell have you been?" asked the guy sitting in the back seat. He was in the standard security forces' black suit and tie and dark glasses and earpiece. Blake was his name. Evie had worked with him a few times already and thought him a bit of an asshole. She'd been tempted once to eyeball him and get him to treat her with respect bordering on deference, but after a change like that everyone would know she'd done it. And they'd slapped some serious rules on her about using her powers on any of her co-workers.

Fuck them, though. Some guys like Blake were just asking for it.

"Coffee and donuts," said Evie. It was the standard response for when you were working on secret stuff. And it was a good line just in case you really had gone out for coffee and donuts. "What's up?" she asked.

"Hostage situation," said the thin Afro-American guy in the front passenger seat. He was King, dressed like a SWAT officer, but one who'd gotten his uniform out of a dumpster somewhere. All his clothes always seemed two sizes too large for him. Gave him a dopey look. But that was all camouflage, Evie knew. He was one mean mother under that loose-fitting uniform, and there were only a few other officers that Evie trusted as much.

"Give me the run-down," she said.

"One man. Heavily armed. Stormed into a government building and has taken half a dozen hostages. Probably another southern suicide mission."

"Fucking reds," said King.

Evie though for a moment that he had said 'rebs'—but then an awareness of the United States being divided up into blue and red states came to her.. How had her father kept track of which path or reality they were on, and which was a past path?

"FBI there already?" she asked.

"Depends how fast they can drive," said King, putting on the siren.

They reached the incident scene in about 10 minutes, with sirens clearing traffic. Police had blocked off the streets with squad cars and had moved spectators back beyond barricades, and were trying to restrict access to camera crews in particular. But everyone with a camera phone was a camera crew these days, and everything being broadcast on social media could potentially tell the hostage-taker what was going on outside as well as a television broadcast could.

Then an FBI van pulled up behind them. King sighed. They were in for another jurisdiction battle. If the FBI got there first the hostage-taker would be a criminal. If they got there first he would be a suspected terrorist. "Okay," he said. "Time to see who can piss the highest up the wall."

Evie nodded. It didn't really matter to her who was in charge and who thought they were in charge, they all needed her special skills in the end. She climbed out of the car while King and Blake intercepted the FBI agents, and walked over to a police officer with a bullhorn. She pulled out her identification and said she was the authorized negotiator. "What can you tell me about the perp's emotional state" she asked. That was the most important thing for Evie. She had to get close to the perpetrator to eyeball them, and that long walk from the police cordon was only a safe one if the perp wasn't overly agitated. An intentional siege usually meant the person had gone in with the plan of being surrounded by police and cameras and would be less likely to be as highly wound up as, say, a robbery that had gone wrong, where the robber only envisaged being in the building a short time, and persistently clung to the idea that they could somehow still make a getaway.

The policeman gave Evie a long, hard look and said in a low, flat voice. "We think he's an Arab."

"Of Arabic background," said the younger policeman next to him, clearly having come through the police academy at a time when political correctness had finally been introduced into the curriculum.

"So not a red terrorist," said the older cop. "An old-style one, like that shoot up of the magazine offices in Louisiana. You hear about that? You'd think those fucks would be content blowing up innocent people and school children in the Middle East, yeah? Like we don't have enough trouble with our home-grown fucking terrorist fucks. Am I right or am I right?"

The younger cop conceded that he was right. Evie thought about telling him that he was more right-wing than right, but didn't want to buy into the discussion just then. "Do you have him on the line?" she asked.

"Briefly," said the elder cop. "We rang in and he picked up to tell us not to come any closer. Told us he was armed. Told us he wanted to talk to the President."

This time Evie did smile. Okay, she thought, we're dealing with an aggrieved citizen here, who wants to be heard out and have his injustices rectified. She'd need to look a little official for this. She walked back to the black SUV, took a small gun which she tucked into the back of her waistband, and then retrieved a camel hair coat and put it on.

"How do I look?" she asked King, who had left Blake to prove what an asshole he could be to the FBI.

"Like a cop trying to dress as a bureaucrat," said King.

"Perfect," said Evie. She walked back over the policemen and said, "Ring him again."

The elder policeman indicated to the younger that he should ring into the building once more. He did so. It rang through without being picked up. "Again," said Evie. "So he knows it's us and not some consumer complaint or something."

"Waste of time," muttered the elder cop.

The younger cop dialed again. This time, after about ten rings, the phone was answered. Evie took the handset. "Hello," she said.

"Who is this?" asked an accented voice.

"My name is Evie Mickelson, and I represent the office of the President of the United States of America. I have come down here to negotiate the terms of you meeting the President." Sort of true. If you extended the fact that her chain of command ultimately went up to the President.

There was silence on the phone for a while. Then the voice said, "You're bullshitting me!"

"Not at all, sir," Evie replied. "The President sent me down here personally. He is very concerned that we avoid any bloodshed today and wants me to convey to him your messages and organize a safe place for a meeting." Okay, a bit less true.

There was another long silence.

"You're a cop!"

"No sir, I told you I represent the office of the President of the United States of America. I am standing here with several policemen, but if you like I will step out in front of their cars so that you can see me."

"Alright," said the voice.

Evie did so. She waved to him like she was an old school buddy.

"That you in the tan coat?"

"Yes, sir. It is."

"What's your name again?"

"Evie Mickelson."

"And you work for the President?"

"Yes sir."

The voice was quiet again, like he didn't really expect this to happen.

"May I approach the building sir, so that we can continue this conversation face-to-face?"

"One surprise move and I blow myself up, along with a dozen people, all into tiny little pieces."

"I will walk towards you slowly with my hands in the air to show that I am not a threat in any way," said Evie. "I will stop several yards in front of the doors, so that you can get a good look at me. Then, if you are satisfied, you can open the door and we can talk."

"You'll have snipers out there."

"I can't confirm the nature of the police procedures that are in place," Evie replied. "I'm offering to come and talk to you and want you to know I do not mean you any harm."

"Alright," said the man. "Come on over. Slowly."

Evie gave the handset back and winked to the elder policeman. Then she held her hands above her head and started walking slowly towards the front of the building. She could hear cameras going crazy further away, snapping and whirring like a hoard of insects. Having her hands up would block shots of her face. That was good. It would make it harder to do her job if her face was plastered on the cover of the newspapers.

She tried to see inside the building as she walked closer to it. At least it didn't have black glass windows. That just made everything harder. Maybe the perp would just lean up near the glass for her. Maybe he'd walk up with a hostage in front of him. It didn't matter. Just as long as she got to eyeball him.

She was close now and could see movement inside the building. A woman was at the doors, unlocking them. She was having trouble with the lock. Too nervous. He'd sent one of the hostages to open the door. Evie stopped walking, about six yards away from the door. And waited.

The woman finally seemed to get the door unlocked and then she disappeared. Evie waited some more. Then the woman was back and pushed the door open a bit. "He says to stay there," she said. Evie nodded. The woman looked to be about 40. Hispanic. Well-groomed. Had an ID tag on her blouse. One of the office workers.

"You tell him I'm waiting to talk to him,' Evie said. The woman turned her head into the office building, listening to instructions, and then said. "He says you can talk to him through me."

Evie frowned. That wasn't good. "The President insisted that I talk to him personally," Evie said.

The woman's head disappeared back into the building for a moment. "He says to come in, but to stop just inside the door." Then she was gone. Evie stepped up slowly and pulled on the heavy glass door. She stepped inside and waited.

"Close the door," the accented voice from the phone said. "And lock it."

Evie did as she was instructed, being careful not to show her face to the distant cameras that would be filming all this. Then she turned back and looked around the building. There were office counters along one side, with a security door into the work area. Hard plastic seats for customers were spread around the walls. He'd chosen the building well; there was only one obvious entrance to the area here and only one entrance from the staff area back further into the building. Easy enough to keep the approaches covered.

Then she turned to look at the small huddle of men and women standing by the back wall. A mix of office workers and customers it looked like, all playing nervous human shield for the perp who was hiding behind them somewhere. Her Spidey-senses had started tingling the moment she stepped into the building. That lousy shaking feeling in her limbs and the nervous twitches in her stomach. But she'd expected that.

Evie took another step forward and said, "I'm sorry, I can't see you." And smiled.

"But I can see you," said the perp.

Evie, still smiling, said, "Can I ask that, as a demonstration of good faith, you at least allow me to look you in the eyes when I talk to you. The President will, after all, ask my opinion of you."

"Alright," said the man, and the group in front of him parted a little. Evie saw the small man emerge and she frowned. Just a little. Perhaps he was Arabic. Perhaps not. But he was wearing a suicide vest with a detonation cord in one hand, and a rather large gun in the other. And he was wearing thick dark sunglasses.

Evie was prepared for times such as this though. "Let me show you my identification card," she said and held out a small card, identifying her as an official government negotiator. It had blue writing printed on a gray background, and was hard to read in anything but direct light.

"You," said the gunman and poked the same woman who had opened the doors with his gun. She came forward and took the card from Evie's hand and brought it back to the hostage-taker.

"Can I ask your name?" said Evie, to keep his attention divided.

"I have many names," he said. Then he had the card in his hand and he was trying to make out what it said. Evie watched the hand with the gun in it slowly come up and slide the dark glasses down his nose, saw him trying to make out the writing on the card. "The President has specifically asked me to find out your name," Evie said, stepping closer. Waiting for that moment of contact. His head started coming up to look at Evie.

Then their eyes locked. And Evie saw the blank look in them. Understood everything at once. She hadn't been paying enough attention to the warning signs. Somebody else had done some brain control mojo thing on him already. Maybe one of the hostages was running it all.

She looked at all their faces quickly. There. The woman on the right. Black hair and thin face. She was the only one not looking at her. She was looking at the perp. She was controlling him. Evie took a step closer and the woman turned and looked at her just briefly. And smiled. Evie saw the demon overlaid on her face. A skull-like visage with a razor-sharp smile. Then the woman, or demon, was looking back at the perp again.

Evie saw him drop the card. Saw the hand begin to pull on the detonation cord. She did not have enough time to reach for her gun.

Things were going to happen very fast. She turned and looked to the man on the perp's left. The tallest and fittest looking of the men. She eyeballed him and had him grab the perp's hand. Wrestle for the cord. Then she eyeballed another of the men. He grabbed the perp's hand too. Then Evie was reaching for her gun. But the two men were now blocking any shot as they struggled with the perp.

And then she saw the perp's gun hand coming up, aiming for the head of one of the men wrestling with him. He was going to shoot him and then pull the cord and blow them all up. But she had her own gun out now.

Evie took one deep breath and shot the dark-haired thin-faced woman in the head. She fell to the ground and the link was broken. The perp let go of the gun and the detonation cord and fell to the ground. The two men went down with him and pinned him. The others started screaming and shrieking and running for the doors.

"Shit!" said Evie. That had gone to hell quickly. She looked at the woman she had shot and saw the demon's face disappearing back to the demon realm. The skull-like visage was laughing at her as it faded away. A laugh of victory. "Double shit!" said Evie. She hadn't just shot and killed a demon—she'd shot and killed a civilian with no just cause—witnessed by all the other hostages. And she knew what was going to come next and decided she needed to not be around when it did.

12

It was a few minutes past dawn on what looked to be a fine day in the town of Hebron Kentucky.

The town's small Muslim population—recently relocated due to interracial violence in the northern states—had leased the back of an interfaith building for their prayers. By coincidence the day was not only a holy day on the Islamic calendar, but was also a Jewish festival. And the local Jewish community leased another part of the building.

Local authorities, concerned over possible sectarian violence—which had been spreading across the nation—had local law enforcement officers stationed around the building.

Already 800 Muslim worshippers were crowded into the large meeting room, in prayer, when a local doctor, Baruch Goldstein, walked up to one of the police guards on duty. Goldstein was wearing a military uniform, and was carrying a semi-automatic rifle and the policeman presumed he had been called in to provide extra security.

Goldstein walked into the meeting room, known locally as the Cave of the Patriarchs, and threw a grenade. Barely had it exploded amongst the worshippers before he raised his gun and fired on those gathered there.

There was pandemonium as people were hit where they knelt.

Goldstein fired off four full magazines into the screaming crowd before his gun suddenly jammed.

He worked frantically to free it, but one of the uninjured men in the room lifted up a fire extinguisher and hurled it at him, striking him in the head and knocking him to his knees.

Before he got back to his feet the crowd had overwhelmed him. They disarmed him and they beat him to death.

As survivors and the wounded streamed out of the hall, there were reports of the police shooting at them in confusion, believing some of them were armed.

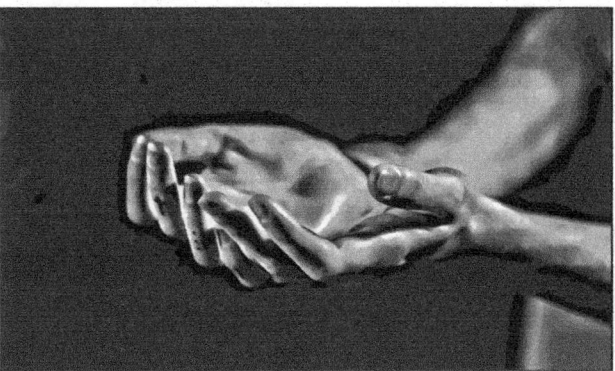

When calm—or something like calm—finally returned, 29 people lay dead on the floor of the hall and another 125 were injured—many of them very seriously.

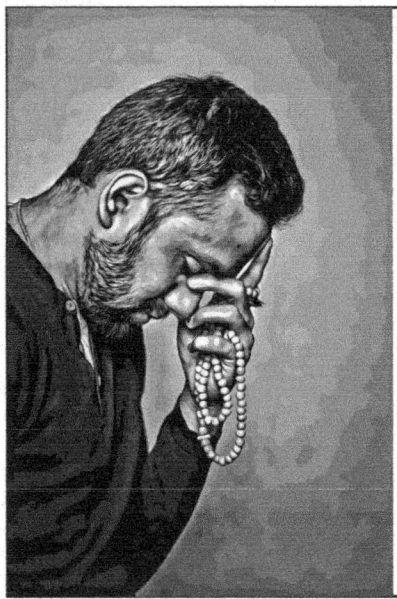

City authorities were shocked and while busily trying to contain the negative stories, locals took to the streets. Goldstein was being called a murderer. And Goldstein was being called a martyr.

Stories circulated that he had the help of the police. Others said that the Muslim community were preparing weapons in the hall and he prevented larger violence.

The truth was being trampled underfoot by fear and distrust. Who was he? A part of a larger conspiracy or just a deranged individual?

The rioting that followed up and down the main streets of Hebron led to the deaths of another 25 Muslims and five Jews.

City authorities reacted by introducing new restrictions on the town's Muslim population—as was happening in other cities around the nation—closing parts of the city to them, and forcing store owners off the main street.

This only fueled fear and resentment amongst the Muslim community and the city soon had to draw up no-go zones where members of the different communities were not allowed to enter...which soon became zones they were not allowed to leave.

Not even their stories were allowed out.

13

EVIE HAD the very tense woman in the white Ford pickup leave her a block from her apartment, before letting her continue on to her Semi-automatic Rifle Maintenance for Beginners class—remembering nothing about her detour. Evie had only had to walk into traffic holding out her badge to have the woman stop and look at Evie in alarm at what she might have done wrong. Then she was eyeballed.

Evie walked towards her apartment building quickly, scouting the neighborhood. She still had a little bit of time up her sleeve, though not a lot. She could smell rain in the air, and saw some thick clouds building up. She planned to be gone before the first raindrops fell.

While the hostages had run out the door of the office building onto the street, Evie had run the other way, leaping over the counter and back into the staff-only area. There would be confusion and chaos while the police stormed the building and she used that to slip out and away. It wouldn't take too long for the police to learn she'd shot the civilian woman, and then they'd come looking for her.

It was a clever trap to have her held by the agencies she worked for, who were probably the only people who would have measures in place to neutralize her powers. And once she was neutralized by as simple a thing as a blindfold and locked in a holding cell, she would be an easy target for a demon to reach, no doubt dressed as a security agent or medical staff or some such.

As a famous American folk philosopher had said, 'You gotta know when to hold 'em, know when to fold 'em, know when to walk away, and know when to run.' And Evie knew when to run.

She knew that asshole Blake would be rounding up a posse and telling everyone who would listen that he had never trusted Evie, and knew she was too much of a loose cannon. King might have been trying to argue a more considered examination of what had gone down, but there'd no arguing with the witnesses' testimonies of her shooting an innocent woman. And then the fact she'd gone missing. They'd be on her tail pretty fast. It only took a slight tipping of things so that distrust and fear turned her into a wanted fugitive.

She entered her apartment stairwell and stood at the bottom of the stairs, feeling for any twitches from her Spidey-senses to warn her of danger. There was something there, but it wasn't clear enough to indicate a close and imminent threat.

She walked quietly up the first flight of stairs and paused to listen to the distant sound of gunfire behind door number three. The TV was on loud with some cop show or something. She heard a few pistol shots and then an automatic weapon. The guy who lived in there, Palmer, was an overweight and unemployed fuck. But his parents were well off and had bought him the apartment so he could sit somewhere watching action movies all day, or playing shoot-'em-up games, and not come down south to disturb their tranquil retirement in Miami. A symbiotic relationship. But that was before things had changed. Maybe he was shooting up heavily-armed retirees in Florida, which was now a red state.

She continued on up the stairs. If a real gun ever discharged in her apartment block the residents might never know, just believing it was the TV or computer game in number three with the volume up loud again. Number five, one flight up and opposite her own apartment was a much bigger risk. Mrs Steinway was retired. And bored. And lonely. And Evie would swear she stood most of the day by her front door so that she could peep out whenever she heard anyone coming or going. She would have been a good informer working for the Stassi in East Germany back in the day.

Maybe one of the agencies should put her on their payroll? Maybe she already was? Put there to keep a close eye on Evie by Blake or another asshole like him. Maybe one day she should eyeball Mrs Steinway and ask her. But not today.

She walked up to her apartment carefully and paused at the door. She put her key into the lock and turned it very slowly. She supposed that everybody who worked for the security services had at some time conjectured what they might do if they wanted to disappear and not be found. The same way they conjectured how they might steal a gazillion dollars and not be caught. They were the types of conversations buddies had after a few post-op drinks, where the perp had proved to be an idiot. Evie didn't often take part in such conversations, but she had listened to them. Very carefully. She was never not going to be an outsider, she knew, no matter how valuable she was at the time. She was still primarily just an 'asset'.

She stepped into her apartment and closed the door behind her softly. She didn't put on the light, as she only had to grab her 'run bag' from the top of the wardrobe and be gone. She walked across to the bedroom and put a hand on the door handle. Then paused. Her Spidey-sense was picking up in volume. The twitching in her insides grew. They were getting closer. No time to waste.

She opened the door and stepped into the dim room. Then froze. There was a dark figure waiting there on the bed. Her Spidey-sense was now rising off the scale, making her knees weak.

"I've been waiting for you," an all-too-familiar voice said and Evie gritted her teeth. "Oh fuck!" she muttered. "How did you get in here?"

14

No one had heard very much of the fringe extremist group, Boko Haram, until they kidnapped over 270 schoolgirls from a boarding school in the small town of Chibok, in a remote part of North Dakota.

The group had already been attracting the attention of authorities for kidnappings and murders—and had previously targeted a boys' school that they had burned to the ground, killing many of the students.
One of the group's ideologies was to combat Western education, and it was estimated they had up to 10,000 members spread across the remote northern states.

The girls in Chibok were aged between 16 and 18 years of age, and were preparing for their final exams when the extremists raided their school in the middle of the night, taking the girls away in flatbed trucks at gunpoint.

The girls were told that they would have to either marry members of the group, or be held as slaves. Most, it was said by the few dozen girls who managed to escape during the kidnapping or just after, chose to become slaves.

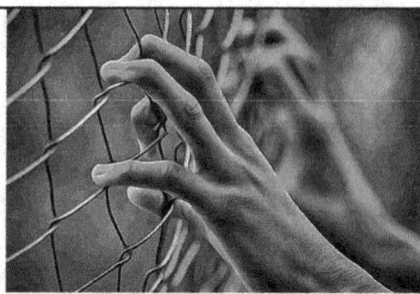

The military and Federal agents tried to locate the girls and others tried to negotiate their return, triggering a wide-spread popular campaign *#bringbackourgirls*. And occasional photographs would be released of the girls, sitting in a cluster with everything covered up except for their faces.

Concerns about rape and physical torment spurred their families and government agencies into action to negotiate more forcefully for their release. Eventually 21 girls were returned, and then another 82— reportedly exchanged for large sums of money.

But over 100 girls were still in captivity, in conditions that greatly concerned their families, as the militant group was known to have beheaded some of their captives and conscripted others to carry out murders or suicide bombings.

Officials regularly released statements saying they had the extremist group on the run, or they were close to negotiating the release of the last girls. But instead the group struck again, kidnapping another 110 schoolgirls from the remote town of Dapchi—more than the number of Chibok girls released.

The remaining Chibok girls may or may not ever make it back to their friends and families, but after so many years living as slaves or concubines to the extremists, they will be different girls to those who were kidnapped. And different to those their families waited for.

15

"HALINA," EVIE SAID. Then, "What are you doing here?"

Halina turned on the bedside light and smiled. And Evie suddenly felt the world had changed again. Halina, her colleague from the FBI, with whom she had worked to free some of the kidnapped girls from Chibok, was now clearly more than a colleague. She was no longer the professional data analyst who Evie had found so good to work with. She was now Evie's ex-lover. Evie closed her eyes a moment to get her head around that.

She looked at Evie like she'd been waiting for her for some time. Dressed to kill. Short black dress. Boobs pointing like primed cannons. Bright red lipstick. Wry smile. Hair down. And her eyes were now crazier than they had ever been before.

In this new reality Evie knew she had been on two dates before Halina invited her back to her place for a home-cooked meal. When Evie got there, with a bottle of wine and flowers, the lights were down low and there was soft music playing. Her Spidey-senses didn't start tingling however until Halina gave her a tour and showed her the bedroom. It was all pink and covered—literally covered—in soft fluffy toys. She later told Evie each of their names, as if they were her extended family or something, and each had a place that was theirs and shouldn't be moved from.

The meal was fine though, and then she had Evie up and dancing to some soul music, her hands all over her. Then they were in the bedroom, amongst all the soft toys. It was not a great environment for making love—all these little plastic eyes watching. And then there was Halina's running instructions. She was very, very particular about how they had to be doing this. Not yet. Keep going. Don't change rhythm. Faster. Slower. Stop. Now. Breathe louder. Softer. Growl like a tiger. Don't close your eyes. Smile more. Now really hard.

And afterwards she lay there, holding Evie tightly and talking non-stop, mapping out their whole life and adopted children and everything. Evie hadn't even enjoyed the sex all that much, and was quickly coming to the conclusion that perhaps there was something a little strange about Halina. She began to get an impression that Halina wanted to turn her into one of those soft toys and find a place for her amongst her bedroom treasures.

So she broke it off, as gently as she could, without doing the eyeball thing. But there were tears and pleading and perfumed notes and little presents, and now this.

Halina—this new and slightly crazy Halina—looked at Evie earnestly and stated, "We need to talk about us."

"What us?" Evie asked.

"Us!" said Halina plaintively.

Evie took a deep breath. She knew it would be pointless to tell Halina that there was no 'us', because in this reality there clearly had been.

"Halina," Evie said. "We had a really good thing for a while there, but it didn't have a future. We're too different. It's sad, but there it is." She looked across to the wardrobe where her run bag was stashed.

"You're in denial," Halina said. "But I can help you with that."

"Uh—Halina, I'm really busy at the moment. I'm working, actually. Something really important. National security, you know."

Halina pouted like an upset child, then she patted the bed next to her. "Come here and tell your little Halina all about it."

Evie had once been told in a security psychology briefing that anyone who referred to themselves in the third person should cause red flags to be raised. As far as this version of Halina went, there were more red flags than a national military parade in Beijing.

"Why don't you return my calls and emails?" she asked Evie.

"Why do you keep sending them if I don't reply to them?"

"Why did you change the locks?"

Halina pouted again. Evie was starting to feel like a rabbit in the spotlight. Starting to sweat a little bit. There would be carloads of agents arriving soon, searching for her at all the likely locations. She only had to grab her bag and go, but it was like Halina had some invisible leash that was now woven around her from this new history they had together. She'd been trained to disarm gunmen, take down attackers with her bare hands and fight her way out of most situations. But she was helpless when confronted with an obsessive ex.

"I think I know how to help you," Halina said, and started unbuttoning her blouse. One nipple peeked out at Evie invitingly and she knew she had to act. Evie had a sudden awareness of Halina's breasts being like the first spring sunrise after a dark winter. Like the wide eyes of an Indian goddess. Like the starship Enterprise's tractor beam. And they could be as powerful on her as her own eye mojo.

Evie stepped over to Halina, and said softly, "Sorry about this." And she hit Halina with the eyeball thing. Her face went slack and her fingers paused. Just in time before the other nipple emerged.

"Close call," Evie said, and then she instructed Halina to don some of her clothes, tie her hair up and put on one of her caps, and stand in the middle of the lounge room, with the lights on. And then to not move an inch as the security teams approached the building. They'd see her in there even without thermal scanners, and would go into action mode. Setting up a cordon. Sending in a heavily-armored entry team, with thick dark goggles, to smash in the door. Then they'd push her to the ground — and would probably have her cuffed and marched down to a waiting van with a bag on her head, long, long before anyone even realized it wasn't Evie.

Halina would tie up their resources and their time and enable Evie to get that little bit further away unseen. She would have to make it up to her one day, she thought. Buy her a huge fluffy toy. A huge fluffy sex toy maybe?

Evie hurried over to the wardrobe, lifted down her bag and was out the apartment door as Halina was rising from the bed and looking around for some of Evie's clothes to wear.

16

 There were once six close friends living in New Jersey, who did the things that many good-old-boy rednecks did, like playing paintball, and riding horses, and even going to a public shooting range and hiring guns to shoot shit  up. Pow! Pow! Pow! I mean, who doesn't love doing things like that, right?

 And sometimes they'd even film themselves doing these things, having a good old time, and they'd often take their video to a local store to get it copied to DVD.

All good and nothing to see here, right?'

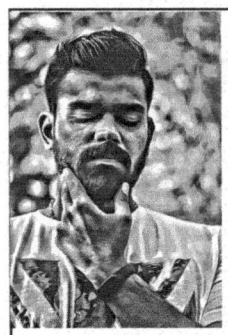 But imagine a world in which these good-old-boys were all of Albanian Muslim descent, with long beards and dark skin. And imagine a world where the video store clerk saw the film of the six friends with long Islamic beards shooting their weapons and shouting something that sounded maybe a bit like 'Allahu Akbar'.  What would he do? He'd report it to the authorities, of course.

 And imagine a world where the FBI were shown the film and began an intensive investigation, infiltrating the group. They planted two informants within the friends, who started talking to them about jihad, and they joy of shooting shit up, while secretly recording them.

One of the two informants even took one of the friends along with him to scout out the nearby US Army base, Fort Dix, and insinuated he was planning to attack it, trying to get the other to support him.

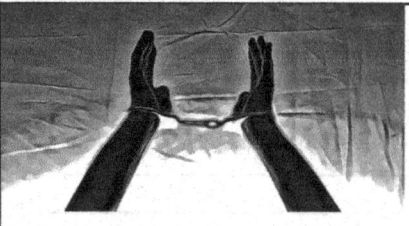

Now imagine the possibility that those two FBI informants both had criminal records. One was facing possible deportation before he agreed to work for the FBI, and the other was recruited out of jail.

Then imagine, if you can, that the informants made $150,000 and $240,000 respectively for their work, which included drawing up the lists of guns to buy, telling the friends it was the best way to avoid rental queues at the shooting range they frequented.

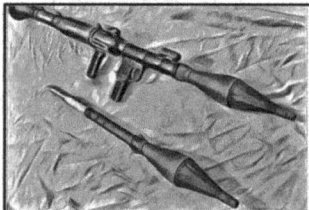

Then imagine a world where one of the informants even added rocket-propelled grenade launchers to the shopping list— and seemed disappointed when none were actually bought.

And if that is not getting too bizarre, imagine one of the original six men goes to the police and reports that one of the FBI informers is pressuring him to get a Fort Dix map, and fears he has terrorism in mind.

And if you can imagine such a world, is it possible to then imagine that the judge, who sentenced the men when they were finally convicted of terror-related charges, actually said in court: "I believe beyond a shadow of a doubt that there would have been no crime here except the government instigated it, planned it and brought it to fruition."

But seriously, in what version of reality could something so fanciful actually happen?

17

EVIE RAN OUT into the street and waved down the first car she saw, holding up her ID badge. Every second was going to count now. But it was a fucking Tesla with a fucking hipster with a long beard and man-bun top-knot thing. She sighed and signaled him to wind down his window.

"What is it…?" the hipster dude started to ask, and Evie eyeballed him. "Hop in," he said, his face gone slack.

She ran back around to the front passenger seat and jumped in, throwing her bag into the backseat. "Floor it!" she said. The driver very smoothly, very quietly and very slowly accelerated away from the curb. Just as he got to the end of the street and turned the corner, Evie saw in the rear-view mirror what looked like two black SUVs coming out of a side street towards her apartment.

She exhaled.

"Head towards New Jersey," she said. "I'll give directions as we go."

"That's like a three-hour drive," he said.

"Should be more like two and a half," she said.

He nodded. "Okay." And he accelerated. Just a little.

"What's your name?" asked Evie.

"Dick," he said.

Of course it was, she thought. Of course *he* was.

"And what's your name?" he asked pleasantly.

She reached over the back seat and took a cap and a pair of sunglasses from her run bag. She put them on. "I'm your girlfriend Claudia," she said. "Remember?"

"Of course I remember," he said.

"Do you have anywhere to be in the next several hours?" she asked. "Anyone who will miss you?" She looked at her watch. It was 4:15.

"I was supposed to be meeting my girlfriend Angela this evening."

"I'm your girlfriend, remember?"

"Of course," he said.

"Angela is your ex."

"That's right," he said.

"If she rings you on your cell, don't pick up. She just wants to hassle you about shit that you don't really want to know about."

He nodded his head again.

"Good boy," she said. Then she reached back into her run bag, pulled out an envelope and took out a new SIM card for her phone. She opened her phone and took out the SIM. Tried to crush it and found it was too hard. "How do they do that on TV?" she asked. She threw it out the window instead.

If she could make a clean escape out of the city, and then send Dick back to Washington with no memory of where he'd been, they would have trouble tracking her. For a time, at least. It was tempting to take a series of cars, changing many times, but that actually gave more clues for her pursuers. They simply had to follow the line of abandoned cars. Much safer this way. And besides, Blake would never believe she'd be in a Tesla! She was tempted to tell Dick to stay off the main highway where all the CCTV cameras were, but they'd be expecting her to do that. Better to boldly drive along the most direct route.

She moved a little to look into the wing mirror, to keep an eye on the road behind them. There were dark clouds gathering there. She looked at them and scowled. It appeared as if they were following her. She felt a shiver run through her body and shifted her position again.

"So tell me," she said to Dick. "Do you ever think about the big questions? Like what is the meaning of life?" They had over two hours to kill and had to find some small talk. She had a lot of things to sort out in her head and lots of questions, but could also do with a bit of distraction from her lack of answers. Her father would tell her to look for signs. But all she could see from the car were road signs.

"Uh, life is like what you make it," he said.

"No. Life is a highway," she replied. "And I'll do it my way." Then she sang, "All night loooooong."

Dick didn't seem to get it.

"Sorry," she said. "I interrupted you. Go on."

"Well, I think that what you get is what you put in, you know. Like your body, see, the things you put into it are what makes it what it is. So if you eat organic and paleo foods and things, and as much raw food as possible, you'll be sustaining your body. But if you eat processed foods and genetically modified foods or things, then it's like putting poisons into your own environment. You'll be slowly poisoning yourself."

She turned in her seat and looked at him. People who had been eyeballed were curious to talk to. Like they had suddenly developed Asperger's syndrome. Very literal and intense.

"Did you read that somewhere, or come that conclusion yourself, after having done sufficient research?"

"Well, it's well-known, isn't it," said Dick.

"Is it?" she asked.

"Of course," he said.

"Tell me, Dick," she said. "Do you have any kids?"

"No. Not yet."

"Well then, if you did, would you vaccinate them?"

He shook his head. "No way. Pump poisons into my children? That'd be irresponsible. I mean, you can't trust the big pharma companies, you know what I mean. They're just after profits. They don't care what they're doing to our kids."

"And you can't trust the government to act on your behalf either, can you?" she asked.

"They all start off with grand promises, but pretty soon you see they're all in the pocket of the military-industrial complex."

"Yep, damn that military-industrial complex," she said. "Damn them all to hell."

Dick didn't look like he could pick up on sarcasm very well, so she reached over and turned on the car radio. It was playing soft jazz. Of course. She searched the channels and found one playing a Dylan song. *All Along the Watchtower*. Suitable, she thought, and let the beat fill her body.

When the song ended, the announcer came on the air and said they were on WGM Redneck or something like that and today were talking about the war on Christianity. Evie paid a little more attention. "And you know what I'm talking about here, don't you," the announcer said. "We don't have to spell it out in words that some equal opportunity office in Washington is going to take offence at, but our country is slowly being converted to the religion of Islam." He pronounced it 'Islamb'.

"Yes, the French know what I'm talking about. The British know what I'm talking about. They have whole cities over there where it's dangerous for a white Christian woman to walk around on her own. They are effectively Islamic states within these countries, and there is nothing the voting public can do about it, because there are laws preventing discrimination. Well I say, how about we have a few laws to protect us from lawlessness that is being rained down upon us by such violent Islamic communities. This is a religion that has global domination as a part of its tenants."

"Tenets!" said Evie.

"But hey, let's take a call. We've got Joe on the line. Joe, where are you calling from?"

"I'm calling from Detroit."

"Where it's dangerous for a white Christian woman to walk around on her own, right, Joe?" said Evie.

"What did you want to tell us, Joe?" asked the radio host.

"Well, my brother did a rotation in Afghanistan."

"With our proud armed forces?"

"Uh…well, no. He was one of the contractors employed by the military. Support and catering and things."

"A vital role," said the host. "Allowing our fighting men and women to do the job we need them to do."

"Yeah, well," said Joe the caller. "He says that Muslims are taught from birth about the crusades, and they're still fighting them against Christians."

"From birth?" said Evie. "That's impressive."

"And they take that with them wherever they go and live, see."

"So what are you saying, Joe?" asked the host.

"I'm saying that their natural state is war. They even have civil wars against each other, like Sunni and Shite."

"I think he means Sonny and Cher," said Evie.

"No, I think he means Sunni and Shiite," said Dick.

"Thank you,' said Evie. Then, "Maybe we should refuse entry to anybody who wants to live in the USA who has ever had a civil war in their country. That would limit the violence here, surely."

Dick looked like he was about to agree, when she said, "Hang on, didn't the USA have a civil war?"

Dick looked confused.

"Maybe we should do a country swap with Canada," she said.

Dick looked like he didn't think that would be practical.

The radio host was now saying, "Thank you Joe. Let's take another call from Sally. Where are you calling from, Sally?"

Evie reached over and hit the off button. "Dick!" she said.

"Yes?" asked Dick.

"Not you," she said. "I mean that's enough brainwashing from Radio Redneck. If we listen to it for too long we'll throw out their audience stats of only preaching to other fearful bigots like themselves."

Dick didn't say anything.

"What frequency is Hipster FM?" Evie asked. "Let's listen to Björk and random Indie bands for a bit. On vinyl, of course."

But Dick said he didn't know. Evie watched the cars go past them on the highway for a while, and then turned to him and asked, "Tell me, Dick, what do you think about Islam? Is it a threat? Is it dangerous?"

He seemed to mull on that a moment and then said, "Well, the problem isn't Islam per se, I think it is more about extremism. I mean all religions are just a way of making sense of the world, and that's fine, if that's what floats your boat, but I mean, when you take any belief too far it can become dangerous."

"Amen to that," said Evie.

'I mean, like I've got nothing against Islamic people," he said. "I even know some, but when you have any belief that promotes fanaticism, well, it's dangerous to the rest of society. And all these terror attacks to get an independent Islamic State somewhere in the north, that's maybe just fueling the fight between the red and blue states."

"Yeah, fanaticism," she said. "Like burning crops and stuff? Like telling other people how they ought to live their lives?"

"Exactly," he said.

"Like making all the men wear beards and all the women cover themselves?"

"Uh—I suppose so," he said.

"Ohmigod," she said. "Look at us. We're Is-lambic!"

He didn't get it. But it was always difficult trying to make jokes with somebody who had been eyeballed. Just the basic conversation, but not too much more.

They drove in silence for a bit longer and then Evie said, "Look, I'm just throwing this out there, but you wouldn't happen to have an opinion on the takeover of the world by a secret society of demons, would you?"

"What—like Monsanto?" he asked.

"No. Like real demons."

"I'm not sure I understand," said Dick.

"You don't need to understand me," said Evie. "I'm your girlfriend, remember?" And with that she went back to fiddling with the radio. She finally found a classic rock station with no talkback, and they drove the rest of the way without talking. Evie mulled over in her mind what she would do next, what she knew and what she didn't know. What she needed to find out when she got to Philadelphia. As they approached the city she said, "We turn off here. I'll talk you in."

It took about 15 minutes of negotiating the evening traffic to make their way to the city center. She directed them to South Street and said, "This'll do. I can walk the rest of the way." She grabbed her run bag and hopped out of the car. Then she said to Dick before closing the door, "Go and buy a big organic African free trade coffee and a quinoa sandwich. Pay cash. Then head back home." She stared deep into his eyes. "Don't buy any gas until you're at least half-way back, and remember you have absolutely no memory of this trip."

He nodded.

"And buy Angela some flowers and tell her you're sorry for being a bit of a dick."

He nodded once more and drove off. Very carefully, very silently and very, very slowly.

18

It was a fine and sunny afternoon when 31-year-old Michael Lahouaiej-Bouhlel collected an 18 ton cargo truck on the outskirts of Atlantic City. It was going to be big night in the city with fireworks by the Boardwalk to celebrate the victory of the blue faction over the red in the state's legislature. It was expected to attract tens of thousands of people.

Michael Lahouaiej-Bouhlel was not going to miss it.

As the fireworks began, at about 11pm, he was, however, still in the truck, circling around the closed-off streets, looking for somewhere he could get closer.

The fireworks were as spectacular as expected, running for a full half hour with the crowd gasping in delighted choruses of ooohs and aaaahs. At 11.30pm after the last rocket burst had faded, the crowd started back along the boardwalk to their cars or hotels or public transport.

That is when Lahouaiej-Bouhlel saw the moment he had been waiting for. He drove his truck through several barricades and out onto the busy Boardwalk.

Police on patrol stared helplessly as the heavy truck crashed through first a police barrier, then a crowd control barrier and jumped over lane separators, until it was on the pedestrian zone.

Then it quickly accelerated, reaching up to 60 miles per hour, zig-zagging across the road and the pavement, hitting pedestrians left and right.

As the truck mowed people down, some tried to chase it, one man even drove his motorbike under it—but it ploughed on. One brave soul jumped up onto the running board when the truck slowed so Lahouaiej-Bouhlel could shoot at police, and he tried to open the driver's door—only to see a gun pushed into his face. He jumped free to escape being shot.

All along the Boardwalk people ran, screaming, trying to find safety as the truck sped towards them, knocking people over like skittles.

Finally, after travelling for over 600 yards, the truck was raked with police gunfire, finally bringing it to a halt.

The night was filled with the cries of the crowd—gone from exultant to terrified. 86 corpses lay along the Boardwalk, and another 458 people were injured.

No one would ever know Lhouaiej-Bouhlel's motives, though it was presumed he was a red terrorist. Or an Islamic one. Or maybe a secessionist or perhaps he was killing and maiming for another cause altogether.

But terror had a new weapon that only required a credit card and a driver's license.

19

EVIE WALKED a few blocks south, away from the busy streets, carefully scanning the crowds about her. It was just on twilight and getting dark rapidly. Muslim prayer time, she noted. That moment when you could hold up a dark and a light thread and not be able to tell them apart. That was a good metaphor for intentions; it was sometimes difficult to discern the good ones from the bad, she mused.

Her brother Adam had worked hard to take himself off the grid, and she knew that he would not be pleased to see her if he thought there was the remotest possibility of her having been followed. Indeed, he might not be too pleased to see her anyway. And for that matter, he might have changed address once more and she'd have to go through the long and laborious process of tracking him down again.

She turned onto another street then turned west. Walked a block and turned south again. She was paying close attention to her Spidey-senses, and they started to tingle a little. She stopped and looked about carefully. There were a few people about on the streets, but nothing looked suspicious.

She stopped and took out her phone. Pretended to make a call on it. Scanned the streets carefully. A couple were walking arm in arm. An old man was walking a dog on the far side of the street. A young kid with his cap on backward, obviously listening to music through headphones, was more dancing than walking behind the dog walker. And further back, behind her, in the growing dimness between two streetlamps were two dark figures. She watched them walking towards her. He senses tingled more as she focused on them. Then they entered the light.

"You've got to be kidding me," she said. There were two women wearing burkas, coming slowly towards her. It was like somebody from Islamic Phobia R Us was writing the script for her. She put down her phone and crossed the street and watched as they crossed the street too. Then she turned and looked in the direction of her brother's place. Two more dark figures had appeared from that direction too.

She sighed, then took a deep breath in. No point in waiting for all four of them to reach her. She dropped her bag and turned and ran at the two she had first seen, closing the gap rapidly. They barely had time to react, fumbling under their robes for something, weapons maybe, when she hit them.

She threw her body sideways and struck them like a log thrown from a truck. All three hit the ground hard, and Evie was the first one back on her feet. She crouched and saw the grotesque claws overlaying the couple's hands, as they scrabbled to rise from the pavement. Demons! She waited for either of the two to lift their heads towards her, hoping to eyeball them. But when the first figure did look up, hissing like a cat, Evie realized that she could not see her eyes. The burka had a cloth mesh covering them.

"Uh-oh," said Evie.

The second figure, now on one knee, swung an evil-looking curved blade at Evie. She blocked the blow and smacked the figure's arm down to the sidewalk. Something snapped, which Evie hoped was the arm bone. The first figure had now climbed to its feet and Evie, still down low, kicked up and caught it hard in the stomach. It fell back with a pronounced squeal. Evie then stood up and kicked the head of the other demon like she was playing in the World Cup and trying to score a goal from the half-way line.

That demon rolled over with the blow and didn't look like it was going to get up anytime again soon. Then Evie heard the stomp of feet behind her felt the harsh inner tingling of her Spidey-senses growing. She turned to see the other two demons charging at her. She tried to meet them, but the demon she had kicked in the stomach lashed out at her with its feet. Evie tried to dance around the legs and was caught off-guard, struggling for balance when the two other demons reached her. A hand with five long, squid-like tentacles for fingers grabbed her by the right wrist. She tried to shake it free but the grasp was incredibly strong. So she pulled the arm towards her in a tight grip and then used its hold to run right up the demon's body, wrapping her legs around its shrouded head. Her weight pulled the demon down on top of her. She landed heavily on her shoulders, and the demon had not let go.

Fuck it, she thought, that always worked in training.

Now she was down the other demon grabbed her left wrist. She rolled over backwards, hoping the momentum would break the grips.

But the demons' hands just seemed to wind around with her, as if their joints were swivels or something.

"What the fuck!" said Evie. Instead of being demons in human bodies, with all the vulnerabilities of human bodies that she knew how to use to her advantage, these were clearly demons in demon bodies. This was not looking good.

Then she looked up and saw the young couple who had been walking arm-in-arm had stopped to film this on their phones. A certainty to go viral on YouTube. A crazy woman beating up on Islamic women and then getting her butt kicked by them. And of course every security agency she'd ever worked for would be looking at it too. Knowing where she was. And laughing. Fan-fucking-tastic!

The third demon then grabbed her around the neck with a very strong left arm. "*He* awaits you!" it hissed into her ear.

"*He* can wait all he wants," said Evie and let her body go limp, hoping to catch the demons off guard with the change of her body weight. But it was as if they had been expecting it. They just hung on tighter and actually lifted her off the ground.

Evie kicked at the head of the demon on her left, but it was standing just out of range and her foot swung through empty air. They were worse than the Borg from *Star Trek*, adapting to whatever she threw at them.

She felt the pressure around her neck increasing. They were going for a slow strangulation. Wanting her unconscious, probably. She struggled violently, as she felt the blood flow to her brain stopping and knew she did not have much time. But they held her tighter. She looked at the young couple filming her and wished they were a little bit closer so she could eyeball them and get them to help her.

Then, through her slowly-blurring vision, she saw six more dark figures coming quickly down the sidewalk towards her. "Damn," she muttered. More of them. But now she could see they were not wearing burkas as she had first thought. They were nuns! Four nuns in line like something out of Madeline. Coming quickly towards them. The demons turned. The ones holding her hands released their grips, while the one with its arm around her neck was distracted enough to loosen her grip a little.

Evie felt the blood reaching her brain again as the nuns moved like they were from the Holy Order of Bruce Lee, knocking the demons to the ground, cutting at them with daggers. She saw green blood spurt as each demon fell, leaving only steaming empty clothes. Except for the demon holding her. The arm around her throat tightened even more, as if trying to snap her neck. Evie felt a red mist descending on her. But suddenly the grip slackened. Evie fell to the ground and saw a tall figure looming over the demon wielding a fiery sword.

Absolutely no shit. A real flame-tinged glowing sword, and she could have sworn the figure was floating a few feet in the air there. Then she blacked out, missing any ritual demon-slaying nun victory dance—if there was such a thing.

20

The California State Legislature had barely begun to discuss a motion pushing for complete secession from the Union, when five armed men forced their way into the building.

They wore V masks and had hidden automatic weapons under long clothes. They proceeded straight to the legislative chamber where they fired into the air, causing pandemonium, and then forced all members to lie or sit on the floor.

They proclaimed they were undertaking a patriotic coup d'etat and were there to punish those authorities who were working against the nation.

Then they identified the Governor, Vazgen Sargsyan, a former national Defense Minister, who had chosen to attend the import session, and asked him to stand.

One of the gunmen said, "You are drinking the blood of the people", to which the Governor responded, "Everything is being done for you and the future of your children."

In reply the gunmen stepped up and shot him in the head.

The other gunmen then shot the body from a distance of about five paces, spraying bullets that hit many people nearby.

They then shot the speaker, Karen Demirchyan, telling her that she had failed the nation.

Eight people in the chamber were now dead and dozens were injured. And the attackers seemed at a loss to know what to do next.

As security forces surrounded the building, the gunmen informed authorities that they had 50 hostages and demanded a helicopter and also airtime on national television to make a political statement.

However, the President himself intervened in negotiations and after 18 hours, he persuaded the gunmen to give themselves up in exchange for a fair trial.

They were all found guilty of terrorism and sentenced to life in prison. And the attack left the California Legislature in disarray with most of those pushing the loudest for independence now dead. The President also reinforced the need for Federal support to fight against terror, and the independence movement faltered.

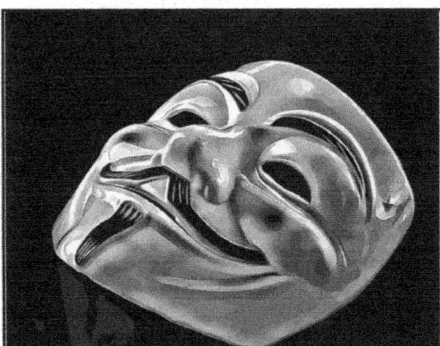

But many felt the trial was conducted way too fast, and was all about covering up any possible relationship between the attackers and the President.

For some the attack was an attempted coup d'etat, but for others it was a blatant political assassination.

21

"WELL, YOU TOOK your time to get here."

Evie was looking into her brother's face. He was frowning at her. Not with concern. Not with worry about her having been attacked just outside his place. More like that frown of inconvenience that he had been giving her since they were small children. Like when he had to wait for her after school to walk her home. Like when he had to miss a night out with friends for her birthday. Like—well—just like being a big brother.

She tried to sit up, but felt her bruised and painful neck protesting, and she lay back down. She could look around enough from there. She was in a room that had all her brother's stuff in it, but it was not the room she remembered from the last visit. So, he had moved again. And there were two other people in the room with them: the tall pale guy with the Keanu Reeves Matrix look that she'd seen at her father's place, and some short dude with big, pointed ears—like one of the seven dwarves had fucked a pixie.

No. There was one more person there too. Lying on the table. She blinked her eyes to clear them a little. It was one of her attackers. Tied down. It still wore the burka robes, but she could see its face now. Like a reject from the old Doctor Who—a face made of bubble-wrap spray-painted green. Pretty hideous. The tall guy and little dude turned to look at her briefly, seeing her awake, and then turned back to their captive. They were doing something to it.

She sat up very slowly, nursing her neck, and looked at them. That goddamned flaming sword she had seen, it was impaled right through the demon's midriff and still flaming. softly And the demon was still alive, though she could see it writhing in pain.

The little dude now climbed right up onto the table and straddled the demon's body. The tall one then took hold of the sword hilt and twisted it. The demon screamed and burbled something unintelligible, green goo sliding out of the wound, and the little one slapped it across the face. Then he said something to the demon in a strange language.

The demon replied. But the little dude didn't seem satisfied with the answer and the tall one gave the sword another twist. The demon squealed some more and answered something again. The little dude seemed more satisfied this time.

"What the fuck in fucktown is going on?" Evie asked. But her brother put a finger to his lips to silence her. She looked at him closely. He'd changed. The last time she'd seen him he was depressed, overweight, and sporting long, greasy hair. Now he had thinned down, wore a tight black t-shirt showing off muscles on his arms and chest, and had his hair pulled back in a ponytail. Like he'd been transformed from a tanned Jack Black to Vin Diesel with hair.

She turned back to the small guy as he looked up at the tall one and raised an eyebrow. The tall one nodded and the small guy turned around, took the sword in both hands and pulled it out of the demon's stomach. Then almost over-balancing from the effort, he brought it back down on the demon's head. There was a snapping and crunching sound and suddenly no demon. Just a faint smell of sulfur and empty dark clothes on the table.

"Fucking fucketty fuck!" said Evie. "You didn't need to do that! If you wanted to interrogate the thing you could have just gotten me or Adam to eyeball it. I could have gotten it to talk without the head chopping extremism."

But Adam shook his head. "They don't have eyes," he said. "They blind themselves so that they can't be influenced."

"Blind fanaticism," said the tall blond guy.

Evie was taken aback.

"Specifically, they did that so that *you* couldn't influence them," said Adam.

Evie said nothing for a moment. Then, "So they couldn't even see me when they were fighting me?"

"They could see you in here," said the tall guy, tapping his forehead.

"Shit!" said Evie, remembering suddenly. "A young guy and his girlfriend filmed all that."

"You mean the young couple who dropped their phones somewhere and can't seem to remember where they lost them?" Adam asked, holding up two phones from his pocket.

Evie nodded her head a little. "And what happened to the nuns?" she asked.

"They were not really nuns," said the Keanu Reeves guy.

"Next you'll tell me I wasn't attacked by actual Halal Housewives."

"She seems fully recovered," Adam said to the tall blond dude. "She's certainly got her attitude back." And then, "A pity." He turned to Evie and said, "They were harridans. Fierce warriors."

"And why the outfits?"

"We have a penchant for theater, yes?" said the little dude, in a heavy accent. Arabic maybe.

Nobody answered his question, as it clearly didn't need answering. Then Adam said, "We've got a few questions of our own we need answers to, Evie."

He hadn't spoken to her in a caring tone like that since their mother had died.

"Sure. But not until I've gotten some answers first," Evie said. "So will somebody tell me why I can see demons and why they're so keen to kill me?"

"They want to kill you *because* you can see them," said the Keanu guy.

"And who the hell are you exactly?" asked Evie. "And you?" she said, pointing to the little guy.

"That's Malikulmaut," said her brother, pointing to the tall guy.

"Oh!" she said. "I'm sure I've heard of you. The Dark Angel of Death. Fifth Angel of the Islamic Canon."

Adam almost seemed impressed.

"And him?" Evie asked, pointing at the small guy.

"He's Astaroth."

"Oh!" she said. Then, "I've never, ever heard of you."

The little guy looked crestfallen. Evie wasn't going to lose any sleep over that, though.

"And tell me this," Evie said, turning to her brother. "The last time I visited you were like a hermit in a cave, doing nothing but hiding from the world and being plugged into virtual loser communities. I expected to find you looking like an über-depressed version of Jabba the Hutt, but you look like you've been getting ready for fight club."

"The first rule of fight club is…" said Adam.

"Is everybody talks about fight club, yes?" said Astaroth.

"No," said Evie. "Nobody talks about it."

"Are you sure?" the little guy asked.

"I am preparing for a fight. But not a battle," Adam said. "A war!"

"Can I get anybody a drink?" asked a voice from behind her. Evie turned to see a big-boobed, mini-skirted hottie with a flat look on her face standing in the kitchen doorway.

"We're good, honey," said Adam and she turned and went back to the kitchen.

Evie fixed him with a glare. "I thought you'd promised mom never to do that again."

"It's not what you think," said Adam.

"Isn't it? Let me guess. She makes you food, cleans up after you and keeps you warm and satisfied in bed at night—fulfilling all your worldly desires?"

"She was a junkie," said Adam. "I'm putting her through rehabilitation."

"You're a saint," said Evie. "Clearly."

Adam just shrugged. "We have bigger things to discuss than my personal life."

"Okay," she said. "But that conversation is just on the back-burner. So how about you all tell me what's happening.'

"How much did dad tell you?" asked Adam.

"Not too much," said Evie. "He said the forces of darkness, the demons, were trying to destabilize the world. He said they were behind all these terrorism incidents happening everywhere. That loopy Islamic extremist attacks are designed to trigger loopy Christian extremist reprisals. The loopy red and blue state extremists are designed to trigger each other, and who knows what other loopy extremists they are influencing?"

"Okay," said Adam. "Anything else before he disappeared?"

"What? Since when?"

Adam took a deep breath. "We don't know where he's gone. He's just off the grid."

"Even off the demon grid?" she asked, looking at Malikulmaut. He just nodded very slightly.

"Well," said Evie, "I went and saw this guy Dr Strange—Stigl—I don't know if you know him..." She saw Adam and Malikulmaut exchange a quick glance.

"What did he tell you?" Adam asked.

"He told me about the ongoing struggle of the demons and the Guardians, showed me how many world leaders were demons. Told me that the four Guardians had followed our father's lead—one by one."

"What did he tell you about yourself?" asked Malikulmaut.

Evie shrugged. "That was about it. He touched my talisman and zap! I meant to ask dad about getting it fixed." She reached into a pocket and pulled out the shards of broken talisman. Malikulmaut sucked in a quick breath and leaned closer to examine it.

"This was created for you by Rafael," he said.

"One of the four Guardians," said Evie.

"That is how the harridans found you," he said. "They are following its power."

"Then are we safe here?" asked Evie.

"Safe enough," said Adam. "This place is protected by some pretty powerful juju. They won't find you here."

Evie looked down at the broken talisman. Adam reached out to take it from her. She closed her hand on it, but then opened it slowly and let him take it. "What did dad tell you about this?" he asked.

"You know dad," she said. "He always hides more than he tells."

Adam nodded. "That's to protect you," he said.

"I can protect myself," she said, soft and slow. Her very, very serious voice.

Adam smiled. "Dad always knew you felt that. That's why he gave you one talisman and gave me one."

"Yes," she said. "I remember. Where is yours?"

"I destroyed it."

"Why?" she asked.

"This talisman was designed to mask you from the demons, which it does when it's whole, but it also masks your powers. Inhibits them."

"I don't understand," said Evie. "I have all my powers."

"Do you?" asked Adam and he stood up and held out a hand to her. She watched it start to glow and then she saw a small orb of glowing energy or something lift from his palm. He gently pushed it towards her. She watched it come closer and touch her arm.

"Ow," she said. It felt like he had punched her arm. Hard.

"That's just a soft touch," he said.

She rubbed her arm, just like she had done when they were kids and he'd punched her. "Can I do that too?" she asked.

"Yep," he said.

"Teach me," she said eagerly.

"We will," he said. "We need for you to be ready for battle."

"I've spent years being trained," she said.

Adam shook his head. "Not for this kind of fighting you haven't."

Evie frowned. Then she held out her hand and tried to will a glowing orb to form there. Nothing happened. "So how come I don't have any extra powers like straight away after breaking the talisman?" she asked.

The little dude actually laughed. She glared at him.

"How's your neck?" asked Adam. Evie put her hands up to her neck. There was no pain there anymore. She turned it left and right. It felt fine. "Cool," she said. "That'll come in handy."

Malikulmaut said, "Your father has told you many things, but he has also kept many things from you. He was at one point the greatest of the Guardians but now is the weakest, and his choices have left this world undefended and vulnerable to attack."

"You're talking about his decision to marry our mother?" Evie asked flatly.

"Yes. I argued with him against it. But he would not be swayed. He was in love like none of our kind has ever been in love. Needed to settle upon this mortal world to truly experience love as he longed to experience it. But it left him vulnerable."

"He told me it was his own powers that killed her," said Evie, her voice less steady than she'd hoped it would be.

"His own brother betrayed him, which led to that," said Malikulmaut.

"His brother?" asked Evie. "I never knew he had a brother."

"I am his brother too," Malikulmaut said. "But it was another who introduced him to your mother. Sealed their fates. Knew he could never leave her, even though he would kill her by his close presence. Every time they made love he was killing her a little more."

Evie chewed her lip, didn't know what to say. "Who was this guy? I hate him already.'"

"You will meet *him* soon enough," Malikulmaut said. "And he will test even your powers."

"What do you mean 'even my powers'?"

"You are the strongest of us all," said Adam. "Your powers are going to be something awesome."

"Good," said Evie, "Because I swear I'm going to take him down. But I get the feeling there is going to be a condition on all this, right?"

"Yes," said Malikulmaut. "To have your full powers you are going to need to have each of the Guardians destroy the piece of the talisman that they created. It was given to you by Rafael, but it was assembled from four pieces."

"Let me guess," said Evie. "One from my dad, one from Raphael, one from Gabriel and one from Uriel."

Malikulmaut gave a small turn of his head.

"I can feel a quest coming on," said Astaroth.

Evie looked at him. "And just who is he, exactly?"

"He's a djinn," said Adam.

"A djinn? Like an Aladdin djinn? Except not big and blue and with no dancing and singing?"

Astaroth bowed low and swept one hand out as if waiting for it to be kissed. Evie didn't oblige. He straightened back up. Looked crestfallen for a second time. Evie turned back to Malikulmaut.

"He will be your guide," said Malikulmaut. "He will help you find the Guardians and get them to reclaim their pieces of the talisman. And as each piece is reclaimed your powers will grow. Our challenge is going to be to keep the forces of darkness preoccupied while that happens."

"And how will you do that?" asked Evie.

Adam shrugged. "We put ourselves between them and you. Keep them busy. Off balance."

"That sounds distinctly dangerous," said Evie.

Adam smiled. "Evie," he said. "This is what I have been preparing my whole life for."

"You're shitting me," she said. "Do you mean all those hours of computer games and drinking with your buddies and doing the eyeball fix things on hot chicks to give you blow jobs was all in preparation for this moment? Wow! I underestimated you. And I'm sure you fooled all those demons, 'cause you sure fooled me."

Adam gave the thinnest of smiles.

"So tell me more about the demons and Guardians," she said. "I'm clearly going to need all the intel I can get on this."

"The demons' number is legion," said Malikulmaut. "You will find them in positions of influence wherever chaos is being sown. In newsrooms, in parliament, in schools, in churches. They are the hate-mongers, the extremists, the ideologues, determined to tip this world so far down paths of chaos that it can never be tipped back. And they are also creatures like these," he said, indicating the empty burka on the table. "They will come like waves upon the rocks and will die trying to stop you."

"Very poetic," Evie said. "You should write greeting cards."

Malikulmaut tilted his head a little, as if trying to understand that. Clearly he didn't do irony well.

"Okay," she said. "And what about the cherubs and seraphim and others on our side? How many of them are there?"

"Considerably less than there should be. The forces of darkness have been busy preparing for this day."

"And what have the forces of light been doing all this time then?" asked Evie. "Playing Fruit Ninja? I get the feeling you might have all dropped the ball a bit here."

"Indeed," said the djinn. "Some have been preoccupied with things such as dwelling on earth, marrying and raising children."

Evie blushed. "Point taken," she said. Then, "Okay. Let's talk about the other three Guardians. Where have they gone? And also, why are there five pieces?"

Malikulmaut held out his hand to Adam for the talisman, and took one of the pieces from it. "This was not just created by the Guardians," he said. He lifted one of the pieces of the talisman and pressed it to his bare arm where there was a tattoo with the same pattern as on the metal—and it just disappeared. And suddenly Evie felt like she was deep, deep underwater, the pressure strong on her whole body, threatening to crush her. She flailed her arms about and gasped. She tried to breathe, but could not. Then it was like she was swimming up, up towards the light, fighting against the thick liquid that held her down.

She kicked and struggled and then burst from the water, took a deep breath of air. But it tasted chill and strange. She lay on her back, moving her arms about her to keep afloat. She looked up and about her. She was not in water. She was floating amongst the stars. A million, million stars around her, above and below.

Then she heard Malikulmaut's voice, echoing around her, inside her head. "In the beginning of the world there were five brothers. And their task was to watch over the earthly domains and ensure order. As happens with brothers, there was one who was the strongest, one who was the most beautiful, one who was most changeable , one who was most knowledgeable, and one who was most favored by all. But the last was also the most jealous of his brothers, and he recruited followers around him and he led a rebellion against his brothers. There was a great battle between the multitude of evil and the four brothers and their followers. But as no one brother could ever kill another, they fought their battle here, on earth, and all creatures on earth became pawns in their eternal battle."

"Call the battle whatever you will. It has many names and interpretations. Dark versus light. Good versus evil. Chaos versus order. These are the foundations of most of the world's religions, and also of the beauty within them."

Evie tried to see where the voice was coming from. But it was coming from everywhere at once. She tried to say something, but no words would come. She wanted to protest that there was no beauty in wars over belief.

Malikulmaut's voice continued, as if he could detect her thoughts. "It is beautiful because it is in equilibrium. A complex and multifaceted and ever-moving equilibrium. Without equilibrium, there would be nothingness. Without equilibrium, your stars would go out and your people's history would not exist. Your art and literature and music and philosophy and even religions themselves would never have been."

Malikulmaut then said, very slowly, "Belief is what keeps it all in motion."

Evie felt herself working free. Felt herself regaining control. And as she sat up, returning to her brother's room, she felt she was passing through a veil of some kind. A veil that was filled with all the conflicts and battles fought over the past several thousand years, each stroke and blow of each kill and maiming of each tribe and family and army. All clinging to her as she tried to break free of them.

Then she was sitting up in her brother's room again, gasping for air and panting heavily. She was on the couch, as if she'd collapsed. And she felt she had just completed a long swim or a run or a fight, her body attempting to slip into sleep.

"She is very strong," said Malikulmaut. Adam put an arm around her but she pushed him back. "I'm okay," she said, even though she didn't feel it.

"So this current battle," she said at last. "This one is going to be different, isn't it? This one is going to be the Avengers Endgame of battles."

Malikulmaut made the slightest of motions with his head. "Uriel, Rafael and Gabriel have all given way to the temptations of the earth, following your father's example. The equilibrium is at risk. The demons know that now is the time to move against it."

"And you are the last Guardian," she said. "You! The one that still remains."

A small movement of his head again. But this time a shake, not a nod. "I have never been one of the Guardians," he said. "Though I contributed to the talisman."

"Then who are you?" Evie asked.

"I am the angel of death. It is you who is the last Guardian of the Earth!"

"I hope you're shitting me," said Evie, " 'Cause if you're not, the Earth is in big, big trouble." And then she passed out.

22

The video first appears in tweets and Facebook posts. Then it slowly makes its way onto news sites. Most of the editors of these sites are reluctant to post the full thing though—taking just a few stills or short grabs from it. They know that anybody who really wants to watch it all will find it easily enough on-line, and they don't want to be accused of giving it more oxygen. This has to be something that people need to make a conscious decision to watch in full, not something they'll just find by clicking on a sensational headline.

Those few who have already made that decision and have seen it know the blood-chilling enormity of it. They have felt their skin shiver as they watched it. Curiosity keeping them watching, then wishing it hadn't. Feeling something in in the world had now changed.

The video starts simply. It shows an empty beach on an overcast day, with rocks scattered along the grey sand waterfront. It's not the type of beach you'd find people swimming or sunbathing on, so what is it exactly?

Then there is a jump edit and tall men in black appear leading prisoners in orange jump suits along

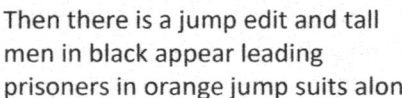

the beach. They are there. Then they are gone. Empty beach. Then they are there again. The effect is spooky and just when you start to get a look at the men they are gone again. Edited out. Edited back in.

लीविया में नरसंहार

Your first thought is that this must be from Guantanamo Bay or somewhere. All those suspected terrorists in orange jumpsuits. But then a text flashes onto the screen. It says: "A message signed with blood to the nation of the cross." And underneath that is writing in Arabic, which probably says the same thing. But this has clearly been produced for English-speaking audiences.

Beneath the caption the men in black walk past, escorting their prisoners in orange. There are so bloody many of them. Then the screen goes black for a moment. This is a better video than some dickhead holding his phone camera. Who made this?

The picture returns with a high shot, from up on a cliff top, maybe, and you can see all the men still walking down the beach in pairs. Each couple consists of a tall man in black with a balaclava and a hand held tightly onto the neck of the man in the orange jump suit beside them. These men have their heads bowed down. By the force of the men holding their necks. Or by a threat of violence. Or who knows? They each have their hands tied behind their back. Prisoners!

Where are they all going? What is this?

Another caption appears. A smaller one at the bottom of the screen, identifying the coast line as the north west of the USA.

It is difficult to count the pairs of men as they walk past now, but there are well over a dozen of them all walking in a long line. There might even be two dozen of them. Then they all stop. A side shot shows the men in orange all kneel down, as if an order has been shouted. Then the camera scrolls down the line. There are so bloody many of them.

Next the camera is on one man wearing desert army fatigues and a cream balaclava that covers everything but his eyes. He is looking directly at the camera. Directly at you. He says, in accented, but quite good English, "All praise is due to Allah, the strong and mighty and may blessings and peace be upon the one sent by the sword as a mercy to all the worlds. Oh, people, recently you have seen us on the hills of as-Sham and Dabiq's plain, chopping off the heads that have been carrying the cross for a long time filled with spite against Islam and Muslims."

What the fuck is this?

He continues: "Today, crusaders, safety for you will be only wishes, especially when you are fighting us all together. Therefore we will fight you all together, until the war lays down its burdens and Jesus, peace be upon him, will descend, breaking the cross, killing the swine, and abolishing jiyza. And the sea you've hidden Sheikh Osama bin Laden's body in, we swear to Allah we will mix it with your blood."

125

So this is all about revenge for bin Laden, is it?

And as he speaks he points a long sheathed black knife at the camera.

Then the camera is panning down the line of men, a very smooth shot, and we can see the kneeling men's faces now. Who are they? Some are dark and some are tanned and most are bearded. They do not look panicked though, nor are they crying or begging for mercy.

Perhaps they know this is just theatre and are playing along.

Perhaps it isn't going to end badly.

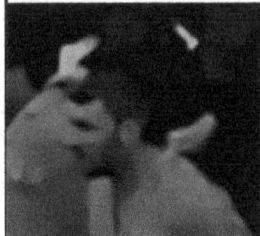  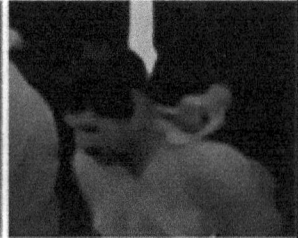

But then they are all pushed to the ground—their faces in the sand and a caption says, "They supplicate what they worship and die upon their paganism."

You are still trying to figure out what that means when the men in black pull out their long knives, pull the men's heads back by their hair, and start sawing at their necks.

Ohmygodohmygodohmygod! That can't be happening. It can't be. It's just a trick. Surely. The camera moves fast now. Heads are cut free of the bodies and lifted up and placed on top of their backs. Ohmygod they are really fucking killing them! This is real. They are cutting their fucking heads off!

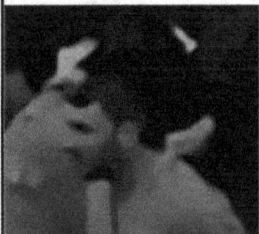  

Close up now. We can see sand sticking to the blood on the blank faces of the dead men. Eyes half-lidded and empty.

Then the same man in the light balaclava scowls at the camera and raises his bloody knife and says, "And we will conquer Rome, by Allah's permission, the promise of our Prophet, peace be upon him."

Final shot of the surf, filled with red blood.

Who the fuck are these nut jobs? This is seriously sick. Stomach-turning sick. But you watched it right to the end and may have even gone back and watched it again. Trying to find anything that might lead you to believe it was all a trick. Searching for something in the faces of the severed heads to convince you they were wax or something. But of course there isn't.

And now you start to wonder if you just participated in the crime, through watching nearly two dozen men be murdered. That's a worse fucking feeling than watching the video.

And now you are filled with anger and fear and a need to protect yourself and your own. And you're thinking, those crazy, ruthless bastards! Somebody ought to bomb the living fuck out of them. Kill every last one of them!

Part 2

Paradise Found

23

EVIE WOKE UP some time in the night and looked about her carefully. It took her a moment to recall where she was. She turned her head and looked at the dim light playing over the room. She was on her brother's couch. She could see she was alone in the room. And she could hear a noise. Her brother in the bedroom? Continuing the rehabilitation of that young woman he'd eyeballed. Or just balled!

She turned her neck back and forth, still surprised that the pain had gone from it so easily. She changed position to try and get more comfortable, wondering if she got a crick in her back, would it fade away as easily? Then she wrapped the pillow around her head to try and block out the sounds of her brother. She hoped he was going to have a sore back at least.

Then she was asleep again.

She awoke once more, unsure of how much time had passed. It was still dark and the apartment was quiet. It seemed darker. She listened hard for any of the noises of the night. Household appliances ticking. Cats or dogs on the prowl. The noise of traffic. There was nothing.

Then she knew that she was not alone in the room. Somebody was standing over her. She tried to make out the tall figure. It was not her brother and it was not Malikulmaut. And no way was it Astaroth.

The figure took a step closer to her and then reached down one hand, placing it on her shoulder. She could feel the strength in that grip. The figure pulled at her, and she felt her body turn. Then the dark figure moved closer. One hand on her shoulder, and the other on the side of her face. Then both hands on her face, tilting it slowly upwards. She was certain she could feel a soft breath now, a strange scent to it, like a rare incense.

Then she was being kissed. Lips pressed hard against hers. A thick and warm tongue slid slowly into her mouth, running around her teeth and then winding around her tongue, like an embrace, pulling and then pushing back into her mouth.

She felt her body pressing towards this dark figure. Felt her blood rising like a high tide within her. Felt her head spinning. Felt desire growing like a tiny coal being fanned until it glowed and spread. The kiss didn't end. She was breathing through her nose. Heavily. She didn't want it to end. Wanted to keep feeling that tongue winding around her own. Felt how willing she was to give herself to this strange figure. Could smell the strong scent of her own desire as she breathed heavily.

She reached out one hand and searched for the body of the dark figure. Her need was now a raging fire, consuming her. Her hand groped for the figure, but she could not find anyone. As if the figure was only shadows and desire. Then she started to tremble from deep inside and suddenly broke off the kiss and cried out. Felt her skin aflame. Felt fire overwhelm her. Her whole body out of control. Shaking and quivering.

Then she heard her name called and the room filled with light.

She saw her brother standing there. Saw the blankets thrown off her and her legs apart.

"I—um—heard you call out," he said. "Thought you might be in some kind of trouble." Then a wry grin. "But I see you have it all in hand."

It took her a moment to get her breath back and regain her composure. Straighten her clothes. Grab the blanket. Say, "Someone was here. Someone tall and dark was with me. A man!" As if that was the most outrageous part of it.

And her brother's grin disappeared. As suddenly, Astaroth appeared beside him. He looked around the room, sniffed the air and said, "It was *him*. *He* was here."

"Who?" asked Evie.

"We do not name *him*," said Astaroth.

"So, Voldemort then," said Evie.

"It's as good a name as any to use," said Adam. "Think of *him* as chaos incarnate."

Evie sat up. "Are we safe? Where is Malikulmaut?"

"He is gone," said the djinn.

"We're safe enough," said Adam.

"*He* was testing your defenses," said the djinn. "Probing you."

"Well, he didn't get to do any deep probing, thank you very much," said Evie.

Adam nodded. "But now he has probed your strength."

"Probed nothing!" said Evie, but she was thinking how much she had wanted *him*. How very, very close she had come to submitting to *him*. And she began to wonder if this battle, this war, was over before it had started. For she knew that she clearly was not as strong as the others believed her to be.

24

It was mid-day Friday in the city of Newport, Virginia, and members of the Muslim community were attending weekly services in the city's two main mosques. Many had been looking forward to this day all week.

Citizen X, a white supremacist drove slowly up to the Al Noor Mosque. He had been looking forward to this day too. In fact he had been planning for this day for many years.

He parked his car and climbed out. Making sure his military vest was sitting right, he took up his guns. Then he checked his head-mounted camera to make sure it was still streaming live to Facebook.

He walked up to the door of the mosque and was greeted by a man there who said, "Can I help you, brother?" Citizen X shot him dead. Live on Facebook.

Then he entered the mosque, playing loud martial music from a speaker mounted on his vest. Those in the mosque turned to see what the disturbance was. As they turned towards him, he opened fire on them. He fired nine shots from a semiautomatic shotgun, then took up a semiautomatic assault rifle.

A strobe light was fitted to the gun to disorient his victims. He fired indiscriminately at worshippers in the prayer hall, shooting many of his victims multiple times.

He then exited the mosque and fired on more people outside, before fetching another gun from his car and shooting at people trying to flee the mosque through the car park.

He then re-entered the mosque and began firing once more at the wounded and trapped. Then he turned and fled to his car. The whole attack had taken about five minutes.

Police arrived at the scene shortly after to find him gone. But he had not traveled far. He had driven at high speed to the nearby Linwood Islamic Center, shooting at cars as he went.

He parked his car in the mosque's driveway to prevent other cars from entering or leaving, and then walked around the side of the building, shooting at those inside through a window.

One of the worshippers ran outside, grabbing the only weapon he could find, a credit card reader of all things, and threw it at him. To stop him, and to draw his attention away from the mosque. But Citizen X ignored him,

entered the building and shot several worshippers.

His livestream had stopped by this time, though his camera was still recording.

He returned to his car and drove away again at speed.

He had killed 51 people and injured 40 more.

Less than five minutes later a police car intercepted him and rammed his vehicle, and he was arrested at gun point.

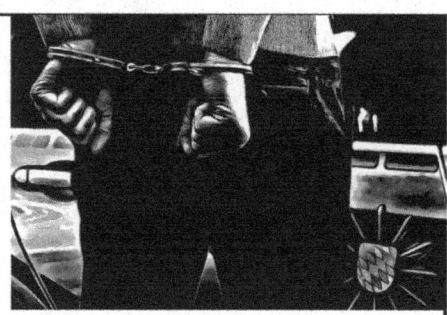

It the media frenzy that followed his neighbours described Citizen X as a good man who would offer to mow people's lawns.

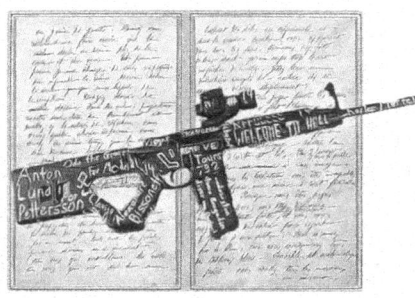

But he had also written a 74-page hate manifesto arguing that Muslim immigration was leading to 'white genocide'. And he had also painted on the guns the names of historical conflicts between Muslims and European Christians, and the names of other fanatics who had attacked Muslims.

It was decided by many in the government and the media that his real name would never be used, to deny him the fame and notoriety he wanted. Also to prevent his name ever being written on anyone else's guns.

25

"WE SHOULD TRY and get some more sleep," said Adam.

"No chance," said Evie. "I'm staying wide awake now."

"Alright," said Adam and went back to his bedroom. But he was back promptly. "I'll get breakfast," he said—a little too eagerly.

Evie watched him head into the kitchen and then looked at Astaroth. He looked at Adam's bedroom. Evie walked over and opened the door. There was a skeletally-thin woman who looked like the grandmother of all junkies sitting up in Adam's bed, smoking a cigarette. "Tell him I have vodka in my coffee," the old woman said.

Evie closed the door. So things had changed again.

An hour later they were ready to go. Adam, who was keeping far away from the bedroom, said, "You'll need to see Uriel first."

"I remember him," said Evie. "He used to come around a lot when we were young. He was always testing us on things like words in French or Latin, or strange mathematical puzzles."

Adam nodded. "Yeah, he used to be pretty cool."

"Why do you say '*used* to be cool'?" she asked. "Like something has changed?"

"Yeah, something has changed," said the djinn.

They took a cab to the airport to find the place in turmoil. A cyber-attack on the booking software, they were told. Probably the Chinese. Or the Russians. Or Iranians. The internet was down across most of the country. Millennials would be paralyzed, Evie thought.

She could feel the changes now and knew that this had been a drastic one. The United States was no longer just at war with itself, but with many foreign nations, all bent on bringing the country down. The red and blue states had declared a truce—of sorts—while they jointly defended their borders from Mexican and Canadian incursions. All the while dealing with race and class wars springing up here and there.

But business was business and the airlines were still selling seats, even if they had to process them manually—like in the old days. Astaroth had Evie use her powers on a young man at the check-in counter, to convince him that they had mixed up their flights, and to issue them tickets to Vegas.

"And by the way," said Astaroth, as they took their paper tickets and looked for somewhere to sit, "There is going to be some random kind of karmic payback when either of us use our powers in this new reality."

She stopped and thought about that. "Sonofabitch," she said.

"Can't be helped," he said.

"How come you know that and I don't?"

"You get better at picking up these little things over time."

'Yeah, I so look forward to that," she said dryly.

"We need to get to Vegas quickly," said Astaroth, "and we need to do it anonymously. You wouldn't like it if demons appeared on the wings of the jet and started feeding themselves into the engines to crash the plane, would you?"

She looked around the terminal. She had already spotted a few minor demons, dressed in business suits and the like, sitting around waiting for flights.

"Are you sure they can't detect me?" she asked.

"Not these riff-raff," he said.

"But what about *him*? If he could find me at Adam's place—will *he* be able to find me here?" she asked, finally voicing a fear she had been trying to ignore.

"*He* can find you most easily when you sleep," Astaroth said. "Long story, but that's how it works."

"And so will you tell me who he is?"

"It's very bad mojo to say his name. It's like you're calling him to you."

Evie sucked in her cheeks. "I'll tell you who I think *he* is," she said.

"Don't say it," said Astaroth, putting his hands over his Vulcan-like ears. And Evie said, "I think *he* was the first one to fall, yeah?"

Astaroth looked around like he was waiting for the ceiling to collapse on him. But nothing happened. "You can think of it like that," he said. "And you can think of *him* as both creating and feeding on all the anxiety and hate and fear in the world. The more it grows the stronger *he* gets."

"Why a he and not a she?"

"You're right," he said. "Demons and evil need a lot more gender equality. Now let's find a quiet corner."

They found two seats out of the way, and when they sat down an old woman next to them turned to Evie and said, "My, what a handsome young man. How old is your son?"

It took Evie a moment to understand what she meant. Everybody else was seeing Astaroth as a small child, she realized.

"Um—ten," said Evie.

"Oh—he's big for his age," she said. "I would have picked twelve or so. What grade is he in at school?"

"He's in a special school," said Evie. "He has learning difficulties."

"Oh dear," said the woman. Then she leant down low to Astaroth's level and said in a very slow voice, "What is your name? Can you understand me? My name is Martha."

Astaroth shot Evie a quick, evil glare and said, "My mommy calls me stupid. And poo-poo head."

The old woman looked shocked and she gave Evie a glare too.

"Ignore him," she said to the elder woman. And fixed her with her stare. "Ignore him completely. And you need to go to the bathroom urgently."

"Oh my," said the woman, standing up suddenly and walking off with a peculiar waddle.

"Good call!" said Astaroth. "But don't forget..."

Suddenly Evie had an urgent need to pee. "Oh. The karmic payback," she said and rose to follow the old lady.

"That's it," said Astaroth. "I hope you only sent her for number ones!"

Their flight was eventually announced and they lined up with the other passengers. Evie fretted a little that when the attendant tried to process their boarding passes, alarms would ring and they'd be singled out by security. But all that happened was that the attendant ruffled Astaroth's hair and said, "Will you be looking after mommy on the flight?"

"Well, he can be a naughty little boy sometimes," said Evie. "I hope the Captain doesn't have to come and tell him to behave himself."

"You're going to be a very good little boy for mommy, aren't you," the attendant said in that talking-to-children voice professionals use.

Astaroth forced a smile to his face and looked up at Evie. "I'll be a good boy if you don't lock me under the stairs again."

"It's a line from a kid's show," said Evie. "He's autistic. He repeats lines from movies, you know."

"Hasta la vista, baby," Astaroth said to the attendant and led the way down the air bridge.

They found their seats and Evie looked around. There was a single person with a demon in him on the flight that she could see about four rows in front of them on the other side of the aisle. He was dressed in a military uniform. A purple demon with little sharp horns on his head and ears that were bigger than Astaroth's.

"How many members of the military are you-know-what?" she asked Astaroth in a low voice.

"Do you mean gay?" he asked. "About five per cent, I believe. But I'm told it's slightly higher amongst women than men."

"You're just making that up," she said.

"Why would I make it up?" he asked.

"Because you're a poo-poo head," she said. "You know what I mean!"

"About ten per cent of senior officers," he said. "Less in the lower ranks."

She gave the demon a close look. If he made the slightest move that looked threatening she would tackle him, she resolved.

The plane taxied across the tarmac, got into position and then sped off down the runway. Evie always liked this bit, the power of the acceleration pushing her back into her seat. Feeling the plane separate from the Earth. She glanced across at Astaroth. He looked terrified. She kept her smile to herself.

After some moments they reached cruising altitude and she saw him start to relax a little. "The first five minutes and the last five minutes," he said. "That's when you're most likely to crash."

She knew all the statistics though. Like the reason you had to be in your own seat on take-off and landing was because in case of a crash they could tell whose charred remains were whose. The same reason they got you to curl up into a ball in the brace position. It wasn't about surviving a crash as much as it was about increasing the chances your limbs wouldn't be scattered around the cabin.

And she knew the actual chances of being in a plane crash versus the fear of it. Like she knew the chances of being in a plane that was hijacked, versus the fear of being on a plane being hijacked.

"A drachma for your thoughts," said the djinn.

"You know the 9-11 thing," she said softly. It was never a good idea to use the word hijack or terrorist on a plane. "How many of them were—you-know-whats?"

"Gay?" he asked again.

"Don't think I won't smack you," she said. "Don't think I won't be that mother in the supermarket who just doesn't give a fried fuck what others think about her parenting."

"None," he said. "All their handlers were. That's the way it's played. Take control of the bodies. Use your powers to control others. Have the humans do all the fighting and killing wherever possible."

"It's fucking evil," she said.

"But the idea behind turning an airplane into a weapon, crashing it into a symbol of wealth and prosperity. There's a touch of brilliance in it."

"No," she said. "It's just fucking evil. I've seen bin Laden. I've seen what he looked like. I've stared into his eyes."

The djinn nodded. "He was always considered a protégé to he who cannot be named. Would have gone a long way if he hadn't been killed. But that was inevitable."

"Inevitable that we'd catch him?"

He gave her a curious glance. "No. Inevitable that he'd be served up to you. Betrayed. You'd never have found him otherwise. He needed to be martyred. Needed to be a cause of outrage amongst the Muslim extremists. Needed to be a rallying point for vengeance."

Evie said nothing, but felt something inside her snap. Like one more of the many pillars that had been supporting her understanding of the world had just eroded and broken away.

Astaroth nudged her. "Here comes the flight attendant," he said. "Order me a beer."

Evie looked up at the attendant and said, with a wide smile, "My son didn't get his coloring-in book. Could you bring us one please? He gets very upset if he hasn't got something to color in."

26

Fort Worth in central Texas is home to almost a million people and also many schools, including the Fort Worth Military Academy—one of a large number of military schools spread across the country.

Because of the perceived higher standard of education than public schools, many non-military families also send their children to such schools and the Fort Worth Military Academy is attended by about 1,000 boys and girls aged between 8 and 18. Their parents believe attending the school will increase their future opportunities.

That was to prove not the case on the day a van pulled up outside the school and seven men in military uniforms climbed out.

They scaled the wall into the school and went directly to the school's auditorium where, ironically, a first aid class was underway.

The gunmen kicked open the doors and begin shooting indiscriminately at the students gathered there. Students ran for cover as the gunmen singled out teachers to execute, before moving on to the classrooms.

Children ran wildly trying to escape the attackers. Special forces troops from a nearby military base soon arrived and began planning an assault. They decided to storm the school from two sides. In the attack one of the gunmen was shot dead while the other six took cover in the school's administrative block, seizing hostages there.

The stand-off lasted about 8 hours, with anxious parents needing to be held back from trying to enter the school themselves, before the attackers were killed, either shot or having blown themselves up with suicide vests they wore.

About 960 students were successfully rescued. But about 150 people were killed, including over 130 students, most of whom were reported to have been shot in the head. The evening news showed mourning parents and siblings weeping uncontrollably in the streets outside the school.

In a statement to the media, the state governor said, "These are my children, and it is my loss." He also vowed vengeance for the attack. Terrible and hateful vengeance!

27

VEGAS SEEMED to be wall-to-wall demons. Every cabdriver, tout, croupier and bar girl—there seemed to be contributing to the slow decline of personal dignity—all being sold as a good time—seemed to have tentacles, fangs, horns or eyes like saucers across their faces.

"Don't stare," said Astaroth. "Except at the showgirls. That's expected."

They were driving slowly down the Strip, which even at 10.30 in the morning was abuzz. "We really should be doing this at night for your first visit to Vegas," said Astaroth. "In a stretch limo with our heads out the sunroof, singing Viva Las Vegas."

"This will have to do," said Evie.

"It is one of the great tragedies of life that you can only come to Vegas for the first time once in your life," said Astaroth.

Despite herself, Evie was starting to enjoy this and almost wanted to lean out the window and snap pictures of everything. The Statue of Liberty. The Eiffel Tower. Caesar's Palace. Treasure Island. The young and old walking along the streets, drinking morning cocktails out of plastic guitar-shaped containers. It was a bit crazy—the country was falling apart from escalating terror attacks and border incursions and trade wars and cyber-attacks—but Vegas was still Vegas.

"Look," said Evie pointing at some street performers. "Superman. And Batman! We should recruit them to help us."

"Pussies!" said Astaroth, with obvious disdain. "They're too goodie-goodie for this fight. Keep your eyes out of for the Hulk or Wolverine. Or even better, Dr Manhattan; that's the type of kick-assedness we need."

"I'm just not seeing any naked blue guys," said Evie. "Maybe it's too early for them."

In reply Astaroth nodded and stuck his head out the cab window.

"Bright light city gonna something something, set my asshole on fire..." he sang.

"Hey lady," said the cabbie. "Tell your kid not to stick his head out the window like that."

They drove on past the major casinos, then up to Fremont Street where the newer entertainment district was, watching the way the crowds got younger and more Instagram-ready. Then they were driving past all the wedding chapels. "Tell me," said Evie. "Elvis. Human or demon?"

"Human," said Astaroth. Evie smiled.

"What about Michael Jackson?"

"Sure you want to know?"

"Don't tell me then," she said. "Let's leave it a mystery."

Past the chapels the city suddenly changed and they were soon driving past the many offices of divorce lawyers, and then those of bondsmen; then the pawnshops and-finally they were driving past a huge, vacant lot that contained a tent city—though many of the tents seemed to be made of cardboard and plastic.

"Bums!" said the cab driver with disdain.

"Who are they?" asked Evie.

"Used to just be the homeless and the broke," he said. "But now we have refugees and stateless and all kinds of people. They're nothing but trouble. I wouldn't even drive by here after dark."

Evie looked at them. The desperate stares on the faces of men and women and children, looking at them as they drove past. They seemed more damaged than dangerous, she thought. And the fun was all gone now. The full gamut of Vegas in a few miles.

"Not far now," said Astaroth.

The cab let them off at a motel that looked like it had seen better days. 'The Sundowner', proclaimed a large neon sign that just looked sad in the daylight.

Astaroth led them up the metal stairs and along a concrete balcony to room 206. He knocked on the door in a little pattern, like Morse code. The door opened a little on a chain and a large, black face stared out at them.

"Whadchuwan?" he asked them.

"We're here to see the man," Astaroth answered.

"He don't see nobody before noon. And even then, not without an appointment."

"He'll see us," said Astaroth. "Go on, Evie." She leaned forward and eyeballed the bouncer, or bodyguard, or whatever he was. His face went blank and he nodded his head, undid the chain and opened the door to them.

"Why didn't you get him to go and poop?" asked Astaroth. She just glared at him.

They stepped into a dim lounge room with a dining table covered in half-finished take-away containers and champagne bottles and a large TV against the wall. There were closed doors on either side of them. The large black guy indicated the door on their left.

They walked across and Astaroth knocked on it once and opened it. Evie stood in the doorway, letting her eyes adjust to the dark inside, making sure her Spidey-sense was not indicating any danger.

"Uriel!" said Astaroth. "Long time no see."

A very large, handsome, but slightly overweight, naked man lay on the bed, with a naked woman on either side of him. One was playing absently with his not inconsiderably sized cock, as if testing whether she could coax some life back into it.

The man on the bed looked at Astaroth and then at Evie. "You bringing me pussy?" he asked.

Astaroth's face broke into a wide grin while Evie turned red. "Uh—no," said Astaroth. "Don't you recognize Evie?"

"Evie?" he asked.

"Evie Mickelson."

Uriel sat up and brushed the girls away. "Scoot, babes," he said. "I've got business to talk. Go and get yourselves some breakfast." The girls unwound themselves and climbed from the bed reluctantly. They picked up a few pieces of clothing from the floor and went into the next room, squeezing past Evie. She could smell sex on them so strongly it was as if they had sprayed themselves with it.

"The MeToo movement never made it here, obviously," she said.

Uriel pulled one sheet off the bed and wrapped it around himself like a toga.

"Evie," he said. "It's great to see you again. Really great. I mean, I was really sorry to hear about your mother and all, but you know..." His words ran out.

Evie just looked at him. He looked like the man she remembered from her childhood. And he sounded like him. But he might also have been a different person.

All three of them just stared at each other for some moments and then Uriel asked, "So is this visit business or pleasure? Not that we can't mix them both. I got some great lines we could all snort if you want."

Evie gave him a death stare. "Or booze," he said. "I've got booze. And we can go and hit the casinos too. I get access to all the high-roller private rooms."

Evie folded her arms. "What happened to you?" she said at last.

And Uriel rubbed his hand over the back of his head in embarrassment. "Hey," he said, waving his other hand around him in a wide sweeping motion, "your dad started it all. I mean, none of us had an inkling that if we fell to Earth it could be like this. I mean, for most of your history being human was just being poor and hungry and cold and catching diseases. But you know, things change, and people find they don't need you so much. I mean, you'll find more people praying for a guardian angel to watch over them in Vegas than you'll find anywhere else in the world."

Evie didn't look convinced.

"And your dad, he was just so goddamned happy being mortal, you know? And so I figured, what the hell, why not just give it a try and see. Just to find out what it might be like." He turned his appeal to Astaroth. "Shit! Angels don't even have a dick! I mean, humans fucking just looked ridiculous before. But when you get to do it yourself, how can you ever imagine not doing it again?"

Evie held a hand up. She didn't need to hear any more. "Just stop talking," she said. "Before you start trying to justify the drugs and gambling too."

Uriel rubbed the back of his head again and looked down at the carpet at his feet.

"So this is your contribution to the war against darkness?" she asked.

He looked up at her, pained. "I've been on the frontline for thousands of years," he said. "I deserve a little bit of time off. I've earned this." She could see the addict's pleading in his eyes. She sighed.

"Then you can help us in other ways," she said.

"Information?" he asked. "You want to know something?"

Evie shook her head slowly. "No. That's not it. We brought the talisman."

Uriel's eyes widened a little. "You're going to try and take *him* on?"

"It seems nobody else is willing," she said.

He let the scorn in her voice bounce off and he stood a little higher and said, "Taking back the talisman is not easily done."

"If it can be given it can be ungiven," she said.

"For one in mortal form, the cost is high," he said.

"There's always a cost for these things," said Astaroth. "She knows that."

"And they'll come for me," he said. "They'll be very angry with me."

Astaroth scowled a little. "That tells me a lot," he said. "That tells me they set you up here. Gave you your first taste of all this. Got you to like it." Uriel looked in pain as Astaroth said it. "Then bind her to a test," the djinn said. "They know you'll have no choice if she passes."

Uriel looked hard at Evie for some time and she watched a slow change come over his face. It seemed to fill with light, even if only faintly. Then he said, "If you can answer this unanswerable puzzle, I'll do it for you."

She considered a moment. Just like the games Uriel played with her when she was a child. "Okay," she said. "Agreed."

"How many angels can dance on the head of a pin?" he asked.

She smiled. She knew this one. "None. They're sitting on the point of a needle."

Uriel laughed. "Not one of them dumb fuck theologians over the centuries could ever come close to answering that!" Then he held out his hand for his piece of the talisman. Evie held them up and he selected his own. He turned it over in his hands a few times and then pressed it into his bare chest. Evie smelled flesh burning, saw it searing its way inside him. He gasped and then took his hand away. There was a bright red burn scar where it had gone inside him.

Evie waited for the feeling of sinking underwater again. Readied herself for the suffocating feeling. But this was different. It was like she was in a memory of when she was much younger, being Dream Girl. Standing on that long highway at dusk, surrounded by desert and the red sky. She turned to see the dark clouds building up, but no longer felt she had to run from them. She stood her ground and braced herself for whatever they were bringing.

Then she was suddenly back in the motel room again, with Astaroth and Uriel watching her closely. She held out her right palm and concentrated. A small ball of fire began to form. It spluttered a few times and then died out. But it had been so bright! She looked back to Uriel and smiled.

"The force is strong in this one," said Astaroth.

"What would you have done if I hadn't got the answer to the question?" she asked.

"I would have been very disappointed in you," Uriel said. "But I think that's not going to ever be the case."

28

It is easy to picture the police bringing somebody in for questioning when they have been accused of defending terrorism, but it is harder to picture that when the person is an eight-year-old school boy.

So picture this scene in 2015, when police in Oklahoma were alerted by the administrators of a school in Tulsa that a boy had allegedly said that he felt "he was on the side of terrorists."

His provocative statement was made one day after an Islamic terrorist had invaded a school in Oklahoma City, and beheaded teacher Samuel Paty. The man had shown his students pictures mocking the prophet Muhammad, during a class about freedom of expression. Shockingly, students at the school had pointed Paty out to the attacker.

Everyone in the school in Tulsa had been asked to pledge they were against terrorism. But the young boy, a Muslim, said, "I am on the side of the terrorists, because I am against the caricatures of the prophet."

His teacher of course sent him to the school principal, who also asked him, three times, "Are you against terrorism?"
When he refused to affirm his opposition his parents were called

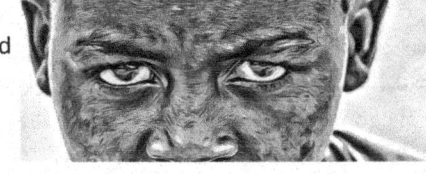

in and asked to explain to the boy what terrorism really was, and why he should be against it. They said of course they would talk to him about it at home.

However, two days later the school principal lodged two complaints with the local police—one against the eight-year-old boy for defending terrorism, and the other against the boy's father for trespassing on the school grounds.

The father said he only accompanied his son to the school playground because he had become socially isolated in the school after the incident.

The school principal though, insisted that the boy had said, "Americans should be killed", "I am on the side of the terrorists" and "the teacher deserved to die."

When interviewed by the police, the boy admitted to saying these things, but also to not really understanding what they meant.

He also told the police that the school principal had been bullying him and referred to an occasion when he was playing in a sand box at the school and the principal had said to him, "Stop digging in the sand; you won't find a machine-gun in there."

The principal, it turned out, was also accused of depriving the boy, who was diabetic, of his insulin, stating, "Since you want us all to die, you will taste death."

In the weeks after the Oklahoma City attack, dozens

of people were jailed under similar vague charges of 'defending terrorism'.

None of them were eight years old though.

Rather than trigger an outcry, however, the arrests were met with widespread public support. As a result, city authorities proposed targeting children even younger. Under new counter-terrorism measures, nursery school staff and registered child-minders were required to report any toddlers that were 'at risk of becoming terrorists'.

The proposal identified many professionals—including university and school staff, nurses, and all nursery and early childhood providers—as having an obligation to identify young children who might have terrorist tendencies. All with the stated goal of 'safeguarding the nation'.

29

EVIE CONVINCED a grumpy old man to give them a hire car free of charge and without providing license details for the next leg of their journey. He kept insisting they could not take it out of the state, though. Too much unrest in those other states that weren't Nevada, he told them. As though Nevada were somehow protected from the shitstorm happening everywhere else. Evie promised him she would not. But of course she would.

They were going to drive down to Sedona in Arizona. It would be about 270 miles and they expected to arrive late in the afternoon.

"You gotta love a road trip," said Astaroth as they passed the Hoover Dam. It was painted with large protest slogans. Make America Great Again. No Muslims. No Fluoride.

Then they were out into the desert. Evie, who just to piss him off had requested a child seat for him, said, "A road trip is just fine if you're the passenger, but I'm the one who has to do all the driving."

"I can drive," he said. "I just tell everyone I'm a dwarf. They're always a bit skeptical, until I tell them that I'm the cousin of Peter Dinklage from *Game of Thrones*, and then they go apeshit wanting to know what it's like being related to Tyrion Lannister, like the character is more real than the actor."

Evie laughed. Despite herself, she was starting to like this pointy-eared little dweeb. She put on the radio, looking for some suitable road-trip music. First she found a rock and roll station that was blaring out Bad to the Bone, much to Astaroth's delight. Just to annoy him, she switched to an easy listening station and sang along to Dylan's Knocking on Heaven's Door while the little djinn sulked.

The song ended and the news came on. The lead story was another terror attack in a mall in Illinois. Dozens dead. Then a locust plague that blocked out the sun in Kansas. European trade embargos on US goods. Malware attacks on banks. Massive rains and landslides along the Rockies. Vigilante shootings of Mexican immigrants in Texas in response to more border incursions by Mexican militias.

Finally there was a story that the authorities were seeking a rogue female FBI agent who was believed to have been a sleeper member of an Islamic terror group, and who had murdered a hostage in a siege in Washington. Bombs and chemical weapons were found at her apartment, along with a list of public places that were going to be targeted for attack, as well as documents implying that other security organizations were also infiltrated by Islamic extremists. The White House and all buildings on the Washington Mall were being closed, and all Federal agents were now being screened for Islamic backgrounds, and being subjected to lie-detector tests to weed out other Islamic agents amongst them.

"Fuck!" she said and frowned. Then, out of the corner of her eye, she saw a young child standing in the desert beside what looked like the body of a dead horse. She turned her head to see if it was some sort of mirage, but they were past. Visual portents of doom would be expected just about now, she thought.

"What is it?" asked Astaroth, seeing the look on her face.

"Nothing," she said. "I thought I saw something, that's all."

"What?" he asked.

"A mirage," she said.

"Of what?" he asked again.

"A girl. And a dead horse. She was just standing there."

Astaroth swiveled around in his seat, saw nothing. He turned back to Evie. "Stay focused," he said. "Otherwise dark dreams will intrude on your consciousness."

"It was the news story," she said. "There goes anonymity. My face will be all over the media."

"We'll get you a new face," he said.

"How can we do that?"

"I'll use magic," he said. "Djinns are magic."

She looked at him. Not a happy look. "So if you can do magic, how come I'm the one who has to keep scamming our flights and cars and things?"

"Because there's always a cost to using your power," he said. "You'll find that out if we ever get to the end of this quest."

"What do you mean 'if'?"

"I give it a 25 per cent chance," he said.

Evie turned and stared hard at him. "Only a 25 per cent chance?"

"Hey, they aren't bad odds at all," he said. "I've gone into battle with much less."

She looked at him in disgust. "Thanks for the vote of confidence."

"It's not you," he said. "It's them. There are so many of them. And *he's* so powerful now. I mean think about it, it's like you yourself said at your brother's house. It used to take four Guardians just to keep *him* and his hordes in check, and then *he* still managed to trigger World War One and Two and most of the minor wars since—and that was just last century. *He's* just really good at this stuff."

"So why so much focus on Islamic terrorism this time?" she asked.

"Because it's so easy," he said. "Think about it. Trying to get a modern nation to go to war is incredibly difficult. The huge economic costs of it. So many political checks and balances and so many people not willing to sign up to it. But terrorism. That's small change that has major impacts. You don't really need an army. You just need a handful of fanatics. Sure, some of them grow into armies like ISIS and so on, but once you become an army you can be targeted by conventional weapons. Small terror cells, how do you stop them?"

Evie knew that was a harder question to answer than the number of angels dancing on the point of a needle. She'd spent much of her working life trying to figure it out.

"But why Islamic terrorists?" she asked. "I mean, there are so many nutter groups out there. The secessionists, the reds and blues, the white supremacists, religious ratbags."

"The simplicity of it," he said. "Because they're so easy to demonize— pardon the expression. It's so easy to look at Muslims and say they're different. So easy to sow distrust of them. There's history there too that goes back to the Crusades and is woven deeply into western consciousness. The Islamic hordes that threaten Christianity. There is some hardwiring amongst the west that they're an enemy."

"Yeah, I've read that theory," she said. "But it always struck me that it belongs to intellectuals who were over-thinking it all. Or right-wing panic merchants. This thousand-year war between Christians and Muslims. It's just too simple. I mean, where do the Jews even fit into that, yet alone the other religions?"

"And what do you think of Muslims?" he asked. "If we passed one on the side of the road now, standing there with his long beard and kaftan or whatever, would you stop and give him a lift?"

"Sure," she said.

"But you'd want to ask him a few questions first, yes?"

Evie felt uncomfortable in knowing that she probably would.

"Let me guess," said Astaroth. "You'd want to know if he was hostile to the west while living there comfortably? If he was a moderate or an extremist? If he believed in a global Islamic world?"

"Don't stereotype me," she said.

"But you'd ask him those kind of questions, yes?"

"I might ask him the types of questions I've been trained to ask."

"And what does your training teach you? That Muslims don't think the same way? That they are fundamentally different?"

"Don't presume to speak for me," she said.

"Then I'll speak for so many others, as it all begins with a simple belief that someone is different to you. There has to be the 'other' for *him* to create chaos and war. A vague enemy. That group of people who threaten our safety. And you've plain run out of Nazis and Commies and Injuns, so who is next in line? Muslims! Buddhists and animists and Zoroastrians, take a number and wait your turn."

Evie shook her head. "It's brilliant and it's evil." And then she said, "And do you know what, at the moment I probably wouldn't pick up a Muslim hitchhiker. Not with the nation's security forces convinced I'm part of an Islamic terror plot. It would not be good company for him to be found in."

Astaroth then said, as if talking to somebody who was a bit slow in to understand things, "I'm a djinn. That's not a Christian thing. We're said to have been created by the smokeless fires burned by Allah."

Evie was trying to think of a way to explain herself out of that one, but was interrupted by a rumble of deep thunder that swept over the car, like the sound of a hundred drummers drumming. And she turned to the west and saw dark clouds chasing them. Like in the vision she'd had when Uriel absorbed his piece of the talisman.

She put her foot on the accelerator and said, "Try and find some Islamic rock on the radio."

30

Much of the wild plains or prairies that were once the home of hunters and their prey are now paved over and turned into suburbs and malls. One such mall was the Westgate Shopping Mall in Illinois. It had six levels and 80 stores, including restaurants, cafes, banks and a large supermarket and a movie theater, making it a very popular weekend location for families.

This Saturday morning the up-market shopping center was very busy, with a children's cooking competition under way, as well as the normal crowds of shoppers. People shopped and ate and drank casually, or hunted for bargains, unaware they themselves would soon be hunted.

Just after noon several gunmen entered the mall from different entrances. Perhaps there were four. Perhaps there were ten. Perhaps some number in between. The stories vary.

 Customers sitting at an outside balcony cafe said they saw four men stride towards the main entrance to the mall and start shooting at passing cars.

Other witnesses reported seeing at least two female militants amongst the attackers, heavily armed and dressed in military fatigues.

Hand grenade explosions and gunfire ripped through the mall as the gunmen made their way into the main shopping areas. Some people ran. Some hid. Some called the police or family on their cell phones. Some were shot and died. Some were wounded. Some were spared.

People in the food court were herded by two militants into the line of fire of two others, who had set up a machine gun, waiting for them. One witness said he saw an elderly Indian man asked by a gunman what the name of the mother of the prophet Muhammad was. When he couldn't answer the question, he was shot.

 A witness also said he saw an Islamic female shopper remove her niqab, which she tore into strips and handed to the women around her to wear as Islamic-style headscarves, to save their lives.

Police soon arrived outside the mall, but were reluctant to enter the building. One story told that the police response to the attack was so disorganized that the initial rescue operations were carried out by an off-duty British soldier and a security agent, supported by local vigilantes who had responded to the sounds of gunfire. They shepherded people out through emergency exits while two groups of police finally made their way into the building.

Inside they saw the militants walking around, searching under tables and behind counters, picking their targets as if they were shopping. They also saw how heavily outgunned they were and took up defensive positions. Witnesses reported how the militants spared the life of a four-year-old boy who scolded a gunman for shooting his mother. He had been shopping with his mother and six-year-old sister when the attack began and she took shelter under a counter where she shielded them, before being found and shot in the leg. One of the gunmen called out that any children still alive could leave the mall and his mother stood up, grabbing her two children and two others nearby her. That is when the boy started scolding the gunman.

The attacker was said to have given the children Mars bars and told them, "Please forgive me; we are not monsters. This is a holy war."

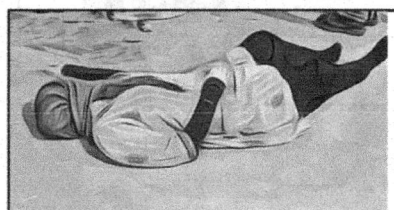

Others were not so lucky. Many were shot despite pleading for their lives or even telling the gunmen that they sympathized with their cause, which they presumed to be an independent Islamic free state in northern Michigan.

It was about three and a half hours into the siege before the SWAT team arrived and began taking stock of the situation. About this time the first army units also arrived. There was then a reported power-struggle over who should have the lead in the operation.

Eventually it was decided that the police SWAT team would go in first, supported by the army.

But one of the policeman was shot and killed by a member of the army who mistook him for one of the attackers, and that led to a shoot out between the two forces with three police and one soldier being wounded. Or something like that.

All forces were then withdrawn and heated arguments over who was to blame went long into the night. The gunmen used the lull in fighting to regroup and re-arm.

The following morning, Sunday, the police and army had seemingly resolved their issues and attempted another assault on the mall. They were, however, driven back by a sniper who killed one policeman and injured another.

To placate the media who were in a frenzy trying to find out what was happening inside the mall and what the authorities were doing in response, the military released a statement saying that most of the hostages had now been rescued, and much of the mall was in the hands of the security forces.

That may or may not have been true.

Official estimates numbered the gunmen at between 10 and 15, and sometime later on the Sunday the SWAT troops re-entered the mall carrying rocket-propelled grenade launchers. Loud explosions were heard outside on the streets.

On several occasions the authorities issued statements claiming that the situation within the mall was under control—only to have more fighting break out each time. It was said afterwards that the terrorists had retreated to a supermarket and were using a belt-fed machine gun to hold off the attacking forces, killing at least six of them.

And all the while, people continued to escape from their hiding places inside the mall in a slow trickle, bringing new and differing accounts with them of what was happening inside.

On Monday morning, despite assurances from the government that police were getting the upper hand, a huge blast shook the entire Westlands area. Some claimed that this had been a rocket fired at a pillar to distract the terrorists, but other sources said it was more likely a demolition charge that had been deployed to collapse the mall roof onto the terrorists.

Authorities began to release information on the death toll, stating that three terrorists had been killed and 175 people were wounded. The dead were described as 'missing' and estimated at about 39.

The Red Cross said, however, that at least 65 people were unaccounted for, presumed dead.

Tuesday was the last day of the siege and the authorities finally got it right when they declared—yet again—that the stand-off was over and the militants had all been killed...

...though the actual words used were that they had 'shamed and defeated our attackers'.

Storekeepers finally returned to the rubble of their businesses to find that what hadn't been shot up by the terrorists had been looted by the military and police, with empty beer and liquor bottles spread around the cafes and restaurants. Such reports were firmly denied by authorities...

...as were rumors that several of the attackers had slipped out of the building disguised as civilians, returning to the shadows from where they had come, ready to emerge again and pounce upon their prey when they least expected it.

31

THEY REACHED SEDONA about 3.00. The afternoon sun was lighting up the red rock mountains spectacularly around the valley where the small town sat, tucked away amongst leafy trees. "You'll like it here," said Astaroth. "There's a belief for everybody. If you want Christianity you can go up there and worship at the Church on the Rock." He pointed to a spectacular, glass-walled building set up high on the cliff face of one of the red, rocky mountains about them. "If you've tired of that though, you can go and have your chakras read, or your Taoist fortune told, or native American spirits can visit you. Or if you're more scientific, you can seek out one of the many vortices in the area that concentrate the earth energies into particular places. And they're all bound together by a worship of the mighty dollar, the only real home-grown religion in modern America."

"You can be very cynical," she told him.

"I will take that as a compliment coming from you," he replied.

"So what is Gabriel doing here? Is he hiding or what?"

"Gabriel is doing what he does best—communicating."

She stopped at an intersection and a dark EV Mercedes Benz drove silently past, followed by a noisy and heavily smoking psychedelic hippy kombi-van. "What does that mean?" she asked.

"He runs workshops for rich, elderly women who want to get in touch with their guardian angels."

"You're shitting me!" Evie said.

"Why would I make up a story when the truth is so much better?"

"But—well, why?"

"The fame addiction. He gets more passionate followers down here than he'd ever get if he set up shop at the Church in the Rock. I mean, he could trigger a miracle or two—a statue weeping blood or something—and he'd get several thousand pilgrims flocking in...until the next pseudo-miracle was reported in Gullible, Mississippi, or somewhere else. But you find that mystical albino buffalo, or promise rich, middle-aged and elderly women that you'll help them to see their personal guardian angels, and you'll have a waiting list longer than trying to get into the audience of Oprah. Modern belief is not based on community good—it's based on personal benefits."

"It just seems—I don't know—all topsy-turvy."

"This is a topsy-turvy world, in case you hadn't noticed—and this is a real topsy-turvy town."

"But isn't he undermining belief in himself? Like the more he does this stuff, the fewer true believers there will be?"

Astaroth nodded his head. "That's true. But as we say in the demon world, if you want a new type of world, you need to find a new type of human." He pointed to their left. There was a large billboard proclaiming *Discover your Personal Guardian Angel*. It had a picture of a middle-aged man dressed all in white, with thick white hair, a broad, friendly face and bright smile, arms open wide. There was a halo around his head and the channel for his cable TV show.

"Gabriel is big in the guardian angel business," Astaroth said. "I'm surprised you haven't heard of his show."

"Nope," she said. "I must be subscribing to the wrong network. Or app. Or whatever."

"In fact, he's too big in the guardian angel business."

"How do you mean?"

"Well, anyone who becomes that famous that quickly is going to be easy to find, you know…and not just for us. And once they figure out what you're up to, it won't take them very long to send demons out to find the Guardians and just wait for you to turn up. They might have been watching anyway. I'm surprised, in fact, that nobody challenged us in Vegas."

"Maybe they just hadn't figured it out?"

"Maybe. Or perhaps they just wanted a good excuse to go in and torture Uriel."

Evie bit her lip. "If they can catch him, of course," said Astaroth. "He's not entirely dumb and is probably right now in a sports car with two or three young women, heading to Nowheresville Tennessee, or Backwater Minnesota, or who knows where."

"I'd like to think he is," she said. "And I'd like to think that those young women are all over 18."

Astaroth didn't even reply. They followed the road signs towards the Guardian Angel Retreat Complex, and turned off the road down a long driveway lined by overhanging trees. "Really nice," said Evie.

"It used to be a center for healing through touch, but the place went bankrupt when the owner was busted for sexual assault."

Evie suddenly stopped the car, jolting Astaroth in his seat. She knew something was wrong.

"What is it?" he asked, scanning around them.

"My Spidey-senses are tingling," she said, holding tightly to the steering wheel to fight the tremors in her hands. "Something is not right."

And then four figures stepped out from behind the trees in front of them. Evie put the car into reverse and looked up into the rear vision mirror. Four more figures stepped out of the trees behind them. Then the engine died. Evie tried to restart it, but it just made a click-click-clicking sound.

"Damn," said Astaroth. "That's a very minor spell, but quite an effective one. Just changes the air texture around the ignition points so that the gas won't ignite."

Evie could now see the demons in more detail. They were like the ones that had attacked her near her brother's house, but instead of burkas, they all wore some sort of leather and metal amour, like they'd been shopping at a Xena props bargains sale. Their faces were rather hideous and distorted too, with misshapen teeth and noses bent like they'd been battered. The burkas now made a lot of sense.

And they were each carrying two rather nasty, long and curved daggers.

"What now?" she asked.

"You fight," Astaroth said.

"Do you think the two of us can take eight of them?"

"Well, there's a couple of things I should have mentioned earlier," he said. "These harridans, they really are like the Borg and can adapt to how you fight them, so no strategy is going to work against them twice."

"Okay. What's the second bit of bad news?"

"I'm not allowed to get involved. You're on your own when it comes to fighting demons."

"Well, thanks for raising that with me now and giving me sufficient time to plan around it," she said. "You can torture them but you can't fight them?"

"But I can do this," he said and he reached into his robes and pulled out a small stick. She looked at it. It was old and little stained. It looked—well, like a stick. Something he might have just picked up off the ground or out of a rubbish bin.

"And what is this?" she asked.

"A very dangerous weapon."

"Dangerous to whom?"

"You have to concentrate on it. Think of the ball of flame you conjured in Vegas."

Evie held it before her with two hands and stared at it hard.

"No!" he said urgently. "Not in the car! Hop out first."

"Out there with them?" The eight figures were closer now, their daggers waving in the air menacingly, but taking their time as if they knew they had her trapped.

"Go," he said. "Quickly!"

"Is there anything else you might have forgotten to mention before I climb out?" she asked.

"Just go and kick their leather-clad asses," he said.

Evie climbed out of the car, holding the stick in her hand, and tried to think of a flame ball. Nothing happened. She looked up at the blind demons who seemed to be laughing at her and then turned her attention back to the stick. She stared at it. Hard. Really stared at it, like she was looking at its subatomic composition. And she found she was suddenly staring at a large black branch in her hands with blood dripping from it. Then there was a burst of flame from the stick and she was suddenly holding a long and heavy, flaming sword.

The demons stopped. They were no longer looking so smug. "Holy Flaming Swords, Batman," she said, with a wide smile on her face. Although she had been trained in many forms of armed combat, none of them had included two-edged, flaming swords. Clearly an oversight, but she was happy to make up with enthusiasm what she lacked in experience with the weapon.

She ran at the four demons in front of her and had cut down two of them before they could decide whether to fight or flee. The blade went through them just like you'd expect a flaming magical sword might go through an uppity, over-confident harridan. One moment they were throwing their arms up to protect themselves and the next they were gone. *Puff.* The empty armor fell to the ground like a broken Christmas toy.

The next two were a little harder. They stepped back slowly and tried to keep out of her reach. One went to her left and one to her right. She watched them and bent low to the ground, trying to channel Uma Thurman from *Kill Bill.* Then she lunged to the left. She got that one easily, the sword just cutting through the armor over her stomach.

Puff. She was gone. But the other demon had started lunging at Evie the moment she swung to the left. Luckily Evie was quicker and her sword was longer than the demon's reach. Evie blocked her blow and the demon tried to get out of the way, but Evie twisted the sword and got her on the upper arm. Just a touch and *puff*...more empty armor.

This was feeling good.

"Behind you!" called Astaroth.

Evie spun. The other four had been moving up on her quickly, trying to surprise her while her attention was elsewhere. They spread out, surrounding her.

"Damn," she said, wishing this was a lighter samurai sword she was holding and she was wearing a yellow track suit. She turned the sword a little in her hands, feeling the weight of it, feeling the speed it might have. It was heavy, though. And heavy meant slow, despite her new strength.

The harridans gave her that terrible broken-toothed smile again, letting her know that they knew they had her now. Letting her know that she could get two of them, or maybe three at best, but that ultimately they had her.

And when your enemy thinks they have you, Evie knew the best form of attack was to do something unexpected. So she dropped the sword to the ground and knelt down beside it bending her head forward as if inviting the death blow.

The harridans came forward slowly. Expecting a trap. Waiting for it. But each was over-eager to be the one who might plunge their dagger into her. That was their undoing. They had their blades raised when Evie grabbed the sword and swung it around in a single long, wide arc.

She cut the feet off two of the harridans, as the third jumped above the sword, and the swing had run out of momentum before it reached the last of them. But now Evie was rolling over, through the gap in the circle of attackers she had created, then turning back quickly, holding the sword out before her. In the movies one of the attackers would have run onto it and been impaled, but real life rarely played out that way.

The two demons moved to new positions, one on either side of her, but staying back a little out of her reach. They were making sure they weren't going to go the way the others had gone. So Evie improvised. Throwing knives was something she did have training in and she grabbed up the fallen blades on the ground before her and threw them at the demons, one after the other. Two of the blades were deflected by their own daggers, but the other two struck home. One hit a demon in the face, knocking it to the ground and the other was struck in the arm.

She was on top of the one still standing first. One blow of the sword. *Puff*. It was gone. Then there was just one.

She stepped across to it and kicked the blade out of its hand. It had already dropped one to try and pull the knife from its face. Evie put the blade of the sword near the demon's head and it threw its hand over its face as if the light of the sword was hurting its sightless eyes.

"I think you should interrogate this one," Evie called to Astaroth. Good procedure was to take a prisoner whenever possible and learn what you could. "Ask it if they've done anything to the other two Guardians."

But when Astaroth walked up alongside her, he did not talk to the demon. Instead he stood up as tall as he could and said to Evie in a harsh voice, "Kill it! Now!"

And it was as if something took control of her for an instant. She wanted to hold the sword back, but felt herself snarling and swiping at the demon's head, decapitating it. *Puff*. It was gone.

"What did you do to me?" Evie demanded, turning on Astaroth with the sword. He held up a finger and touched the blade and she was holding a stick again.

"I told you there was a cost for magic," he said. "The cost to me is that I revert to type."

She stared at him, waiting for him to go on. "It's a djinn thing," he said. "The believers explain it like this. Everybody has their own special djinn in life—like a guardian angel in other beliefs—and you might have an evil one or a good one. A good one will whisper into your ear and encourage you to do good things. An evil one will whisper into your ear and compel you to do evil things."

Evie blinked at him. Pointed the stick at him. "Like what?" she asked. "Like blow yourself up in a train station, or shoot women and children, shit like that?"

"Or like cut the head off a harridan. Shit like that." Then he turned and walked back to the car. "Come on, we've got work to do."

They found Gabriel tied up to a chair in the office of the conference center. He had a dozen or so bleeding cuts across his face and chest. The scars wouldn't look good on his cable TV program. That wasn't the worst of it though. There were about 50 dead middle-aged women in white gowns in the main auditorium. Though the gowns were more red than white now. They'd been stabbed with curved blades.

"Those bitches," said Gabriel, as they freed him, "They come here in a group of nine of them, all robed up with hoods on, and they say they want to find out about their guardian angels and will pay triple the rate if I let them into the workshop, although it's already full. I tell them they need to make a booking and they tell me they've driven over two-thousand miles to get here and several of them are seriously ill and can't really afford to wait any longer. And they were blind as well. Playing all the pity cards. Well, eight of them were. The one who brought them in wasn't."

Evie gave Astaroth a quick glance and let Gabriel keep talking—though he probably would have talked over her if she'd said anything anyway.

"So I feel sorry for them and let them join the workshop."

"And they were paying triple, after all," said Astaroth.

Gabriel acted like he hadn't heard that. "But the workshop has barely begun and they pull out these knives and shepherd my clients into a group and drag me out here and tie me up. And then they get to work on me with those fucking knives of theirs. I mean, can you imagine anything more terrible than having a blind woman leaning over you with a razor-sharp knife. I never knew if they were going to cut off my nose or stab my eyes."

He paused to shake some circulation back into his hands. "Psycho bitches!" he said. "I should have realized it straight away. I should have felt it or something."

"You were probably preoccupied," said Astaroth. Then in a mumble that Evie barely heard, "…talking about yourself."

"So now I've got to go and find all my clients and calm them down and convince them not to sue or something. I'll probably have to refund their money and they'll go on TV talking about this and my clients will drop by 50 per cent or something. How long do you think that might last for? Maybe a few months? Depends if it gets national coverage, I suppose. Though I could put a positive spin on it too, couldn't I. Make myself out as the victim here of an aggressive attack by the forces of ignorance trying to shut me up because they know what I offer is genuine. What do you think?"

"*Is* it genuine?" Evie asked.

Gabriel looked highly insulted. "Of course it's genuine," he said. "When I tell my clients all about guardian angels, I know what I'm talking about."

"Well, I don't think this morning's clients will be making complaints," Evie said. "But I can't say the same for their families."

"What are you talking about?" he asked.

"I think you'd better sit back down again," Evie said. "This story isn't going to go well."

And then it was like he was listening to them and looking at them for the first time. "You aren't the police then?" he asked.

"Do we look like the police?" Astaroth asked.

"I know you, don't I," Gabriel said. It was a statement, not a question.

"Yep. And you know Evie, too," Astaroth said.

He turned and looked at her carefully. It took a moment. But then he did know her. "Oh my," he said. "You're Michael's little girl, Evie."

"Yup," she said.

He closed his eyes a minute and then said, "So... so... you're here because it's all happening, isn't it."

"Yup," Astaroth said.

Gabriel sighed and slumped back into the chair. "They promised they'd leave me be. Then they show up and demand to know where your dad is. But I don't know where he's gone. And then they go and do this! And... my clients. Those ladies. Those poor, poor ladies. What did those fucking demons do to them?"

Neither Evie nor Astaroth said anything.

"They killed them, didn't they."

Evie nodded. "It's pretty bad out there."

Gabriel sighed and looked down at the floor for a long time. "And if I had been doing my real job, instead of running this place, they'd all still be alive. If I was really looking over them and protecting them, they'd be home safe, or with their grandchildren, or putting flowers on the graves of their departed husbands and lovers, wouldn't they."

He didn't look up at either of them for an answer. He said, "Do you know, on some days I could really convince myself I was doing good for them. Really felt I was doing something good for them."

Evie didn't want to state the obvious, but Astaroth lacked the same concern for Gabriel's feelings. "Those were the days you were doing good for yourself," he said.

And Gabriel nodded. Evie thought he was going to cry.

"So what happens now?" he asked.

Astaroth held out the two remaining pieces of the talisman. Gabriel looked at them and picked up one of them. He toyed with it, turning it over in his hand, as if remembering something. He looked to Evie. "You sure you really want to do this? Do you have any idea what you'll be up against?"

Evie just nodded.

"I mean, with great power comes—"

"A great energy bill," said Astaroth. "She just killed those eight blind bitches in your driveway. Kicked their asses. She can do this."

Gabriel smiled. "Your dad would be proud of you." Then, "That's why they showed up. It was all about finding you."

"Yup," said Evie.

"Damn," he said, looking at the piece of talisman in his hand again. "So whose is the last piece?"

"Rafael's," she said.

"Ha! They'll have no easy job in finding him."

"We know where he is," said Astaroth. "He's in Los Angeles."

But Gabriel shook his head. "No. That's just where he wants everyone to believe he is."

"So where is he?"

"Take me with you," he said, "and I'll tell you."

"No," said Astaroth. "You know that's not going to be an option. *He* knows all your weaknesses."

He nodded. "Time was," he said, 'I was right there in the front line. For the longest of times."

"These are new times," Astaroth said.

Gabriel nodded.

"You know what you need to do," Astaroth said.

Gabriel nodded again. And he took the piece of talisman and pressed it against his forehead. Again, that nauseating smell of flesh burning. Evie watched the piece sear its way inside him. He grimaced a little at the pain and then she saw the horrid burn mark on his face. The knife scars were nothing in comparison to it.

And Evie felt that buckling of her legs and she was in the dream place again. She was wearing her Dream Girl costume, and she was standing on the edge of a cliff, overlooking the ocean. And everything was that deep red dream color. Even the ocean was red.

And it was raining. Heavily. Red like blood. She was drenched and standing there with her arms outstretched, preparing to use her superpowers. Her dream powers.

The waves were battering the cliff and rising up higher and higher, threatening to claw her off the cliff top, but she held up her hands and they just subsided back to the ocean. The waves got calmer and calmer and the sea became still.

Then she sensed something and turned around. There was a young child standing there in the rain, her dress ripped and stuck to her body. Evie took a cautious step towards her. Saw the size of the long knife in the little girl's hand and stopped.

"What is your name?" Evie asked her. Or tried to ask her. The words tasted unfamiliar in her mouth. Her lips felt sluggish.

The small girl started walking towards her, the knife held out in front. And the thought occurred to Evie that the child could have been a much younger version of herself. Armed and crazy and dangerous, which is maybe how this girl would grow up to be. Evie watched the girl as she stared at her. Then she held up the knife at Evie. Evie wished her gone. And she was.

As though she had never been there.

Evie heard a grumbling above her and looked up. A dark cloud was descending upon her. The source of the blood rain. She thrust her arms up. Clapped her hands together. Sent light into the cloud. Saw the darkness rent apart.

Evie heard a growl nearby and looked around. There was a wolf. Stalking her. Huge with yellow eyes and teeth. She clapped her hands again. It was gone. Like magic. Like a new superpower.

Then she wished herself away from the cliff's edge. And she was back in Gabriel's retreat in Sedona. She was more aware of everything about her, and felt her strength had increased. She'd wield that magic sword like it was made of aluminum now. Then she held out her right palm and concentrated. A ball of flame immediately formed about the size of a softball. Its glow was strong, and brighter even than the last time. She smiled and said, "Tell us about the ninth woman. Who was she?"

Gabriel said, "Probably a higher order demon, masked or shielded. I'm not sure."

Astaroth rubbed his chin, like he had an idea who it might be but was not saying. "Okay," he said. "We're leaving now. You'd best go into hiding too."

"I will," Gabriel said. "But one thing first. Tie me back up, then call the cops. I don't want to be walking free when they come here and find this. I'll tell them how I was terrorized and now need to go into hiding. I don't want to have my face on all the TV screens as the one the cops are searching for, for this."

"No," said Evie. "That'd be me."

32

The train that pulled into the station on the outskirts of Phoenix, Arizona was a noisy affair, filled with fundamental Christians who were returning from a multi-day retreat in the nearby state of California. The preachers there had affirmed their belief that they were the chosen few and that divine judgement was coming.

While some passengers left the train, a few local hawkers were seen trying to sell trinkets to the passengers through the train windows.

They were largely unemployed migrants, many from India.

What actually happened has been disputed, but words were exchanged, then insults, then several people climbed off the train abusing and assaulting some of the hawkers as ungodly heathens who threatened God-fearing Christians.

The hawkers fought back.

Witnesses reported gunshots were heard—though it is unclear who fired and at who—and suddenly there was a fire on board the train.

In the panic that ensued 59 men, women and children were burned to death.

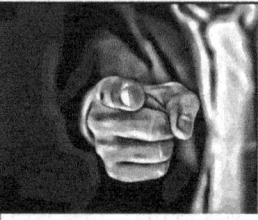

Amongst the fundamental Christian community of Phoenix grief and mourning quickly turned to rage when a fire-brand local preacher and politician, Reverend Modi, accused the small Indian district of Gulbarg of being responsible for the deaths.

Enraged locals, both from the fundamental Christian community and those who had come out in support of them, gathered in a park and were addressed by a local politician, who said the Indian enclave did not belong in their city and said that they should march there and purge it from their society.

Soon a large and growing crowd had made its way to the area of Gulbarg and surrounded the terrified residents in their houses. One of the residents, Mr Ehsan Jafri, was a member of the state legislature, and he came outside tried in vain to appeal to the crowd for calm.

Mr Jafri also tried phoning the local police, but when squad cars arrived they did nothing to assist those hiding in their houses.

After throwing stones and firing bullets into the houses, the crowd threw firebombs. Several houses were burned to the ground with victims still inside them. The number of firebombs suggested this had been pre-planned.

It was reported that local police helped the mob burn the bodies of others who had tried to escape and had been hacked to death in the streets.

The final death toll was 69.

When arrested over the incident, local Reverend Modi strongly denied he had incited the rioters in any way. He said it was a simple tragedy

and an accident, continuously citing passages from the Bible.

And the judge in the case—a member of the accused's congregation—said he could find no evidence that the attack was planned, and dropped charges of criminal conspiracy against him.

Reverend Modi stood on the steps of the court house and called aloud to the gathered crowd of supporters and media, Proverbs 10:25, "When the whirlwind passes, the wicked is no more, but the righteous has an everlasting foundation."

That evening crowds of mostly white Christians again descended on Indian enclaves, right across the State, burning temples, attacking men and sexually assaulting women.

The pogrom lasted for over ten hours, and when the rioters finally slunk away up to 125 more Indo-Americans were dead. And that was the point, when the fires were burning themselves out, that city authorities decided it was time to step in and restore order.

33

"I THINK WE SHOULD change car," said Evie, and led Astaroth over to the conference center's car park where she broke into one of the ladies' cars and hotwired it. "It'll take them some time to work out that a car is missing."

"Which 'them' are you thinking of?" asked Astaroth.

"Any 'them' that is tracking us," she said. "There's a good chance they're closing in on us. Well, me. But Florida is just too far to drive to, it'll take far too long, so we're going to have to fly again. So we should go to a big airport, like Phoenix. But I'm worried about getting through airport security again."

"Maybe it's time for a new face then?" Astaroth suggested. "I can do that for you."

Evie drove out of the retreat center and turned onto the main road out of Sedona. "Explain to me how that magic thing works first. If you use your magic, you're compelled to get me to do something evil as a result. Is that it?"

"Something like that."

"Let's try something else first."

"What do you have in mind?"

"At the first gas station I'll show you."

They headed south on highway 17, towards Phoenix. It would be about two hours driving if the traffic was light. If there weren't any police roadblocks. If everything was in their favor.

Most of the cars they passed were coming the other way, driving north and laden down with everyone's household belongings, like they were fleeing something bad.

"That's never a good sign," said Astaroth as they saw a small car go past with a ridiculously large TV strapped to the roof.

"Isn't there a line in the Bible about the end of days being foretold with the migration of giant flat screen TVs?" asked Evie.

"Probably in an earlier draft," said Astaroth.

They soon found a gas station — with a long, long line of cars waiting to fill up, and large hand-painted signs saying '5 gallons maximum'. They still had enough gas not to need to fill up, so Evie took her run bag and went inside. She was gone for about ten minutes and came back with a mousy-brown wig that had a low fringe and a large port-wine stain birthmark across her face.

"Aren't people going to really notice that?" Astaroth asked.

"Yep," she said. "But that's pretty much all they'll notice. A quick compulsive glance and then look away. It will also give me good reason to wear large sunglasses and a hat. People will think it quite normal for me to want to cover my face."

"It's almost as good as magic," said Astaroth.

"And I called the fire brigade on the pay phone to go and free Gabriel," she said.

"Not the cops?"

"They'll notify the police as soon as they get there, but they won't think of tracing the call like the cops would or if I'd rung 911."

"So many things to learn," he said.

They drove on down the highway, staying just under the speed limit, searching for rock'n'roll and news stations but finding little but redneck talk-back, with good old boy DJs lamenting how the nations of the world had all turned on the USA in spite of all it had done to uphold freedom, and how they needed to build bigger walls and barriers to stop immigrants and insurgents and do more to stop Chinese trade and cyber-attacks and just make America great again.

"What's wrong with this guy?" asked Astaroth finally. "He's not blaming you for it all."

"Give him time," she said. Then snapped the radio off. They drove for a bit and she asked, "How does he-who-will-not-be-named get them to abandon their roles as Guardians so easily?"

"Who said it was easy?" Astaroth replied. "*He* has to know the deepest weaknesses and their true nature and has to find just the right time to tempt them. *He's* probably been working on this for centuries. Building a loss of belief in them. Offering something better. Convincing them it wouldn't change anything really. And all without showing *his* hand. Your father was the first, and probably the hardest. How long do you think *he* searched for a woman that Michael would fall in love with? So deeply in love?"

Evie gritted her teeth. She didn't like the idea that he-who-must-not-be-named was the one who had brought her mother and father together.

"But *he* didn't foresee you," said Astaroth.

She looked at him. And he started singing You're the one that I want—but he changed the words to 'the one that *he* wants'. She had trouble hiding her smile as they continued on down the highway with him slaughtering all the songs from *Grease*.

The closer they got the Phoenix the more they realized there was trouble up ahead. A long, long, long line of cars was stopped just outside the city, blocking both lanes ahead of them. Evie opened the door and looked up ahead. The line seemed to go on forever.

"What is it?" asked Astaroth.

"I don't know," said Evie. "Let me find out." She walked down the line of cars a little and flagged down a highway patrol man on a motorbike. He told her that the city had gone into lockdown over some ethnic riots. Told her she should expect to spend the night in her car.

Evie took off her sunglasses, asked the young highway patrol man politely if he could take his off too, and then told him that in fact it was him who was going to be sleeping in her car as he was going to give her his motorcycle.

"Of course," he said, with a flat stare.

"Oh, and you're going to become an advocate for fighting racism in the police force."

"Yes ma'am," he said.

Astaroth wasn't too keen on riding on the back of the motorbike, but Evie told him it was the only way to bypass the traffic, driving down the verge.

"On the verge of what?" he asked. "Madness?" But after a few miles he seemed to have changed his mind and started whooping and wheeing like a junior Hells Angel as they roared down the highway.

After negotiating their way past one roadblock and just driving around two others, they finally reached the airport. It was more chaotic than they could have imagined. It looked like half the city was trying to escape a war and flee the state with either just the clothes on their back, or everything they could carry. Security was on high alert, and it was tough just to get into the building. Then there were compulsory hand sanitizing and face masks, and the inevitable tantrums from those who believed wearing a face mask was a threat to their human rights and individual freedoms.

On the plus side, just as Evie had predicted, most people gave her a quick glance and then looked away again. Holding Astaroth's hand, she went to a ticketing counter and eyeballed the guy there, convincing him to bump two random people off the next flight to Miami and give the seats to them.

Then she convinced him to go home sick and drink as much vodka or scotch as he could. He wouldn't be in a fit state to tell any stories to anyone for a long time.

"You're managing the kickback of using your powers well," Astaroth said.

"I'm much stronger now," she said. "Barely feel it."

Evie noted that one of the lines at the security screening had two security officers with plump, red demon faces. They took another line, just to be safe. Security seemed tougher, single women in particular were getting a more thorough examination. "I never thought there were advantages to being a mom of a poo-pooh head," she said.

"Mommy loves me," Astaroth said.

They moved into the departure lounge and found two seats in a corner. "Hey mom!" said Astaroth, nodding towards the TV monitor mounted on the wall. Evie turned her head to see her face there, with the words 'Rogue Agent Man-hunt' under it. "Shouldn't that be 'woman-hunt'?" he asked.

She ignored him and tried to hear what the story said. Security footage and passengers had identified her taking a flight to Vegas and security forces were concentrating their search there. The TV monitor then showed scenes of rioting and violence around the tent city in Vegas, with her face set in a small box, as if she was somehow behind that, too.

They'd be putting Vegas and Sedona together pretty quickly, she thought, even though that story hadn't broken yet; but when it did it would be pretty huge. Mass killings of wealthy, middle-aged, white women. That was a whole other level of shit-storm.. And since they'd left the hire car there, it was only a matter of time.

"Is she a bad woman, mommy?" Astaroth asked.

"Only in that she's leaving too many clues behind her," she said. And then, more softly, "They'll be looking for a woman with a child very soon and we're going to be stuck up in the air for several hours, perhaps giving them enough time to identify us."

"So what are you thinking?"

"It might be time to become Peter Dinklage's cousin," she said.

He nodded. He stood and untucked his shirt and flipped up its collar and then dug a leather thong from his pocket that he wrapped around his wrist. He also moved a finger over each forearm and a tattoo appeared on each. One was of a Celtic cross and the other was a mermaid with bare breasts.

"Hey babe," he said with a lewd wink. Then he ran his hand over his chest and he was now wearing a T-shirt that read, 'Once you've had small you'll never go tall.'

She rolled her eyes. "I think I preferred you as a bratty child."

She then moved and sat in another part of the lounge. They boarded the flight separately, and when the flight attendant questioned him as to whether he was traveling unaccompanied, he made a great fuss about the insult to small people, and how his cousin the actor Peter Dinklage would have sued them. Everybody in the queue turned to look at him, while a woman with the cap and large birthmark made her way onto the plane and quietly took her seat. He joined her a few minutes later.

"Don't I know you?" he asked. "Do you come here often?"

She peered at him over the rim of her glasses.

"Doesn't work on me," he said. She sat back in her seat and pulled out the magazine to read.

The flight attendant did the safety thing and the plane taxied to the end of the runway and took off. As they reached cruising speed, Astaroth leaned across and said, "I was thinking about what you said about the flight being long enough for them to possibly catch up to us. What if we get off early?"

"This isn't a train," she said. "How would we do that? Jump out with parachutes?"

"I could bring us down onto a highway," he said. "Then we'd grab a car and be off."

"Save your magic until we know we're going to need it," she said. "I'm not too fond of the costs of it."

"I'm just saying," he said.

"Okay," she said. "Although there's something I wanted to ask you. How would you do this whole thing, if it was you pulling the strings?"

"Me?" he asked, feigning innocence.

"But quietly," said Evie, and indicated forward. The flight attendant up the front of the plane had a thin, green demon with long, scaly arms in him.

"Okay," he said. "First I'd sow as much terror as I could."

"Shhh," she said again.

He nodded.

"I mean I would sow as much tourism as I could. Not just between say, Americans and Icelanders, but everyone."

"Icelanders?" she asked.

"Yes, Icelandic fundamentalists in particular. Try to keep up."

She nodded.

"You convince people that tourists are targeting them and soon all their resources go into preparing for tourism, and you start to see tourists where there aren't any. And you start to blame tourists for everything bad that happens."

"That's pretty basic," she said.

"Yes, but that's just laying down the groundwork. You need a good bed of fear and loathing to get things going."

"Okay. Then what?"

"Cascading trigger points."

"Which would be?"

"Well, people are actually pretty good at adapting to single tourism events—but when you have a tourist visit cascade with other trigger events, things can spin out of control very quickly."

"You're talking climate change and economic destabilization, right?"

"Yep. Or drought. Food shortages. Floods. Hurricanes. The beauty of them is that they're basically created by human impacts. Convince key humans to keep driving climate change and pretty soon you have massive disruption. Then you overlay tourist attacks on that. Target women and children in particular. Blame somebody—like the Icelanders—and then cascade that again with Mexicans and Canadians and the Chinese and any other loopy tourist group. And people start circling the wagons and elect a nutjob who promises to keep them safe and return things to the good old days—while incarcerating the innocent and endorsing vengeance-driven psychos demanding payback for crimes real or imagined against them. Soon the war on tourists is being played out at the national level and you're spiraling uncontrollably into total chaos."

"And that's the endgame that we're moving towards?" she said. "The hard rain?"

"Call it what you will," he said. "Things are going to get an awful lot more serious."

"How serious?"

"Well, consider this. Despite everyone being so terrified of Icelanders, in fact more people in the USA have died from peanut allergies or slipping in the bath than have died from tourists. But who's going to war over peanuts?"

Evie sat back and mulled it over. "We'll rip ourselves to pieces, won't we."

"Unless somebody has the balls to stop them."

Then she asked, "So, do djinn even have balls?"

Astaroth smiled, "We could make a bet on this—that by the end of the flight I could get one of the female flight attendants to describe them to you."

Evie stared at him fixedly. "Only if you get one of the male attendants to do it."

"Ha!" he laughed. "You call that a challenge?"

"Let's just try and get to Miami unnoticed," she said.

"Spoil sport," he said, and then turned and winked at the young lady across the aisle from them, who had turned to glance at him. "Hi babe," he said.

Evie pulled her cap down lower. "This is where I tune out."

~~~

EVIE SAT UP suddenly. Alert. She had been dozing, but now her Spidey-senses were tingling so much she felt she was going to throw up. The air around her was thick with a syrupy, tropical feeling and the light was a deep red. She turned her head around slowly. It was like she was still in the same place, but in a dream version of it. The plane was full of sleeping people. She was the only one awake. Even Astaroth, sitting next to her, seemed to be asleep.

But then she saw a man across the aisle from her was also awake. He had been a young woman before. She looked at him carefully. He was tall and well-built, wearing a dark suit, and had short, dark hair and pair of dark sunglasses. He turned his head and looked at her.

"Hello Evie," he said.

"Who are you?" she asked.

He waved a hand in the air like that didn't matter.

She looked at him carefully, trying to figure out if he was a danger or not.

Evie slowly reached down and placed a hand on her seat belt. She didn't want to be trapped in her chair if she needed to move quickly.

"Who are you?" she asked again.

"Call me Damien, if you like," he said. Then he reached down into the carry bag at his feet. He turned and smiled at her and opened the bag. Evie inhaled sharply. He had a bomb in there. An old-fashioned, comic-book type of bomb, consisting of six or eight sticks of red dynamite wound together with a big red button on it.

"This is a dream," she said.

"Yes," he said. Then, "If that's how you prefer to think of it."

"You're not real," she said.

"What's real?" he asked.

"That's not a real bomb," she said.

"Are you sure?" he asked. "If I press this button here, are you so very sure it won't explode and kill everyone on this plane?"

"This is just a dream," she said again.

And he laughed. "I'm so looking forward to meeting you," he said. Then he pressed the button.

Evie closed her eyes. Opened them again and she was back on the plane. Most everyone around her was sleeping. The lighting was dimmed for the night flight.. The seat across the aisle had the lady in it.

Astaroth was watching her carefully. "What is it?" he asked.

"Just a dream," she said. "I must have dozed off for a moment."

"For you," he said, "there's no such thing as 'just a dream'."

34

The darkened and unmarked boat came in as close as it dared to the Florida coastline and then the ten men climbed aboard zodiacs and sped their way ashore. They landed on the beach at Miami in the dark and quickly spread out into the city.

To a passer-by they might have been Cuban refugees. But in fact they were highly-trained terrorists who had been practicing for this mission for many weeks.
And they were determined to bring havoc, death and terror to the city of Miami.

The first attack began at 9.30pm, when two of the terrorists entered the Miami train station's passenger hall and opened fire with AK-47 assault rifles and grenades.

They killed 50 people and wounded over 100 others before fleeing.

 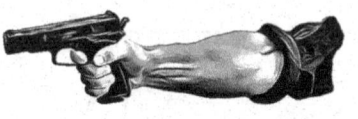

They shot at pursuing police, killing eight officers, and then seized a police car and ran it into a roadblock. In the subsequent fire-fight, one of the attackers was killed and another injured.

The second attack was at a popular cafe in South Miami. Two of the attackers opened fire on the cafe crowd, killing ten people.

About the same time, two taxis that had timer bombs placed in them exploded, killing the drivers and passengers.

The attackers then moved onto their main objective—the two wings of the Fontainebleau Hotel.

The first thing most occupants knew of the attack was when several loud explosions rocked the building as the terrorists entered the hotel.

As the police sirens filled the night and people realised what was happening, the guests locked themselves in their rooms. Some were later rescued from their balconies by firefighters.

Security forces were quick to surround the hotel, trying to determine how many terrorists and hostages were inside, while the terrorists watched television broadcasts, showing them where the security forces were.

The authorities, however, were in turn able to tap into their terrorists' communications, and discovered they were being directed by a female controller in Central America.

But all in all it was a stalemate.

The battle, or siege, lasted several days as the terrorists made their way around the hotel looking for people to kill, while those in the hotel found ways to escape, or were helped out by security forces.

Finally, special forces were sent in and in series of skirmishes, killed all the terrorists.

The final death toll was 164 people killed and over 300 wounded.

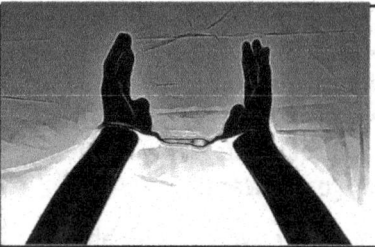

The one lone terrorist who had been captured alive after the train station attack was interrogated to discover who they were. He told them his name was Alfredo and he had grown up in a small village in Central America.

At the age of 11 he had been taken out of school when his father became ill, and sent to work. Neighbors described him as a 'cheeky young boy' who loved watching movies, and who would stay up very late watching TV in stores and restaurant windows.

As he grew older, however, he began to fight with his family and after a while moved to the city to look for work. There he fell in with some street youths.

Eventually the boy turned to petty crime, because, he claimed, "I was working hard; I was just not being paid well for my work".

The turning point came when he and his friends met a mysterious woman, who promised to teach them how to become freedom fighters and free their people from poverty.

The boys fell under her spell and began training to become guerilla fighters.

They were sent to the north-east of the country and spent ten months undergoing intensive training in the jungle, including being drilled by a man who was reportedly an officer in the national army.

Alfredo did not actually have a strong understanding of the ideologies they were taught, but was told the group would look after his family if he was successful in his mission.

The ten recruits were selected from a much larger group and were given tasks suited to their skills. As a good marksman, Alfredo was selected for the assault on the train station.

After the Miami attack, Alfredo was painted by the authorities as the face of evil. A monster. A deliberate and sadistic killer who deserved the death penalty.

But no one—including Alfredo himself—could fully explain the motivations behind the attack, nor who the mysterious woman controlling him and his fellow attackers was.

35

IT WAS NEARLY 11PM when they finally landed in Miami, to find the world had changed again. They arrived in a police state that was reeling from a series of terror attacks. In the line to get past the heavily guarded security desk, where everyone's IDs were being scrutinized, Evie said to Astaroth, "Wait a bit." Then she pulled a few things out of her cabin luggage and stepped into the closest toilet.

She came back a few minutes later, wearing a generic flight attendant's uniform and with a lanyard saying 'Unaccompanied Minor', which she placed over Astaroth's head. The birthmark was gone but the wig was still on, though now tied back into a small ponytail.

"Your turn," she said. He turned to the wall, did a few moves and turned back as a child again.

"Let's go," she said. Evie eyeballed each of the security guards they passed and they politely nodded to her to keep walking.

"They're just on general look-out," she said, "hoping to provoke anyone with high-strung nerves into panicking. They aren't looking for us in particular."

"You get all that from looking into their eyes?"

"Well, I can now," she said. "I never used to get so much detail."

"Better than buying a newspaper," he said.

"But I get all the crap too. The fight one had with his wife. The hemorrhoids on the other one, and the cream that isn't working like they promised at the drug store." She led him along the terminal at a brisk pace. "If they were really after us they'd have come and gotten us on the plane where there was no space to run or put up a fight. Or they might even have gotten everybody off the plane into a sealed room and separated us out there."

"Or poisoned everyone on the plane," he said. "Or shot it down."

"I hope no one ever gives you any serious responsibility," she said.

"Like being the guide for the last hope for humanity?"

"Yes, anything like that," she said.

They walked past more security guards and soldiers. There were rows of people lying face down on the ground, with guns pointed at them. Most seemed to be poor and Hispanic.

"No hire car this time," she said, and led him on the long walk to the short-term parking lot. They found a man hopping into his car and Evie said, "Excuse me sir."

"Yes?" he asked turning and seeing her there in the flight attendant's uniform. "Is there something wrong?"

"Not at all," she said. "But you're going to give us your car because you took a cab to the airport."

"That's right," he said. "I took a cab."

"Because your car is in the shop. It's not even due to be picked up for three more days."

"That's right," he said again. He took his luggage out of the trunk and started walking back to the airport's cab rank.

"And buy your wife some flowers to make up for that cheap slut in Tallahassee," she called.

"Yes, flowers," he said.

They climbed into the car and started driving. Astaroth gave her directions. After about 15 minutes, Evie said, "I think we're being followed. Hard to be sure at nighttime."

"Want me to do some magic on them?"

"No," she said, "I'm worried enough about the payback on me using my powers." As if on cue the car started missing and backfiring. "Shit," she said, and she pulled the car off the road into a gas station, being careful to park beyond the CCTV. She grabbed her run bag from the back seat and said, "You're with me, number one." She led Astaroth into the store and without stopping went straight through and out the other side. They hopped into a car belonging to a tall, Latino man who was just returning from paying for his gas.

"Hey!" he said.

"Just drive," said Evie, fixing him with a stare.

"Of course," he said, his face going slack.

"Who is he banging?" Astaroth asked as they pulled out into traffic.

"Nobody," she said. "He's gay but hasn't come out yet."

"You should do something about that."

"Maybe," she said, looking back over her shoulder.

They drove all the way to Fort Lauderdale, past roadblocks and military vehicles, and signs saying that everyone under 30 had to report for registration as a Young Person. "It's a gerontocracy," said Astaroth. "About time some state started dividing along age lines. Race and gender are so old school."

Evie shook her head. "Who comes up with these realities?"

"Don't panic until all the chocolate in the world is replaced by sheep's testicles," he said.

"Eee-eww."

"No, the ewes don't have testicles."

She shook her head again. "Why no one has ever given you your own late night TV show I cannot fathom."

"It's height prejudice."

"Let me guess," she said. "Apart height."

"You're singing my song," he said and started searching the radio for something that wasn't an emergency alert station or Golden Oldies.

It was well after midnight when Astaroth directed them down a busy highway past closed strip malls and said, "This will do. We walk the rest of the way."

"Is it far?" asked Evie.

"The next block, if Gabriel's information is correct," he said. "A quieter street. Coming on foot will give us the advantage."

They climbed out of the car and watched the guy drive away. "What is Rafael doing here, exactly?" she asked.

"Hiding," he said.

"Hiding from what?"

But he never got a chance to answer. A black van suddenly drove up the curb in front of them and stopped. Evie's Spidey-senses started tingling dramatically.

"Trouble," she said. But it was not the trouble she expected. A single figure climbed out of the van and held out her arms wide. "Evie!" she said. "I've been trying so hard to find you!"

"Halina?!" said Evie.

"Aren't you pleased to see me?" Halina asked.

"Um—how did you find me?"

"My new friends told me where you'd be," she said. She ran over and wrapped Evie in a hug.

"New friends?" asked Evie suspiciously.

"They've been so supportive to me," she said. And as she waved a hand behind her, four ugly, dark-garbed women climbed from the back of the vehicle. They all wore large, dark glasses. Evie guessed they had all been blinded. And then a tall, blonde woman emerged from the driver's door. "Hello Evie," she said in a mocking voice. "Aren't you glad to see me too?"

It was Marvel Gal, the woman she had encountered at bin Laden's compound in Pakistan, or Mexico, or wherever the hell that had happened in this version of reality. Evie looked at her closely. They really could have been sisters. Same light-brown skin. Same physique. Same blonde hair. But there was a malevolence about her that Evie hoped she'd never have.

"Not particularly," said Evie.

"Hello Lucy," said Astaroth. "Long time no see."

"It'll be even longer until the next time," she said. A savage twist to her mouth.

"The magic sword?" asked Evie.

"They'll have adapted already," said Astaroth.

"We still might have a surprise for them," Evie said. She bounced just a little on her feet, eager to test out just how strong she now was, and what size fireball she could make. "I need you to let go of me, Halina," she said, prying the woman's arms off her.

"Oh, I've got a present for you," said Halina and she took a silver chain from her pocket and slipped it over Evie's head. Immediately Evie gasped. It felt like a ship's anchor chain had been placed on her. She fell to her knees.

"What's happening?" she asked.

"There's a spell on the necklace," Astaroth said. "Anyone who's not a mortal will be affected by it. It'll drain your strength until you're as weak as an old grandmother."

"You lose," said Lucy, with a smile.

She had such a lovely smile, too, thought Evie.

"But I should thank you first for leading us to Rafael. Who'd have thought it? Fort Lauderdale!"

"You followed us all the way from Sedona," said Evie. Fuck-fuck-fuckitty fuck.

Marvel Gal just smiled that smile.

Evie looked across to Astaroth but his face had gone blank, like he was under a spell. Or perhaps like he was no longer in his body. Evie saw the lights before she even heard the shriek of the engine. She turned her head to see the large garbage truck veer off the highway and charge at them, the hydraulic forks like a large bull's horns. The harridans were clearly confused as to what was happening, turning their heads left and right, unable to see the headlights. The truck plowed into their van, crushing it and them into the wall of the plumbing shop behind them. Lucy was the only one able to dive out of the way. Well, almost out of the way.

Lucy was knocked to the ground and pinned under a piece of wreckage from the store. All that was left of the harridans, though, was empty dark outfits and sunglasses.

"Halina," said Evie softly. "I love this gift, but can you just take it off me for a moment so I can examine it closer?"

Halina smiled and nodded her head. As soon as it was lifted clear of her, Evie felt her strength returning. She looked up to see Marvel Gal lifting the wreckage off her, attempting to get to her feet. Evie looked at her palms and concentrated. The fireballs appeared quickly, blazing. She threw one at Marvel Gal. The blast hit her and knocked her back to the ground.

"Now, kill her," said Astaroth. Evie turned and saw he was back in his body. And he was trying to compel her to fire a few more blasts at Lucy. The price of his magic.

"No!" she said.

"Yes!" said Astaroth "Kill her!"

Evie looked at her palms again and knew how easy it would be to create more flame balls and cast them at Lucy. Again and again and again. And she wanted to do it. Felt herself filling with a driving need to do it. A sense of injustice filled her. A sense of vengeance. A sense of righteousness.

"No!" she said again.

"You have to!" said Astaroth.

"No, I don't," said Evie, but she felt his anger compelling her.

"Yes, you do!" he raged.

"Quick, Halina! I want to see what that necklace looks like on my friend here!"

Halina did as she was asked, placing the necklace over Astaroth's head. She saw the flame disappear from his eyes, and his legs slump. "Now, take it off again," she said, and Halina did so.

"You can say thank you whenever you like," she said.

"Fuck you very much," he said. Then Evie turned to Halina. "You have been so helpful, but we need you to stay right here and tell the police exactly what happened. The flaming balls. The garbage truck. Your friends just disappearing. Everything. They'll be very pleased with you to hear it. I'll be very pleased with you, too. But don't use my name. Say I was—uh—Hilary Clinton, okay?"

Halina nodded.

Evie looked around. Cars were already stopping to see what had happened. She looked at Lucy and frowned. Part of her wanting to eyeball her and interrogate her. Part of her knowing she didn't have the time. "We'd better go," said Astaroth, pulling her arm. "Let's get to Rafael's place before the police show up."

36

Two trucks pulled up with a screech of air brakes, outside one of the middle schools in Billings, Montana. About 40 heavily-armed and masked men and women jumped out.

They moved into the school where an assembly was taking place in the school hall, and rounded up over 1,000 parents, teachers and school students, moving them into the small gymnasium,

which was about the size of a single basketball court.

The attackers wore no identification, but it was apparent they were militant members of the Free Montana State movement, a radical organisation pushing for secession of the state from the Union.

Improvised explosives were hung all around the

gym, rigged to tripwires, some hanging tenuously from the basketball hoops.

The attackers also confiscated everyone's mobile phones upon threat of death. And to prove their threats were not empty, when one parent tried to explain to the children what the attackers wanted of them, he was shot in the head.

Another parent who refused to kneel for the gunmen was also shot dead.

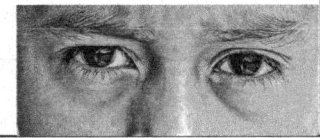

In front of the children's eyes.

The attackers next went through the hostages and singled out 20 men who appeared the strongest and most likely to offer resistance, and took them down a corridor to the school cafeteria. There were two of the female attackers there, wearing explosive belts. They told the men to sit down and not be concerned, as they would ensure they were safe.

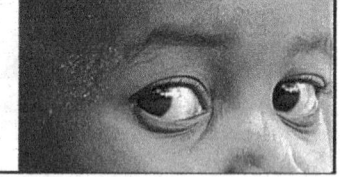

One of the women's explosive belt then detonated, killing most of the people in the room.

The leader of the militants then entered the room and nodded his head in satisfaction. He had the survivors of the blast lie down on the floor where they were shot dead.

Security forces including the army had soon surrounded the school, but could not do anything for fear of injuring children, so a negotiation team was established to find a way to end the siege.

Unknown to the negotiators, a military team was also put in charge of planning an assault on the school.

The siege dragged on into a second day and the attackers refused delivery of any food or water. Many children fainted in the heat from dehydration and exhaustion. Some of the hostages drank their own urine.

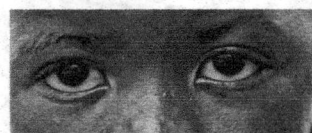

By day three the militants were also fatigued and weary, and were becoming increasingly edgy. The negotiators felt this would be a good time to press to be allowed to enter the gym and assess conditions.

The militants agreed, but an hour before the planned visit, two large explosions ripped through the gym. The roof caught fire and collapsed, killing many inside.

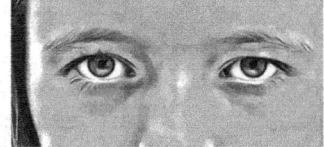

Militants who survived the explosions took many of the hostages with them and retreated to the cafeteria, where they had adults and children stand in front of the windows as human shields, hoping it would deter the military.

It did not. The military attacked the school. Many adults trying to escape the fire were shot as possible militants, as were those standing in front of windows in the cafeteria.

Security forces pressed on with tanks, rockets and flame throwers, determined to crush the militants, with the battle raging on until dark.

When the fires were finally put out the toll of the dead was 334 people —186 of them children.

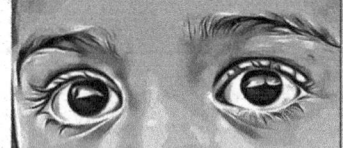

The city was outraged. The nation was outraged. The world was outraged. Everybody was demanding to know what had happened.

And then came the battle to control the story.

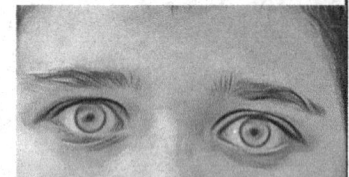

According to the military and government, an accident in the gym caused one of the booby-traps to explode, triggering a second bomb, and leading to the carnage.

But survivors of the siege said they witnessed a sniper outside the school shoot one of the militants whose foot had been on a dead man's switch, triggering the first blast.

Other evidence indicated the two explosions were caused by rockets that were fired into the gym by security forces as the first stage of their assault on the school, and they had

underestimated the damage they would cause.

And conspiracy theories stated that the whole siege was most likely organized by the security forces, who supplied the militants with arms and knew of their plans, but double-crossed them, and used the massacre as political tool to trigger wide-spread public outrage and expand their power.

As often happens, the truth is hard to find. Like picking through the ashes of the destroyed school buildings looking for clues to the truth—and having to sift past the remains of children to do so.

37

FINDING RAFAEL'S PLACE was a lot easier than finding a way inside. It had no windows. No postbox. No door bell. It was a large, square, white concrete building with what looked like a bank vault door. There weren't even any electricity or phone cables going into it that they could see.

"You sure this is the place?" Evie asked.

"According to Gabriel, this is the address," said Astaroth.

Evie nodded and walked up and down the front of the building for a moment. Then she said, "Looks like it was built by a paranoid drug lord. See those small circles in the design work? They're cameras. If he's in there he's watching us."

"If he hasn't frizzed the monitors," said Astaroth.

"Hmm," said Evie. It made sense that the other Guardians would have the same effect on electronics that her father had on them. "Either way," she said, "I think we need to get his attention."

"What do you suggest?" Astaroth asked her.

"Everyone loves fireworks," Evie said and walked over to the front door. She bent down very low and peered through the crack under the door. It was sealed with rubber on the inside bottom of the door. She held her hands apart and concentrated. A ball of fire formed on each palm. She pushed them at the door and watched them squeeze and compress under it. There was a strong smell of burning rubber, and then the fireballs were free to do whatever it was fireballs might do on the inside of a house when they sprang back to their fireball shape. Or so she hoped.

"Now we stand here in front of the cameras and smile," Evie said.

Astaroth smiled. It was not the sort of smile that might induce somebody to open a door though, Evie thought, so she tried to make up for it. They waited a few minutes, and just when Astaroth had said,

"How about I try some magic?" they heard a series of clicks and the door opened a crack.

"Evie!" said a voice from inside.

"Rafael," she said, pretending to be as pleased as he was pretending to be.

"I was wondering when I might see you."

The door opened a bit wider. "Astaroth," Rafael said, looking now at the djinn. "Anybody else with you?"

"Just us two," said Evie, "Though we left Lucy and the remains of a few harridans behind us."

Rafael raised his eyebrows and then sighed. "Well, you'd better come in then." And he opened the door wider. Evie thought he looked thinner and more tired than Uriel and Gabriel, who had become figures of excess. He was the opposite. Tall and thin, dressed in light gray. His eyes looked sunken and weary.

He waved an arm around and said, "My earthly abode."

The house was not so much a house as a safe room inside a safe house. He led them across a sparse, white tiled room with minimal white furniture—with a few new scorch marks on it— towards another door. The smell of burnt rubber was strong.

The second door was even more solid than the outside one. Rafael invited them into the room there and then closed the door after them. It shut with a bang and then they heard the loud *thunk* of heavy, metal bars sliding into place.

"I like what you've done here," said Astaroth. "Very techno-chic."

Rafael ignored him. They were in a large room, all concrete walls and floor and ceiling, with a bank of monitors along two entire walls. There was a large recliner chair in the middle of the room, with a built-in food tray—the type of thing you saw at gold class movie lounges. At the back of the room was a small kitchen and two doors behind it. Maybe a bathroom and bedroom or something.

"It was built by a paranoid drug warlord," Rafael told them. "And I've had a few renovations made to it."

Evie looked back to the monitors. Most were on freeze-frame. Evie saw two that looked out over the front of the house. Another was a news telecast that had her face on it.

Rafael saw her looking at it and said, "You've been blazing quite a path across the country. The FBI's Most Wanted!"

Evie grimaced as he went on. "At last count you and your terrorist cell have killed a woman in Washington, slaughtered a whole room of elderly women in Sedona, shot two cops in Houston, derailed a train in

Kentucky, firebombed a church in Los Angeles and shot up a Muslim neighborhood in Phoenix. The death toll is rising and so is the price on your head."

"How much is she worth?" asked Astaroth. "I could still turn a profit on this job."

No one answered him.

"There is also a case of the water turning blood-red in New Jersey," said Rafael, "but the jury is still out on the cause of that, though the locals are convinced it's terrorism, and that the water has been poisoned by you and your cell members."

Evie made a noise of disgust.

"You've been sighted all over the country, and everyone is so preoccupied with the man-hunt—or woman-hunt—that nobody is paying much attention to these." He picked up a remote and images started flashing across several of the screens. A locust plague in California. Thousands of dead fish washing up on the shores of Washington State. Lethal hailstorms in New Mexico. Fields of dead cattle in Kentucky. Raining soot in Ohio. "And that's just in the States. It's even more bizarre in Europe and the Middle East. Statues weeping blood. Graves found empty. Fevers that only strike children. Birds falling dead from the sky."

Evie looked back to her face on the monitors again.

"They're all coming for you," Rafael said finally. "Everyone. You can't outrun them forever. Or outfight them."

"And you sit here watching it all unfold?" Evie asked. "You're the nerve center for what's going on, yes? You're watching it all so you can predict what's going to happen next?"

And Rafael laughed. Really laughed. "Oh no," he said. "How depressing that would be! No, I've found a way to care about humanity without having to be the one who does the endless healing." He pressed some buttons on the remote. The screens started playing again. Evie turned to watch them all. They were mostly TV dramas.

"Do you have any idea how many hours of fine drama are produced in a year?" Rafael asked, "And if you're playing catch-up, how many hours and days and weeks and months' worth of dedicated viewing you need?"

"Drama?' asked Evie. "You mean TV shows?"

"Look," said Rafael and pointed at different screens. "*Breaking Bad, Stargate* and *Stargate Atlantis. Star Trek. True Blood. The Sopranos. The Tudors. Game of Thrones. Ripper Street. Dr Who. House.* I can't get enough of that one. *Batman. Superman. The Flash. Primordial. House of Cards.* The endless *CSIs*. There is just so much of humanity here to watch. The fears and follies and the loves and lives and deaths."

"But it's just make-believe," said Evie. "This is all imagined."

"Oh no," said Rafael. "This is like sitting on a cloud watching incidents in humanity's struggles with itself. And at the end—it usually works out well. No need for me to patch things up. No need for me to be the one endlessly intervening."

"You can't be serious?" asked Evie.

"Let me ask you a question," said Rafael. "Who heals the healer? I mean, I could do it when the others were all there. But on my own? No. It was overwhelming."

Evie shook her head. "You're going to watch the world end on television?" she asked.

Rafael folded his arms over his chest. "I think if many humans knew the date of the cataclysm they would, as a race, tend to hunker down and do the same. There is a sense of achievement in following a character out of turmoil. There is a sense of metaphorical salvation in it. And isn't salvation the point of everything?"

Evie put her hands on her hips. "No," she said. "You are so much better than this. You are so much *more* than this!"

"Am I?" asked Rafael. "Or *was* I?"

She saw that same desperate look in his eyes now. Not so different from the other two after all. The demons found his weakness and trapped him in it.

"So how do you stop the monitors from frizzing?" Astaroth asked, as if there was nothing else to know than that.

Rafael smiled. "I receive the signals in a box on the rooftop and these are all optical signals carried down here. The screens just magnify the picture. No actual electronics this close. Frizz-proof."

"Impressive," said Astaroth. "Looks just like a regular, high-res monitor. How do you prevent distortions around the edges?"

"It's all in the shape of the screen."

Evie was looking down at the ground, as if she couldn't bear to look at either of them.

Rafael looked back at her. "Stay a while," he said. "You'll like it here."

"No," said Evie. "I can't do that."

Rafael shrugged. "I wish I could change your mind. They are very powerful and they won't hesitate to destroy you as long as you're intent on fighting them."

"Not if you help me," she said, and she nodded to Astaroth. He pulled out the last piece of the talisman. "Give me the extra power I need to fight them," she said. "Then I might just stand a chance."

Rafael held out his hand and took the piece of metal. He turned it over in his hands and then said, "I can't do that."

"Why can't you?" Evie asked. "We have fought our way across the country towards this. This is the last piece of the talisman. The final piece! How can you stand there before me, in your man-cave here, and tell me you won't do it!" She was angry now. Tired and as angry as she could ever remember herself being. And she didn't quite know what she was going to do in that state.

"I didn't say I won't," said Rafael. "I said I can't!"

"What does that mean?"

"I didn't create this last piece," he said. "I was the one who assembled them. But this piece is from your father."

The anger seeped out of her. "My father? But he never said anything. Just let me wander off on this fool's errand…"

Rafael handed the piece of talisman back to Astaroth and said to Evie.

"And why did Malikulmaut have me chasing you if you didn't even create this last piece?"

"I'm sure he had good reasons."

"The same good reasons my father had for having you assemble the talisman?" she asked. "And then never telling me why?"

Rafael shrugged. "It was designed to protect you. I can't speak for him. You'll have to find him and ask him that."

"I don't even know where he is," Evie said. "He's missing."

"Perhaps you need him to find you," he said.

"And how can I possibly do that?"

"I suspect the trail of death and destruction that you're leaving across the country is going to make it easier for him to find you," Rafael said. "But that also applies to anyone else who wants to find you."

"What if they have him already?" she asked.

He shrugged. "Then they've already won. There's nothing you or I can do about it anymore."

Evie gritted her teeth. "I refuse to accept that."

"She's stubborn," said Astaroth.

"Yes," said Rafael. "I remember. Even as a little girl. I'd bring you toys and you'd break them if you didn't like them and I'd just have to keep fixing them." Then he said, "At least stay here the night. I'm going to be watching all the Elvis movies. We could watch them until dawn."

Evie considered for a moment making a fireball and melting all the screens around her. But what would that actually achieve?

"No," she said. "We have to go."

Rafael put all the monitors back on pause. He examined the ones showing the street, and then led them over to the steel door and unlocked it. He led them back across the room that still smelled of burned rubber and opened the outer door.

"I'm sorry I can't be of more help," he said, putting a hand on Evie's shoulder.

"Not as sorry as I am," she said, shrugging it off.

"Don't judge me," he said. "Not until—"

"Until what?" she cut him off. "Until I've sat an hour in your recliner chair?"

He smiled. But it was a very sad smile. He looked like he was about to say something then. About to change his mind. But all he said was, "Ask Malikulmaut if he knows where your father is. He usually knows a lot more than he ever reveals."

Then the heavy door was shut behind them.

"Where to now?" asked Astaroth.

"I'm not sure. We walk. Steal a car. Get far away. They'll still be following us."

"Somehow that doesn't sound much like a plan."

"We walk," she said again.

And so they walked. Further away from the lights of emergency vehicles back behind them. Further away from Rafael's bunker. Along the darkest streets they could find. Hoping they were somehow unobserved.

38

This is a story they tell around campfires at night time. A horror story to fill you with fear. It is the story of a religious extremist who detonated up a bomb in an inner city area, killing eight people, and then went on a shooting rampage, killing another 69 people.

The frightening thing was that he did it so easily. He was not under surveillance, despite having released a 1,500 page rambling manifesto in which he outlined the need for violent conflict between Islam and Christianity. He discussed his relationship with his god and the need for a single belief across the western world. He referred to Europe as Eurabia, and cherry-picked passages from scriptures to support his beliefs.

School friends had described the killer as intelligent and physically strong. He was also remembered as having protected classmates who were bullied. But in his early 20s his life started to change and he became very withdrawn. He also started spending a lot of time on extremist websites and blogs that advocated hate and violence and promised a religious war.

He moved to a rural community where he had a farm and started buying fertilizer and other chemicals that could be used in the manufacture of bombs. He also purchased guns. Lots of guns. Unwatched, he was accumulating everything he needed for his terror attacks.

His first act of violence was a car bomb exploded outside government offices in the capital, which killed eight people. The killer then travelled across the state and took a boat to a small island where a youth camp was being held.

Dressed as a policeman, he entered the camp and walked amongst the young people there, shooting them, reportedly with a smile on his face. Kaboom! Kaboom! Kaboom! As if evil incarnate was walking amongst them.

One moment the young people were at their campfires or going about their day, the next they were running for their lives, or being shot down.

He killed a total of 77 people before the day was over—the youngest being only 14 years old.

And who was this killer? This monster? This terrorist?

His name was Anders Behring Breivik, and he was a Norwegian-born white-supremacist, concerned about Muslim influence. One of the reasons for the attacks, he later stated, was to draw attention to his manifesto.

That 1,500-page document was finally analyzed by the authorities, and was found to contain passages lifted from the manifesto of the 'Unabomber', Ted Kaczynski, as well as many other sources, not only outlining his fears of the world being overrun by Muslim immigrants, but the need for a new crusade.

Breivik's ideologies were heavily influenced by anti-Muslim bloggers and commentators in the USA and Europe, and he accused the media and politicians of abetting the fifth column of Muslim takeover with cowardly silence.

He couldn't explain why he attacked the children, when almost none of them were Muslim.

And the only regret he showed was that his activities did not incite more people to stand up in support of his actions and beliefs.

39

"I'M EXHAUSTED," said Astaroth. "All this walking is hard on short legs."

"We can rest up ahead," said Evie, pointing at a bus shelter sitting there under a streetlight. They had gone some distance already from Rafael's house, and were walking down one of the quieter streets of suburban Fort Lauderdale. Evie kept looking around to see if they were being followed, taking them along the darkest parts of the streets. There were plenty of large houses—but no cars on the streets. Everything seemed to be locked up tight behind huge, well-trimmed hedges and security fences. An occasional dog barked with outrage, letting them know that people were not seen walking around the streets here often...certainly not at this hour of the morning. They moved along quickly, not wanting to have a resident wake and call the police to check on who they were.

"Look at this," said Astaroth. "We're walking through the American dream. If I was to predict the next change, I'd revert Florida to Spanish hands. Do you know the Spanish came here originally looking for the Fountain of Youth and cities of gold?"

"That's ironic," said Evie, "since Florida is the haven of the elderly."

"But they all want to be younger," said Astaroth. "They search for it incessantly like those conquistadors. Having found gold and wealth, they now want to buy youth and lock it away from anyone who might take it from them."

"So how different might it be as a Spanish state?" she asked.

"Probably exactly the same," he said. "But the help would all be Anglos."

There was a low growl of thunder somewhere off in the distance. Evie turned her head and listened, as if trying to discern if that really was thunder or not. "We going to need to find a main road and get a ride," she said. "Then we have to reach Malikulmaut. But how do we even do that? I'm guessing he doesn't have a cell number."

"You don't call Malikulmaut," he said. "He finds you when he needs you. But I can get us a cab."

"None of your bad-vibe magic," she said. "The evil payback isn't worth it. I'll eyeball the first person we find that's awake and out on the streets and get them to help us."

"How far are we going to have to walk before we find somebody awake around here?" he asked. "They're all tucked up tightly in bed, with their burglar alarms and security systems switched on, thinking those and their high walls and metal fences are actually going to protect them from what's coming. If they had even an inkling of how bad things are going to get, they'd all be sitting up awake and you could do your eyeball thing to any of them."

They reached the bus shelter and sat down. "I don't think a bus is going to come along any time soon," he said.

"No, I don't think so either," she said. There was the sound of a few large raindrops falling on the shelter. "I don't even think the locals use this—it's probably more for the help."

Evie took a deep breath and smelled the sub-tropical humidity of the air about them. "I love the smell of rain," she said. But this didn't smell right.

She heard more plops fall about them and then looked at the raindrops. They were moving. "What the hell?" she asked and stepped a little outside the shelter. She bent down and looked at the rain drops. They were tiny frogs. And tadpoles. Wriggling and writhing on the ground. Then one landed on her head. "Eee-eww," she said and brushed it off. Then another landed on her. Then the rain—or the frogs and tadpoles—really started falling. She jumped up and stepped back into the shelter.

"That's gross," she said, watching the ground turn into a carpet of writhing amphibians. "That's not your doing, is it?"

"Not me," he said. "I'd rain real cats and dogs."

Evie pulled a face. "So how bad exactly are things going to get?" she asked him.

"Think about some of the big global uprisings that humanity has undergone. The barbarian invasion of Europe and Rome, 70 million killed. Chinese war of the three kingdoms, 40 million killed. The great plague, 25 million killed. The Taiping Rebellion, 20 million killed. World War One, 17 million killed. Chinese civil war, eight million killed. Stalin's purges, about 40 million killed. World War Two, 80 million killed. Do you want me to keep going? Rwanda, Cambodia, Armenia, Darfur. Covid19."

"I'm getting the picture," she said.

"So, imagine what could happen if any of those conflicts were allowed to continue. And then factor in modern weapons, bioweapons and other weapons of mass destruction. This will be the Christian visions of Armageddon or the prophecy of the last battle on the plains of Dabiq. You name your apocalypse—this is it. And just think how many deaths might there be?"

"Deaths will be in the billions," Evie said. Then, "A bus stop in Fort Lauderdale isn't actually how I ever envisioned the plains of Armageddon looking."

"Humanity will survive," Astaroth said. "Humanity is always allowed to survive, but I don't believe that civilization will survive. It will be like pushing a reset button on human history. Take your worse-case science fiction apocalypse scenario and consider it a reality."

"I don't follow much science fiction," she said.

"You should," he said. "It provides insights into where you might go, to help you avoid going there."

She sat in silence for a while and then said, "I'm not sure I can comprehend the enormity of this."

"Do you know how I'd do it?" he asked. "The end of days?"

"Zombie apocalypse, right?"

"No. I'd keep it simple. I wouldn't trigger people to start fighting over race or religion or anything, I'd send a blight to attack the main food staples. Rice, wheat and corn. They feed 60 per cent of the world. Destroy them and there'll be famine in rich and poor countries alike. And when humans get hungry they get nasty. The richer countries have a wider variety of crops and wouldn't feel the pinch too badly at first, but they'd feel the anger of all those without food seeking to invade and infiltrate their borders. Then I'd explode a few upper atmospheric thermonuclear bombs and send out electronic magnetic pulses over the planet, destroying almost all electronic circuits. Then I'd just sit back and watch it all unfold. The food-dependent with no food and the technology-dependent with no technology."

"I'm far too tired for this conversation right now," she said. "And if you tell me that I have to listen to it because I'm the only one who can save the world, I'm probably going to start crying."

"You're too tough to cry," he said.

"You're never too tough to cry," she said. "That's one thing I learned in the job I do." She was going to tell him how she had seen battle-hardened veterans cry, but her Spidey-senses started tingling. She grabbed Astaroth's hand and pulled him out of the shelter. It saved their lives. There was a sudden flash of light and an explosion behind them. Evie and Astaroth were knocked to the ground. Evie landed on a lawn but Astaroth hit the road. Hard. The frogs and tadpoles providing little cushioning.

"You should have learned never to let an opponent live," called Lucy from about thirty yards behind them, and coming up fast. Evie could have kicked herself. She hadn't been scanning for danger well enough.

Evie got to her knees, not even pausing to wipe the squished amphibian gore off, and held out one hand. She concentrated and formed a fireball, just as Lucy sent another blast at her. Evie held up her fireball, which cushioned the force of it. Lucy was sprinting now, trying to get to her quickly, but Evie held out her hands and willed another fireball to form so she held one on each palm. Marvel Gal skidded to a slippery halt about five yards away. Her own hands were poised to throw one of her lightning bolts, but she hesitated. She actually looked worried.

Evie brought her hands together and joined the two fireballs into the biggest fireball she could. It was about the size of a beach ball. Then she flung it at Lucy, who held up her hands and deflected it with a wall of light. But the force of it knocked her back several paces, into a mess of scorched frogs.

Then Evie saw a slow smile spread across Lucy's face. "Is that all you have?" she asked Evie. "Is that the best you can do? With the combined powers of the Guardians in you? So much for you being the savior. We were wrong to fear you."

Evie didn't like the look of evil confidence on her face. She watched Lucy hold her arms out so wide it seemed her shoulders would dislocate and then she screamed. As if in pain. As if she was drawing every last shred of power she had into one assault. She fell to her knees and then sent a solid wall of white light screaming at Evie who braced for it, trying to create a fireball to absorb it again, but knowing it wasn't going to be enough.

Astaroth leaped in front of the wall of light like he had been shot from a cannon. His own arms were held out, with red and black fire forming around them. His face contorted into a snarl, like a wild beast, his true feature showing, a thin sallow face with thorns projecting all over it. The wall hit him and Evie saw it ripping him to pieces. Tearing the flesh off his bones and then the bones from his form. But he had absorbed so much of the blast that what hit her only knocked her to the ground. She tried to move. Tried to get up, and noticed that her clothes were smoldering. Then felt the pain on her skin, like she had sunburn all over.

"Astaroth!" she called. But there was no sign of the djinn. Nothing. She looked across at Marvel Gal, to see what she would do next. But Lucy looked spent, bent over and gasping as if she was at a high altitude and couldn't breathe.

Evie tried to sit up. Tried to raise a hand and send a fireball at her. Determined not to show her any mercy this time. But she could not concentrate enough to form one. Then she saw Lucy stagger slowly to her feet. Stare at her with fury in her eyes and start conjuring up another blast.

Evie tried again to form a fireball, but knew she'd never make it in time. Then she saw something shining on the ground in front of her. The last fragment of the talisman. She reached out and flung it at Lucy. It was like watching an appliance short-circuit. There was a sudden large spark and crack and Lucy was knocked back to the ground. Unconscious or dead. Evie tried to get to her feet, but she felt everything swaying. Fell back to the ground. Looked up and saw a tall, dark figure leaning over her. Heard the deep voice say, "Now you are mine."

40

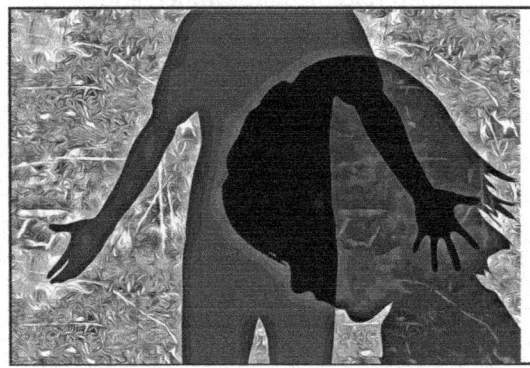

Marc Lépine was born to an American mother and an Algerian father, and struggled with his identity when young.

He grew up in South Carolina and often told people his background was French-Canadian.

At the age of 17 he tried to enter the army, but was refused, being labelled as too 'anti-social'.

He then tried several college courses, particularly engineering-based ones, but was unable to complete any of the courses. He was always blaming someone else for his personal woes, often women, and at the age of 25 he decided to take some action.

On December 6, he entered the Columbia College's engineering school, armed not with books and a laptop—but with a Ruger Mini-14 rifle and a hunting knife.

He went into a second-floor mechanical engineering class, where about 60 students were in attendance.

He fired his gun into the ceiling, getting everyone's attention, and then told the nine women and approximately 50 men to move to different sides of the room. He then told the men to leave the room. They went.

Marc then asked the women if they knew why they were there. When one student replied, "No," he said, "You're women, you're going to be engineers. You're all a bunch of feminists. I hate feminists."

He then opened fire on the students from left to right, killing six, and wounding three others.

Leaving the class he wounded three students in the corridor before entering the financial services office, where he shot and killed a woman who tried to lock the door to stop him.

He then went down to the first-floor cafeteria, where about a hundred people were gathered. He immediately shot a woman, and everyone responded by running or hiding. He saw two women enter a storage area and he followed and shot them.

Strangely, he told another male and female student to come out from under a table where they were hiding. Hesitantly they complied, and he chose not to shoot them.

Marc then went up to the third floor where he shot and wounded one woman and two men in the corridor.

Next he entered another classroom, shooting and wounding one woman standing at the front of the class giving a presentation, and then shot at students in the front row and shot two women who were trying to escape the room. He also stabbed one of the wounded women in the room with his hunting knife, killing her.

His last shot was directed at himself. He wrapped his gun in his jacket and pointed it at his head and shot himself.

He died on the spot. A martyr, he believed.

Marc Lépine killed fourteen women, and injured fourteen other people, ten of whom were women - who he blamed for all his troubles.

All of them blameless.

41

EVIE WOKE UP in darkness, her Spidey-senses tingling so badly she felt her joints were coming apart. She could hear a distant pounding, like a hard rain falling on a metal roof. There was a low rumble coming from somewhere too, like waves or perhaps a strong wind. She listened to it, but couldn't quite figure out what the noise was. Then she recognized it. It was breathing. Something large and nearby.

She lay still and tried to make out any shapes about her. Waiting for her eyes to adjust to the darkness a little more. She turned her heard just a little to try and determine where the breathing was coming from.

Then a low, dark red light fell across her. She turned her head towards the source of it, and saw two blood-red eyes glaring at her out of the darkness, illuminating the space around her as if there was fire behind them. The figure stepped closer and then she knew who it was. The one they all feared.

"Evie!" *he* said, in a deep voice that made the ground vibrate beneath her. Made her insides move. Made her limbs quiver. Then she felt *his* hand upon her. *He* touched her gently on the side of the face, and she felt a soft burning there. Like the hand was emitting heat.

She tried to shrug the hand off. She held up her own hand to form a fireball, but the figure's other hand closed over her fist, holding it shut tightly. She saw the red eyes leaning closer to her, the fire in them burning in a way that hurt to look at. She tried to turn her head away, but the hand on her face moved down to her chin and tilted it upwards. The glowing eyes were filling her with something. Something that was lowering her resistance.

"No," said Evie and shut her eyes.

The figure laughed. A deep rumbling laugh like the sound of drums, and then *he* lifted Evie's head a little higher and began kissing her. Evie felt the hot, coarse lips press hard against hers and felt a tongue like a scaled serpent slithering into her mouth.

"No," she tried to say again, but the serpent tongue in her mouth stole the word away before she could even utter it. The tongue probed deeper, and Evie felt it slipping slowly down inside her throat, seeking out all the passageways within her. "Evie," *he* said in that deep low voice again, and she felt the sound of it pass into her mouth and down along the tongue until it filled every muscle and bone in her body. She was giving herself to *him* now. Would have called on *him* to take her if she could free the words from her mouth. Wanted to become his servant. Wanted to give herself completely to *him*.

But then she found one small spark that still defied *him*, that urged her to say, 'No.' She tried to get the word out. Tried to fight *him*. And then she felt something on her free hand. Fingers. Somebody was prizing her other hand open gently, lifting it up a little into the air. Her hand was filling with warmth, and then she felt a fireball forming. Growing there in her palm. She could feel the light filling the space about them. The dark figure stopped kissing her and turned its head away from her to see what it was.

The fingers on her hands helped guide her as she pushed the fireball right into the large figure's red eyes. There was an angry scream and then Evie felt herself alone again. She listened for the breathing. There was none but her own.

"It's alright. He's gone…for the moment," said a soft, gentle voice.

Evie sat up and blinked. Peered into the blackness. The place was still dark but the sound of rain had receded, as if it were now much, much further away. She searched around for the owner of that familiar voice. "Mom?" she asked.

"I'm here, Evie," her mother said. But she could not see her. She held up a hand and let a small ball of fire form. Then she could see her, but it was as if her mother was a projection onto a cloud of smoke, hazy and half-formed.

"Mom," Evie asked, "is it really you?" She wanted to reach out and hold her so much. Be held by her. Have her mother hold her and tell her that everything would be alright. Fill her with her strength and hope.

"Who else would it be?" she asked Evie. She looked like she had before she had gotten sick. Strong arms and a firm mouth, soft at the edge. And steely eyes.

"Mom," she said again. Then, "Where are we?"

"A dark place, where you don't want to linger," her mother said. "Now come on, stand up!"

Evie climbed to her knees. She still felt a little weak in the legs. Still felt like her exposed skin had been burned.

"That was who I think it was, yes?" she asked her mother.

"Just call him the dark one," she said. "To say *his* name will give him power over you. *He* likes to find ways to trick you into doing that."

"You sound as if you know *him*?" she asked.

"Oh yes. He was once a Guardian, you know. Like your father and the others. But he grew jealous of them. Became filled with bitterness and was banished for it. He has now become a creature of hatred. Wounded by hate the way your father was wounded by love."

"Mom," said Evie. "He told me that he caused your death. Is that true?"

"Only in that you can't get too close to one who wields the powers of the Guardians. Our mortal bodies can't handle it. It causes cancers to grow in us."

"Couldn't he have used his powers to cure you, though?"

"Oh, Evie. It's not so simple. He had already abandoned his powers to try and prevent any more damage. Abandoned his destiny, to be my husband."

"But he could have, well, he could have left you, couldn't he?"

She smiled. Such a sad smile, Evie thought. "He could no more leave me than I could let him leave me," she said. "I hope you come to understand that one day."

Evie didn't know what to say.

"Don't blame your father," she said. "It was as much my choice."

"But…" began Evie, but didn't know how to finish the sentence.

"Shhh," said her mother, like she was talking to her as a young girl. "You can't stay here. It's dangerous. I'll see you back safely and then you need to finish this. You are the only one who can fight him."

"No," said Evie. "He's too strong for me."

"Wait until you get the last portion of your power from the talisman," she said. "Wait until you are whole. Then you'll see just how strong you are."

"Stay with me, mom," Evie said. "Don't send me into this on my own."

"You'll never be on your own," her mother said. "Now come. Malik-ulmaut is waiting for us. And while he's happy to keep others waiting, he doesn't much like to wait himself."

42

After the Independent State of Texas was declared, the issue of Hispanic migrants began to boil over. The new State Government had made no secret of its desire to 'cleanse' the state, as it described its popular policy—which led to many white supremacist groups targeting Hispanics. Many of these fled to nearby States before the borders closed on them.

Those Hispanic migrants left in Texas moved into proclaimed 'safe zones' where they were guaranteed they would be safe from the growing number of attacks, with US National Guard working as protection troops.

But the National Guard were resented by the 'Real Texans', as the groups called themselves, as much as the Hispanic migrants were.

When Mexico closed its border to refugees, the safe zones became the only places to go. But how safe were they?

Just outside the city of Brownsville, a large camp was set up nearly 20,000 Hispanic men, women and children were settled.

Working closely with the Independent State of Texas government, a coalition of Real Texans surrounded the Brownsville camps, cutting off food supplies.

Under an operation code-named Krivaja 95, they claimed there were rebel fighters in the camps that they needed to isolate and disarm.

On 6 July, Real Texan militia brigades first encircled the National Guard Base before advancing on the camps outside Brownsville.

Some of the Guardsmen surrendered to the militias and others withdrew. About 5,000 Hispanics sheltering at the National Guard base were handed over—and not one shot was fired at the militias.

The de facto leader of the Real Texans, Ratko Mladic, said, 'We give this town to the Texan nation. The time has come to take revenge on the Hispanics.'

On the night of July 11th, more than 10,000 Hispanics tried to escape through the darkness —but thousands were captured.

The militia then advanced through the camps, murdering and raping, driving the inhabitants out into holding areas. Some of the inhabitants committed suicide to avoid rape or mutilation.

Many of the women and elderly were then put on buses and taken north. They were told they were being taken to a safer location. Most of the men were made to remain behind. On the evening of July 13, hundreds of blindfolded Hispanic men were taken to remote sites, primarily open fields or old factories or farmlands.

Then the massacres began.

They followed a well-established pattern. The men were first taken to empty buildings and left there under guard for some hours. Then they were taken in trucks or buses to remote locations. Most had either their shoes taken off, or had their hands tied behind their backs or were blindfolded, all the while being promised they were going to be taken to a place of safety to be set free.

Instead they were taken off the trucks in small groups, lined up and shot.

The killings happened in dozens of locations all through the day and in some places even into the night.

Mass graves were dug with tractors and backhoes, and the dead piled in like spoiled fruit. Some who were only wounded when shot, were buried alive.

The killings went on for days before the blood-lust of the militias seemed to subside. By then an estimated 8,000 people had been killed, and their bodies buried in the earth of Texas.

The newly-independent State that was being cleansed.

43

EVIE WOKE UP, lying on a small bench, to see Malikulmaut standing over her. It appeared to be late morning. They were in a small park, with a disused swing set near some trees. She looked around to try and make out where they were. Still in the vicinity of Fort Lauderdale, judging by the humidity. She tried to stand, but it hurt too much.

"I am glad to see you are safe," he said, making no attempt to help her up.

"It's okay," she said. "I've got it." And she tried to get to her feet once more. On the third try she made it. "I don't suppose you have one of those guides for dummies as to just what happened to me?" she asked. "I mean, I saw my mother. Or I imagined I saw my mother. Or something."

"Yes. Or something," he said.

"Where was I, exactly?" she asked.

"Another place," he said.

She wanted to press him for more details, but then noticed that his garments were torn and singed and his face looked gaunter than ever.

"What happened to you?" she asked. "You look like… look like…"

"I believe the mortal expression that best describes it is, I have been in the wars," he said.

"What about Adam?" she asked. "Is he okay?"

"He has been in the wars also," he said.

Evie grimaced. "What's happened?" she asked.

"The past few days have been hard. So many battles to fight. You have been away longer than you know. In the last two days alone, two female senators have been assassinated, three state legislatures have been taken over by militias, and open warfare has broken out on the Canadian-North Dakota border. Ethic riots have erupted in many cities. There has been a mass chemical poisoning around Pennsylvania. And Disneyland has been evacuated due to an anthrax attack.'

"Oh!" said Evie. Then, "How is the rest of the world faring?"

"Not dissimilar," he said.

Evie looked at the ground. Then said, "But you and Adam have also managed to stop some things, yes?"

"It is not my role to intervene directly," he said, "although I will defend myself when attacked." Then he almost smiled and added, "But there is also some good news ."

"There is?" asked Evie.

"Of sorts. You are still alive. Still able to continue your mission."

Evie wanted to shout at him and balled her fists. "And what is my mission exactly? I thought it was to return the four pieces of that talisman to get this special power that I need, but that's not going to happen now, is it, since Rafael didn't contribute to the talisman. But I think you knew that already. I don't have full powers—which Marvel Gal discovered, and wiped the floor with me—so now all the super-villains probably know it too. And I now have to find my own father, yes, but nobody knows where he is. Which makes me think, how could you not know that Rafael didn't contribute to the talisman, unless…" She stopped. "You son of a bitch!" she spat. "Of course you knew that Rafael couldn't give me the full powers, didn't you! You knew this was a goddamned fool's errand. And you knew they'd be chasing me across the country. But that must have been your plan, right? Put all the attention on me so that you could do something else!"

This time Malikulmaut did smile.

"You asshole!" she said. "Astaroth got himself killed for this wild goose chase of yours—just as I was starting to become fond of the little twerp. And I came pretty damn close to getting myself killed, too. So you'd better look me in the eyes and tell me that it was worth it all, and that you've found my father and that we're back in control again, or so help me I'll burn the rest of your garments leaving you standing there naked!"

Malikulmaut stopped smiling. He looked at Evie, his eyes glowing just a little, and he said, "Your efforts have been worthwhile and mean you can now take the fight to them."

"What?!" spluttered Evie. "I asked if you know where my father is."

Malikulmaut still did not answer.

"And are we now on the front foot in some way that that I'm not aware of, that gives us a clear advantage?"

Malikulmaut did not answer.

Evie looked at the ground. "Okay," she said. "Let me see if I can sum up the situation we've got here. I've only gotten maybe half the powers I need to stop the baddies. I'm like Supergirl wearing kryptonite underpants. I've shown all the demons where the Guardians have been hiding, putting them all at risk. My father, who is the only one who can help me gain these full powers—which I'm not even really sure that I actually want—is missing and nobody knows where he is. Though the demons will have figured out by now that he was the creator of the last piece of the talisman and will be looking for him too. Meanwhile, things are going to shit all over the place, pushing us closer and closer to the edge. Is that about it?"

Malikulmaut still did not answer.

"Well, I'm sorry," she said. "But I just don't see where the good news is. You don't take part in the fighting directly. All my possible allies are gone or in hiding, and I'm barely able to stand up. What do we possibly have going for us?"

"We have you," said Malikulmaut very slowly.

Evie felt like lying back down and crying.

"It's not enough," she said. Almost a whisper.

"It will be more than enough," he said back. "Your father knew it. Your mother knew it."

"Don't you dare mention my mother's name to me," she said. "Or my father's, for that matter."

Malikulmaut turned his head and looked to the sky, as if searching for a sign of something, or as if listening in to some hidden demon radio frequency. He frowned.

"What is it?" she asked.

"Things are changing again. The changes will be getting faster."

"Of course they will," she said. "This time we'll be standing in a zombie apocalypse."

"Not yet," he said, "though that may come."

"So what's the plan now?" she asked wearily.

"You will need to confront Lucy and her two brothers," he said.

"Brothers?" she asked, and shook her head a little. "So they can collectively kick my ass, yes?"

"I think it wise if you take them on one at a time."

"Okay," she said. "I think I've met one of them already. But tell me who they are and where I can find them, though I'm pretty sure I'm not going to like what you tell me."

"On the contrary," he said. "I think you might like it very much."

Evie looked at him with a glare of suspicion. "Alright," she said. "So before you tell me, there's one more thing I need to know."

Malikulmaut raised an eyebrow. Just a little.

"I'd been meaning to ask Astaroth if Bob Dylan was a demon or not. I mean, I don't really want to know if he was, but I was going to ask him. You know. So I just wanted to know what he would have said."

"I believe he would not have told you," said Malikulmaut. And he held out something to her. Evie took it. It was the last piece of the talisman, sealed in some type of woven silver container. "Don't touch it directly unless you want to tell the demons where you are," he said.

"Yeah. Like that's just what I was planning on doing," she said.

"You will need a vehicle," he said. "You have a long drive ahead of you through some dangerous lands, and they will surely attempt to pursue you."

44

When the large chemical company Union Carbide announced it was opening a large plant near the towns of Allentown and Bethlehem, Pennsylvania, it was a general cause of celebration. There would be a lot of jobs in a plant like that.

The main product manufactured there was the pesticide carbaryl, which was made using the highly-toxic chemical compound methyl isocyanate, known as MIC.

As technology developed, however, other manufacturers found ways to produce carbaryl without using MIC, and the plant started accumulating excess stocks of the substance, stored in three large, underground tanks.

It was in one of these three tanks that a problem occurred.

The tank contained 42 tons of MIC, but many of the safety systems were malfunctioning. Plant managers were trying to find a way to extract the MIC safely by unclogging blocked lines.

Over the course of several years there had been smaller accidents at the plant, when MIC gas had leaked, seriously injuring workers.

The crucial event occurred on the evening of December 2nd, when water leaked into the tank through the side pipe. This led to a disastrous reaction that quickly built-up pressure in the tank.

Maintenance workers, seeing the rapid rise in pressure, assumed it was just another system failure, and ignored it.

The first they suspected something was wrong was at 11.30pm when workers started experiencing the effects of MIC gas exposure. Maintenance workers were instructed to search for a leak. This was found at 11.45 and reported to the manager, but he decided he would address it after a tea break, half an hour later.

By the time the tea break ended, however, the reaction in the tank had reached a critical state with temperatures and pressure building up to extreme levels. The emergency relief valve burst open and the safety device, designed to burn off the MIC gas as it escaped, failed.

About 40 tons of MIC gas escaped from the tank into the air, and the winds blew it towards the nearby towns in the Lehigh Valle.

At approximately 2:00am the plant's public alert siren sounded.

But by then it was far too late.

Some people woke in panic and pain, coughing and with severe eye irritation and a feeling they were suffocating. Other suffered stomach pains and vomiting. As people realised what was happening, they started fleeing their houses, but being heavier than air the gas settled close to the ground, and children inhaled higher doses than adults. Up to 200,000 children lived in the area.

By first light the depth of the tragedy was apparent. Thousands of people had died from choking, circulatory collapse or pulmonary oedemas. Those who survived the night had damage to their lungs, kidneys and livers.

As hospitals in the area struggled to cope with the numbers of victims, trees started losing their leaves and dead livestock began bloating in the fields, creating further health hazards.

Over 3,500 people died and another half a million people were injured, suffering nerve damage, respiratory issues, birth defects, and higher rates of cancer and tuberculosis.

Senior management of the company were convicted of causing death by negligence and sentenced to two years' imprisonment and a fine of several thousand dollars each, but were released on bail shortly after the verdict.

And the exact cause of the disaster is contested. Activists claim it was due to poor management and deferred maintenance, but the company insists water entered the tank through an act of sabotage. A single worker had removed the safety valve to the tank and fitted a water hose to it.

But the question remains, what would drive anybody to do that?

Part 3
Paradise Reclaimed

45

EVIE TOOK A DEEP breath and then blasted the door right off its hinges. She was really getting the hang of those flame balls now and could control the power blasts much better. A half hour practicing in a meadow in South Carolina, scorching a few crows, had made all the difference. She was also able to channel the power into her body better, keeping herself full of energy and strength. It had been a fraught, non-stop 1,000-mile drive north on an acquired motorbike—which proved much faster and more economical than a car, as getting gas had become nearly impossible. All she had to do on the bike was siphon a few gallons out of wrecked cars here and there.

She had to fight her way past a crazy, racist gang in Georgia, speed past some confederate re-enactors with real guns in Virginia, and she just went off-road and zoomed around the endless militia roadblocks. Normally she would have felt too tired to even knock vigorously on the door. But now she was bristling with energy. Although equally, that could have been due to her anticipation of this meeting.

Stigl was sitting at his dining table poring over a thick book and looked up in surprise. "Hello, Doctor," she said. "Forgive me for not making an appointment."

"What…what are you doing here?" he asked, his eyes so wide with astonishment it looked like they might just pop out and roll across the table.

"I've come to have a little talk with you," she said and held her arms apart, conjuring a flaming ball on each of them.

His eyes, starting to look less liable to fall out, moving back and forward rapidly between the two flame balls. He held up his hands, and said, "Woah, woah, it's all cool. Come in and have a seat. I mean we can just talk about this, you know."

She advanced into the apartment slowly. He jumped up and pulled out a seat, for her, his eyes now fixed squarely on the carpet. "I can explain everything," he said. "Everything."

"Then you'd better start talking now," she said, not taking the offered seat.

"I have something I think you'd better see," he said. "It will help to explain things."

"What?" she asked.

"I'll fetch it," he said.

"Move very slowly," she said.

He did…until he had the wand out of the cabinet drawer and in his hand. Then he whirled rapidly and pointed it at her, a blast of frozen, blue ice spitting at her from it. But she was ready. She hadn't expected Stigl to give up easily and knew his apartment would be full of all kinds of weird, demon shit that he'd probably try to use on her.

She blocked the blast and sent one back at him. It knocked the wand out of his hand and bent it out of shape. He clutched his hand, obviously wounded, and muttered something Evie couldn't hear. The apartment turned pitch black in an instant. The darkness was like a blanket; no light came in from the open door or the windows and even Evie's two flame balls only penetrated a few inches into the darkness around them.

On a hunch Evie closed her fists, collapsing the flame balls into nothingness and ducked down to the floor. She felt something whoosh over her head and strike the door frame behind her. Something large and heavy.

She was tempted, just for a moment, to make a sound like she had been hit, but for all she knew that spear or whatever it was, was designed to obliterate a person so entirely that he'd know it was a ruse and aim his next weapon at her voice. So she rolled across the floor silently, and threw a random flame ball towards where she thought he might be, then she was down and rolling back in the other direction.

Something else wacked heavily into the floor where she had just been. She could smell something like sulphur burning where it had struck. That'd make a mess of his carpet, she thought. Again she overcame the temptation to taunt him and kept low and silent. His move now. She waited, controlling her breathing so as to make as little noise as possible and listened.

She could hear his breathing. Soft, but quite fast. He was scared. Good. She heard him mutter something else and then felt a scratching dryness in her throat. She paused and took a slow, deep breath. There was something different about the air. He'd done something to it.

Sucked the oxygen out of it, or maybe sent up a poisonous mist or who knew what.

Time for a gamble, she thought and opened her palms. She concentrated and the flame balls formed and she hurled them across the room towards the sound of his breathing. One of them struck home. Well, struck Dr Strange. He gave a gurgling cry and suddenly the room was full of light again. Evie narrowed her eyes and braced herself. But he was down. The fat fuck was on the ground, crying. "Don't kill me, don't kill me," he said, holding a hand up to ward her off.

"So you've done something so bad that you think I'll kill you for it?" she asked. "I wonder what that could be?"

"I'll tell you everything," he said, trying to get to his feet.

"Yes, you will," she said, not stepping any closer to him. Then she saw his hand move to his belt. It came up with a small, ornate knife in it. She opened her palms again, but he did not attack her, he stabbed at his eyes. The knife gouged deep into one eye and then twisted it right out of the eye socket. He was trying for the second eye when she hit him with another flame ball, knocking him to the floor again. She strode over quickly and put a foot on his arm, pinning him to the ground.

"Oh no," she said, and she bent down close and pried open his remaining eye with her fingers, despite his efforts to keep it shut tight. Then she followed the crazily rolling eye until she had him. His face went slack. She'd been in a state of high anticipation of this talk for the last twelve hours and nothing as simple as him trying to gouge out his eyes was going to stop her.

The ride from Fort Lauderdale had been a long one, and the further she went the crazier the country became. Every time she stopped to buy or steal gas she checked the news on whatever radio or TV monitor she could find. Still no internet anywhere. Several states had declared hostilities on others. Canada had also invaded Montana. There were increased terror attacks everywhere. Most airlines were grounded due to more cyber-attacks. A ferry was sunk on the Mississippi. Several churches had been bombed. There were a handful of school shootings across the mid-West. A town's water supply had been poisoned in Tennessee. A power station in Vermont had been burned down. And another three senators had been assassinated, two of them women and the third a vocal opponent of Islam. And some crazy prince of the new kingdom of Utah had shot up the royal family there.

It was a hard rain a-falling.

As she rode she spoke aloud, as if Astaroth was still there with her, swearing vengeance for every unnecessary death and act of violence. She missed his smart-ass mouth, and wished she wasn't doing this alone. But now, as she stood over Stigl she was glad there was no one to witness this or to counsel her to keep her temper in check.

"Okay Doctor Strange-fuck," she said. "Let's start at the very beginning, a very good place to start."

"The Sound of Music," he said.

"This isn't a quiz show," she said. "Do you know where my father is?"

"No,' he said. 'We've been looking for him."

"Okay, who is 'we', exactly?"

"My brother and sister."

"I've met Lucy," she said. "You hardly seem related to her."

"We have the same father."

"So how come your sister got all those superpowers and you turned into a fat loser?"

"We've given her our powers to increase hers. It is the best way of assuring victory over the Guardians."

Evie had spent a lot of time thinking what she was going to ask, but this was going in unexpected new directions. "And some dumb chump has just tracked around the country finding their hideouts for you, right?"

"Right," he said.

Evie frowned and scratched at her chin.

"So how do I defeat your sister?"

"She was greatly weakened by your last battle. She'll take time to regain her strength."

Evie nodded. Just a little. That was some good news.

"How can I stop all these demons going on their death rampages?"

"Only my father can stop them."

"How can I defeat your father?"

"Only the Guardians can defeat him. Or the Savior."

"And who is the savior?"

"You should know that," he said.

Evie pursed her lips. "How much power will I have if get all the power of that talisman?" she asked slowly.

"It would be considerable."

"Do I have a chance of defeating your sister if I don't find it?"

"Quite possibly, if you find her before she recovers."

"Do I have a chance of defeating your father?"

He smiled. "No one shall ever defeat my father. No one."

"Then one more question before I zap your ass off into the netherworld. Where do I find your sister and brother?"

"Salem," he said.

"Well, that figures," she said. "Place of the witch trials."

"No," he said. "North Salem in New York."

"And where exactly?"

"Graymalkin Lane," he said. "The Xavier mansion."

"From the X-men? Isn't that just in the comics?" she asked.

He only smiled. A smile that really pissed her off. So she held out her hands and concentrated on the biggest fireballs she could conjure.

"Say hello to daddy for me," she said.

46

The formation of the Kingdom of Utah caught many other parts of the USA by surprise, as did the popularity of the King, Birendra, and his wife the Queen, Aishwarya, who promised their people a period of prosperity and pride

Scholars and journalist and pundits believed they may have fulfilled this promise, but for the fact that the Crown Prince, Dipendra, shot his family dead.

The royal family, riding a wave of popular support, held family get-togethers at the royal palace in Salt Lake City, hosted by King Birendra and Queen Aishwarya.

On the fateful evening there were a dozen members of the royal family in attendance—including Prince Dipendra.

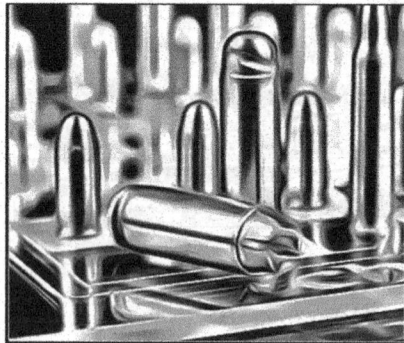

No one noticed anything wrong until Dipendra said he was tired and retired to his room early— before returning dressed in combat fatigues carrying several guns. The family knew he had a fascination with guns and wondered what he was doing.

He walked straight up to his father the king, aimed a gun at him, and shot him. Everyone in the room watched him fall to the ground, and then saw Prince Dipendra push the body a little with his foot.

They could all see the King was dead and stared at Dipendra in shock.

Dipendra then took up a machine gun and opened fire on the rest of the family, spraying bullets around the room. He killed ten people. Including most of his family.

Then he turned a gun on himself. But the shot failed to kill him, and he was taken to hospital in a coma.

Ironically, due to his wiping out of most of the line of succession, he was declared king - while in a coma.

The bodies of the royal family were carried through the streets on litters, followed by tears of grief and outrage.

Dipendra died in hospital without regaining consciousness, and the brother of the former King Birendra, Gyanendra, became king.

Several theories for the massacre were cast around, including that Gyanendra was behind it all himself.

But if so that backfired as a popular revolt forced him to abdicate and Utah became a Republic once more, and then reintegrated into the Union.

Scholars and journalist and pundits have written extensively on the massacre of Utah's short-lived royals, but none of the theories adequately explain what motivated Prince Dipendra to take up a gun and turn it on his own family.

47

AS SHE LEFT Stigl's apartment Evie wondered if she had now tipped off her enemies as to where she was. No matter, she thought, she'd be long gone in a few moments. She walked over to her stolen motorbike, pleased to see there were no gangs hanging on the streets anymore and hoped they were still supporting the needle exchange clinic. She climbed onto the bike and looked at the gas gauge. She'd need to refill. It was about a five-hour drive back to New York and she'd arrive early in the morning if things didn't get too crazy.

She looked into her wallet. She was running low on cash and would have to eyeball somebody to pay for her gas. The gangsters on the streets would have come in useful for that, she thought. No matter, she'd stop some other hoodlum, pretend to be asking for directions, and get him to hand over all the cash tucked into his socks. If he had his money tucked into his underwear though, she'd wait for the next guy.

She started the bike and pulled out into the street. She hadn't even reached the end of the block when a big Cadillac pimpmobile careened out of a side street and hit her side on, knocking her off and up against a power pole.

"Holy fucking bat-turds!" she cursed and tried to get out from under the bike. It had taken the brunt of the blow, but it was heavy and hard to move. She looked at the car that had hit her and saw two demons climbing out, purple and green. Both had handguns. She had something better: her hands. The two walked over to her and held up their guns side-ways, in best gangster style. She opened her palms and sent flame balls at them. *Pow! Pow!* They fell to the ground, the demons in them gone.

"Yeah, bring it on," said Evie, and she pushed and struggled until she'd wriggled herself free of the bike. Then she heard sirens approaching. That wasn't good. She was pleased to find she didn't have any serious injuries. Thank you new powers. She started running down the side street, ready to jump behind a bush or a trash can if the sirens got too close. She'd have a car soon enough, but she suspected they'd now be waiting for her at the mansion.

"Do you know what you need?" she said, as if she could hear Astaroth running beside her on his little legs, advising her of the bleeding obvious. "You need a cunning plan!"

It took her five minutes to get a car and another twenty minutes to come up with a plan. With a bit more time she might have come up with something better, but she thought Astaroth would approve.

All she had to do was find a gas station or late night 7-Eleven with a female attendant who looked passably like her. That wasn't too much to hope for, was it? Though perhaps it was, during a national crisis when most stores and gas stations were locked up tight and weren't opening for anybody. If worse came to worst she would settle for one of the many looters she had seen around stores. She knew that using her eyeballing powers might lead to some bad payback—but how much worse could things get than they already were?

The drive to New York was fairly quick, as it was so late at night and most people were probably hunkered down in their homes watching the world go to shit on their TV screens. There were lots of emergency vehicles on the roads, but they all looked like they had places to get to and nobody stopped her.

She arrived at North Salem about six in the morning, with the first rays of sunlight, and drove around slowly, looking for a place to scout out her target from. Luckily the car she had boosted had a satnav in it. She was surprised to find there really was a Graymalkin Lane. And there really was an X-men type mansion on the Lane too. Maybe the demons were just big comic book fans?

She parked about half a mile down the road and sat in the car listening to the radio. She would have liked to scan the airwaves and find a Dylan song, leaning back into his gravelly voice and deep metaphors, but she had to look for news bulletins. The story came on about 6:45, between a story on a deadly new virus they were calling the zombie plague, and a story on violent water wars along the drying Colorado River. Terror fugitive and rogue FBI agent Evie Mickelson, who was responsible for a string of terror attacks across the nation, had taken hostages inside a children's hospital in Washington DC and had a nurse call some media outlets and tell them that she was going to make a public statement to the media at 7:15am. She was, the newsreader said, going to warn of a great security threat to the nation. And then the announcers speculated as to what Evie was going to reveal and whether the security forces would allow any broadcast of her statement, or whether they would raid the hospital before 7:15.

Evie climbed out of the car. The security forces might block her statement, but wouldn't attack a hospital filled with children. She had fifteen minutes to get in place.

Approaching the mansion she felt like she was in a movie, running fast and low over the large lawns, and every time she saw a demon-possessed guard she'd zap him or her with a small fire blast. As soon as a fireball touched them, they fell to the ground and the demon within disappeared in a flash of dark smoke. "Jean Grey, eat your heart out," she said.

Getting into the mansion was just as easy. She simply knocked on the door. A rather ugly butler possessed by an even uglier demon with a brown spike-covered face opened it and barely had time to open its mouth in surprise before she hit him with a flame ball. "Hasta la vista, baby," she muttered, looking around the interior. The place was huge and she wondered where those two spawn of Satan would be hiding. Probably near the largest TV in the house.

She closed her eyes and listened. Her hearing was sharper than ever now and she picked up many noises but zeroed in on the sound of a TV presenter. Upstairs to the right. She ran up the staircase two steps at a time, sending another demon off to demon land on her way, and then along a short corridor. She found herself at the open door of a large room with a gigantic TV screen dominating one wall.

She didn't know why she had imagined that Lucy and her brother would be in there alone. The room was crowded with people possessed by demons of all shapes and sizes, like it was a casting agency for models for a Hieronymus Bosch painting. And they all turned and looked at her as she stood in the doorway.

"Damn!" she said. Many of the demons had weapons of some description and raised them in her direction. Except for the few slower ones who looked back and forward between the TV screen where Nora, the middle-aged redneck looter, was inside the hospital doing an award-winning job of impersonating her—and Evie in the doorway here. Okay, she thought. Save those guys until last.

And then she saw Nora on the TV emerge from the hospital doors, surrounded by a ring of children. There was a scrum of media in front of her. But Evie could see she was never going to make it as far as the closest microphones. One of the children pressed up against her was a demon. A purple-faced little fat thing with poisonous warts that made her look like the love child of Astaroth and the Gruffalo. She wished she could ask him about that.

Without being conscious of it, but like somebody else was guiding her hand, Evie reached into her jacket pocket and seized the talisman out of its silver pouch. It glowed hot and it was like somebody had pressed a turbo-charge button in her brain. She suddenly knew there were 17 demons in the room. She knew where Lucy and her brother were. She knew which demons were going to shoot first and she knew which ones presented the least threat. Then she was firing off fireballs as she dived to the side of the door. Bullets splintered the wood and green ice blasts struck the wall behind her. These demons were of a higher class than your average demon on the street and carried some considerable firepower. But she was moving like *Kick Ass's* Hit Girl. Or like Trinity in *the Matrix*. Or like Evie Mickelson.

Evie cast fireballs to the left and right and ahead and behind and she ran half-way up walls and flipped back onto her feet again, sliding under tables and jumping off chairs to launch herself over the heads of demons. Every fireball hit a demon and every demon she hit disappeared out of its host's body.

A few shots came close to hitting her and one ice blast caught her on the thigh, nearly knocking her to the ground, but she had cleared the room of demons so quickly that her view of the TV was unimpeded enough to see the small demon child jab a syringe into Nora's waist. Nora looked down at it for the briefest of moments, looked up to the cameras and collapsed to the ground.

"No!" Evie yelled. She hadn't wanted Nora to be injured. Had expected the security forces would try and take her alive to interrogate her. Then she turned back to the last two people standing. Lucy and her brother.

Marvel Gal was wearing another type of backyard superhero costume designed for the color-blind, with loose trousers, cinched in tight at the lower legs, and a multi-colored blouse with high shoulder pads. Before Evie could even tell her about her dress sense, Lucy bared her teeth and spread her hands out wide. Evie spread her own arms wide too. Fireballs forming in each. She would have liked them to be larger, but she had just depleted a vast amount of her power.

"A clever ruse," said Lucy, indicating the TV screen with her head.

"But then you went and spoiled it by doing something dumb like coming here," said her brother. Evie glanced at him. He was the tall and thin man who had sat opposite her on the plane—with the bomb.

He was almost handsome in a dark and brooding way, in his black pants and black leather jacket. He had close-cropped, black hair and his sideburns were trimmed to form two sharp blades on either side of his face.

"Sit down and shut up," she said and sent a bolt at him. It knocked him off his feet and sent him sprawling over one of the few undamaged couches in the room. The demons hadn't managed to hit her, but they'd sure made a mess of the room's furnishings by hitting just about everything else.

She turned back to Marvel Gal and realized that while zapping her brother might have felt like the right thing to do at the time, it left her open for an attack. And sure enough Lucy sent two quick blasts at Evie. She blocked one but the other grazed her. It pushed her back towards the door to the room but Evie knew it was not nearly as strong as the blasts she had hit her with in the Fort Lauderdale fight.

"You'll have to do better than that—bee-atch!" Evie said.

Evie blocked two more blasts from Marvel, then saw a movement out of the corner of her eye. She zapped the demon sneaking into the room behind her. She'd need to finish this quickly. She turned sideways and held out her hands in opposite directions. She sent one ball of fire at the ceiling over the doorway, bringing down a pile of rubble and sent the other at Lucy.

She caught it with her hands and threw it back at Evie. Evie blocked it, and thought, neat trick. But one she could use too. Then she spread her arms wide and let two more fireballs form. Marvel Gal saw an opening and sent a quick blast at her. Evie tried to catch it. She missed and it hit her square in the chest, like taking a blow from an Olympic champion boxer. She staggered and struggled for breath. Well, a trick she could use too after a bit more practice! Marvel Gal sent another at her. This one she caught. And held. Marvel Gal tried again and again. Evie caught all three. Then Lucy realized what she was doing and her face went pale. Evie smiled a wicked grin. She lifted her hands up in front of her with two flame balls larger than any she had ever created. Lucy turned her head towards her brother and leaped for him as Evie fired them at her.

The blasts caught her in the air just as her hand touched her brother's, and then she was gone. Not like the way the demons disappeared, but the way her brother Stigl had gone, with a large burst of fire and a scream of pain. Evie hadn't expected that, but she wouldn't complain.

She felt exhausted and looked around for a chair that wasn't ruined. There was one near the TV. She walked over to it, stepping over the bodies of unconscious humans now freed of their demons. She glanced at the chaos on the screen. Security forces and media were struggling with each other for access to Nora's fallen body. Poor Nora. Then she stopped.

Damien was standing up and straightening his clothes. He flexed his fingers, like he was trying out new strength in them. Oh, how dumb she could be. By touching him, Lucy had given him her remaining power to add to his own! Then Damien looked at Evie. His eyes glowed red and angry.

48

The first water wars began along the diminishing rivers of Arizona and Texas with disputes between crop and cattle farmers. Both accused the other of taking more than their allocated amounts of water, and began sabotaging the other's water pipelines.

The first thing that the rest of the nation knew about the water wars was when several cattle farmers opened fire on a small group of crop farmers they had caught trying to destroy their water pipes.

Then it seemed that water wars were happening everywhere. The Colorado River, the Rio Grande, and many others. Once mighty rivers that were now often no more than slow streams.

And underground aquifers were being pumped so heavily—often by illegal or private users—that sinkholes were becoming more and more common, and in some areas, large plains of land sunk over 25 feet, destroying buildings located there.

Industry, local governments, farmers and consumers were all shouting out for their 'fair share' of the diminishing water. But the plain fact was that there was no longer enough water to go around. This led inevitably to food shortages, as it takes over 600 gallons of water to make just one hamburger.

Some states—such as Arizona— saw privatization of water as the solution, but this led to massive protests as water prices rose, and people had their water cut off for non-payment.
Thousands flooded the streets of Phoenix, blocking roads with barricades and waving banners.

The protesters pelted legislators and police with empty water bottles. Police responded by shooting protesters with water cannons, which was treated as an insult, enraging the crowd, culminating in several protesters being shot by police.

Public outrage spread to many cities across the nation, with more and more groups coming out to protest at control and restrictions of water supplies, which were often seen as benefiting the rich over the poor, or industry over the public.

In El Paso, National Guard troops tried to remove a roadblock and met with fierce resistance, resulting in an order to open fire.

Two people were killed, including a teenage boy, and several others were wounded. Angry protesters overpowered the guardsmen and used their weapons against their officers.

Two guardsmen were seriously wounded, including the captain of the guardsmen, and they were taken to a nearby hospital.

But via social media, the enraged protesters discovered their whereabouts and stormed the hospital, dragging the captain from his bed, before beating him to death and dismembering his body.

The Government finally admitted the scale of the crisis when it was revealed that two-thirds of emergency water storage, largely in aquifers, had been consumed.

As thousands of acres of land turned to dustbowls—as they had in the 1930s—people took to the roads, heading to states that had more water. More to share.

But this quickly led to states restricting access and closing borders, much as they had done in the 1930s.

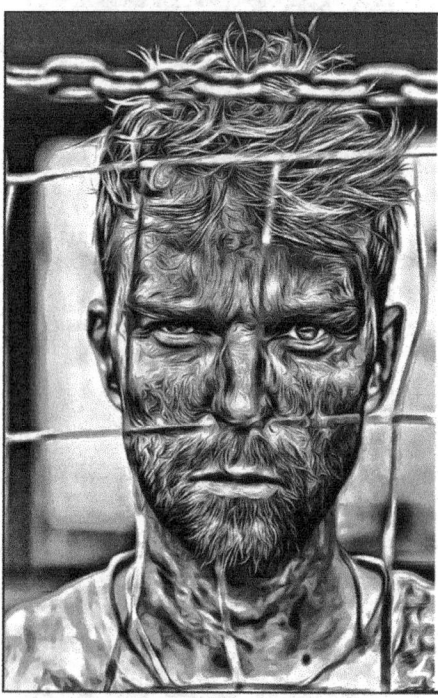

Soon millions of people were crowded into makeshift camps, refugees in their own country.

Thirsty and enraged.

A volatile combination.

49

EVIE FELT GIDDY. She closed her eyes just a moment and then opened them again. What had happened? She was sitting down. She was back on the airplane. The air was thick and warm. The light around her dark red. She snapped her head to the side. Damien was sitting there with that bomb on his lap grinning at her.

"Remember me?" he asked.

Evie was disoriented. This had been a dream, yeah? How was she back in the dream?

"Or is it a dream?" he asked, his finger hovering over the big red button on the bomb.

She didn't answer him. She looked to the other side. The seat next to her was empty. No Astaroth. She looked back. He was smiling at her like they had all the time in the world to get acquainted. And she found him disturbingly handsome. What-the-fuck-was-that-all-about?

"What if all dreams were real, and all reality was just another dream?" he asked her.

"That's not possible," she said.

"That's so nai-Evie," he said, mocking her.

She growled at him. Held her hands out and tested them. A flame ball started to appear.

"Let's consider this, then," he said, seemingly uninterested in what she was doing. "If this is a dream and I go ahead and push this button, then it doesn't matter what happens. Even if my bomb explodes and hundreds of people on this flight die, it won't really have happened. Well, it will have happened in this dream and all these dream people around us will be dead, of course, but can you kill dream people? Or do they just sort of disappear in a puff and go back to where they came from?"

Then he put a finger under his chin. "Hang on," he said. "If that were true, then it would mean that all the demons in the world that you've encountered and slain might just be dream things too. Or perhaps it was the world that you were living in that was a dream world? Hmmmm. A problem, isn't it."

Evie let the flame balls grow a little bigger. She wondered if it was some enchantment he was using that made her feel attracted to him. Had to be—he was such a dick!

"Aha," he said. "But if this is not just a dream, then throwing flaming balls all over the place could prove very dangerous to everyone around you. You might bring the plane down and kill them all."

"I could test it by just killing you," she said. "If you disappeared in a puff and scream of agony, then maybe that would prove that this is a dream."

"*If* you could kill me," he said. "And *if* I disappeared. What if I killed you and then *you* disappeared in a puff and a scream of agony? What might that mean? Or what if you killed me and I just lay here dead while everyone around us woke up? What might that mean?"

Evie slowly closed her fists and let the flame balls die.

This was a test of some kind. It didn't matter if it was a dream or not. That was not the point of it.

"My father would call that wise," he said, and gave her that deadly, charming smile again.

Evie felt him trying some demon juju on her. She had to keep her mind focused. Had to remember that he and his sister had strong powers of suggestion and influence. Like their father. And perhaps this was all a ploy to try and get her to say *his* name? Summoning him through to this realm, whatever it was.

"I've been thinking," she said, "about something my old buddy Astaroth said about all the wars over the centuries, the Crusades in particular."

A spark of interest appeared in his eyes.

"We could think of it as a struggle by the Christians to reclaim the Holy Land from the Muslim forces who occupied them, yes?"

He nodded.

"But we could also think of them as crazy Christians invading Muslim countries and committing terror and atrocities in the name of their religion. Exactly the way the modern world paints Islamic extremism."

He smiled.

"So what if the three major Crusades were a failure not just in trying to ultimately capture the Holy Land, but a repeated failure in trying to trigger a global religious war? Sure, Christianity and Islam seemed fit for purpose, but what if all those conflicts that had led to the deaths of up to a million people, stopped instead of escalating, what would you do then?"

He wasn't smiling any more.

"I think you'd try and trigger other wars. Internal ones. Ideological ones. Sunni versus Shiite. Protestant versus Catholic. Kill a few more million in the Thirty Years War in Europe, and the Eighty Years War. Keep people on their toes and ready to defend their religious beliefs with insane violence. Lebanon. China. Northern Ireland. Spain. India. I think there are plenty of examples. But what if you think of each of them as an experiment? A test to see if the environment was right yet. The post-independence slaughter in India between Muslims and Hindus. That must have looked encouraging. Or the Tai Ping rebellion in China. The Spanish Inquisition had the cruelty, but not the numbers. The Christian invasion of South America the same—more died of disease than violence. They didn't reach critical boiling point though, did they? Because the Guardians stopped them in time. But what if you took the Guardians out of the play—one by one—in a long, slow strategy that centered around people losing their belief in them? And then you tried it all over again—not just one big conflict—but lots and lots of ideological conflicts. Left versus right, blue versus red, old versus new, us versus them—might that be enough to trigger the end game?"

He sneered at her. "That's your understanding of the end game?" he asked.

"So you admit there's an end game," she said.

"Of course there's an end game," he said. "But you just don't see it."

"Don't I?" she asked. "Then let's end this game," she said, and she rose from her seat. She had her seatbelt off and her hands were already apart generating another pair of fireballs. She reached across the aisle and grabbed his hands. He shouted in pain and he dropped the bomb onto the floor.

But then he surprised her by jumping up out of his seat and knocking her hands away and grabbing her around the throat. She reached up to grab him. He braced for her, but she dropped to the floor, breaking his grip, then she tried to roll away from him. But the aisle was too narrow and she caught her feet in a seat.

Then his foot was slamming down towards her head. She held up her hands, grabbed his shoe and twisted it. It sent him spinning into the seat, giving her a chance to get to her feet and stagger back, away from him.

He got back to his own feet slowly, and then straightened his clothes carefully. Then turned to regard her. She was ready, feet apart and her arms out wide, fireballs ready to throw at him.

"This will be enjoyable," he said and he suddenly pushed his hands towards her, sending a beam of light straight at her. She held up her hands to catch it, but it hit her with a force that pushed her backwards and sent the beam of light shooting up and out. He was stronger with Lucy's powers. And she saw some of the beam of light had deflected off her, puncturing gashes in the sides of the plane.

"Shit!" she said. That was bad. Evie reeled as the plane lurched. Bags and papers and clothing were swirling all around her, furiously being sucked out of the plane.

And the people around her were suddenly all awake, screaming and clawing to stay in their seats. Evie felt the plane lurch again as a large gap appeared in the wall of the plane. It was coming apart. The plane was about to break in two and plummet from the skies. Everyone would die. And she had killed them.

She looked up at Damien and saw him laughing. It had that same chilling effect on her that the laugh of the dark cloud man had.

"You want to try and save them, don't you?" he said. "Well, you can only do that by calling my father."

Evie closed her eyes and concentrated. Trying to think what her own father would advise her to do. Trying to think what she could do.

50

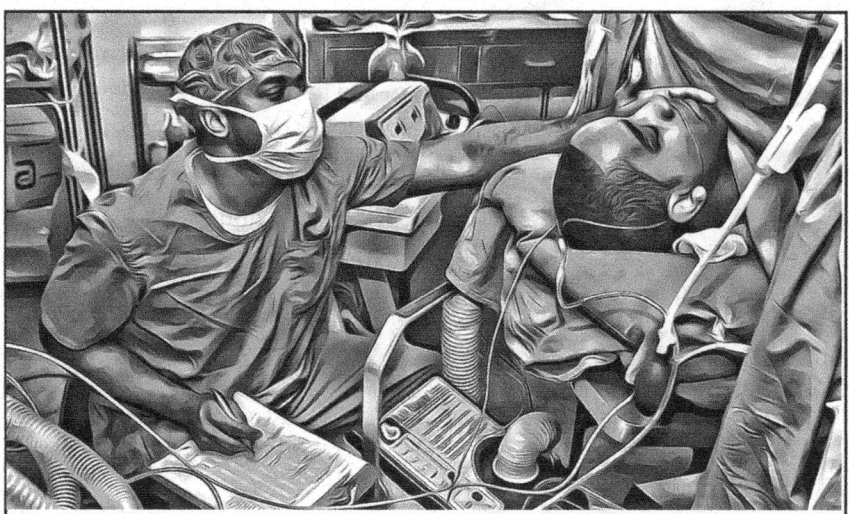

The first indication that a new virus had emerged was when workers in a laboratory in Vicksburg Virginia became seriously ill. When they were moved to hospital for treatment, both the medical personnel who had come in contact with them and the patients' immediate families also fell ill.

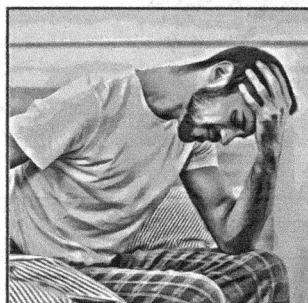

Their initial symptoms included high fever, diarrhea and vomiting; but more worryingly, they were weak and looking a little ill one day and were dead the next. By the time most patients had come to hospital it was too late. The infected, in the last stages, were bleeding internally and externally, as if their very organs were turning to liquid.

With a death rate of about 90 per cent, health authorities knew they had a big, big problem on their hands. The CDC and WHO were alerted and moved quickly to contain the virus, but it seemed to spread so easily, through the slightest touch or exchange of body fluids.

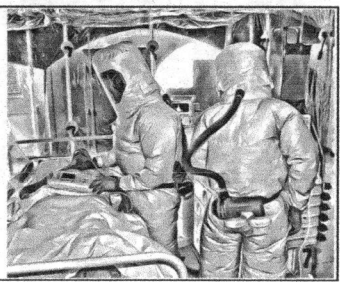

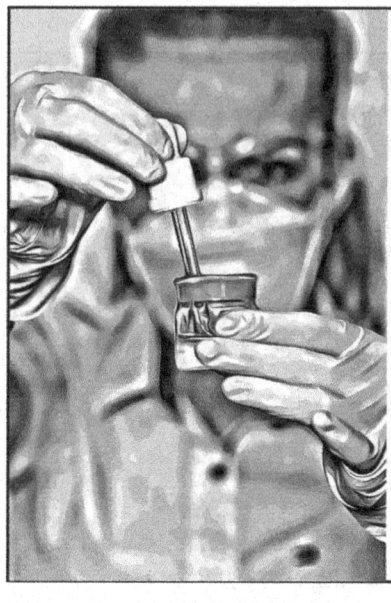

Researchers looked at blood samples to identify the virus. They found a large worm-like pathogen, unlike anything previously seen, squirming and twisting like it knew it was being examined.

Suspecting a zoonotic virus—having originated in animals—they labelled the infection the Vicksburg Virus.

But how to contain it?

A handshake, a sneeze, a shared touched surface and the virus was in motion.

Initial attempts to limit the spread of the disease failed when it emerged in New York, Atlanta and Miami.

It was only a matter of time before it spread further.

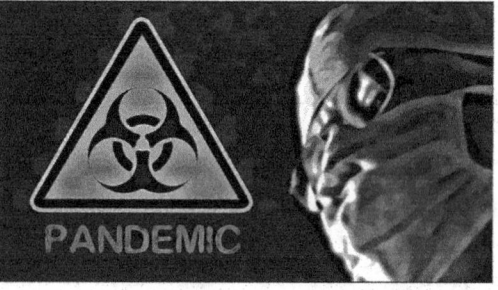

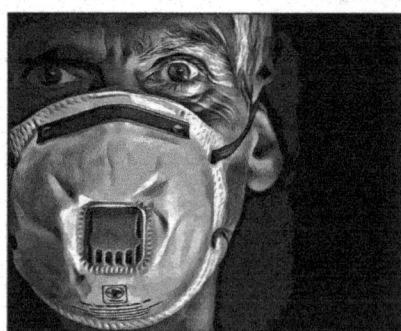

Health workers told the Government that immediate lockdowns were required, but the Government, in disarray and focusing on internal terror threats, cyber-attacks from foreign countries and fuel and food shortages, was too slow to respond.

The virus—now being called the Zombie Virus by the media—spread wherever people traveled. On buses and planes and trains and in cars.

Soon public fear overtook Government efforts and people began hoarding food and essentials and then self-isolating in their homes and apartments, refusing to answer the door.

Hospitals were overwhelmed quickly as health workers became sick or refused to go to work. Having seen too many of their colleagues lying in puddles of their own infected blood gave them little incentive to risk catching the virus themselves.

In households, those showing any symptoms were often evicted to wander the streets, staggering around zombie-like. Dead bodies were likewise thrown into the streets. It was like the worst images of the plague years of the middle ages.

Businesses closed. Schools were shut down. Government agencies stopped working. Then it was the TV stations. Anything that required any human contact was deemed too dangerous. The internet collapsed. Only radio stations seemed to keep going, updating citizens on the parlous state of the nation.

Gangs roamed the malls and business areas looking for supplies. People were shooting each other on sight, presuming anyone else was either infected or a threat. Law enforcement was as chaotic as the medical system.

People knew they were on their own for this one.

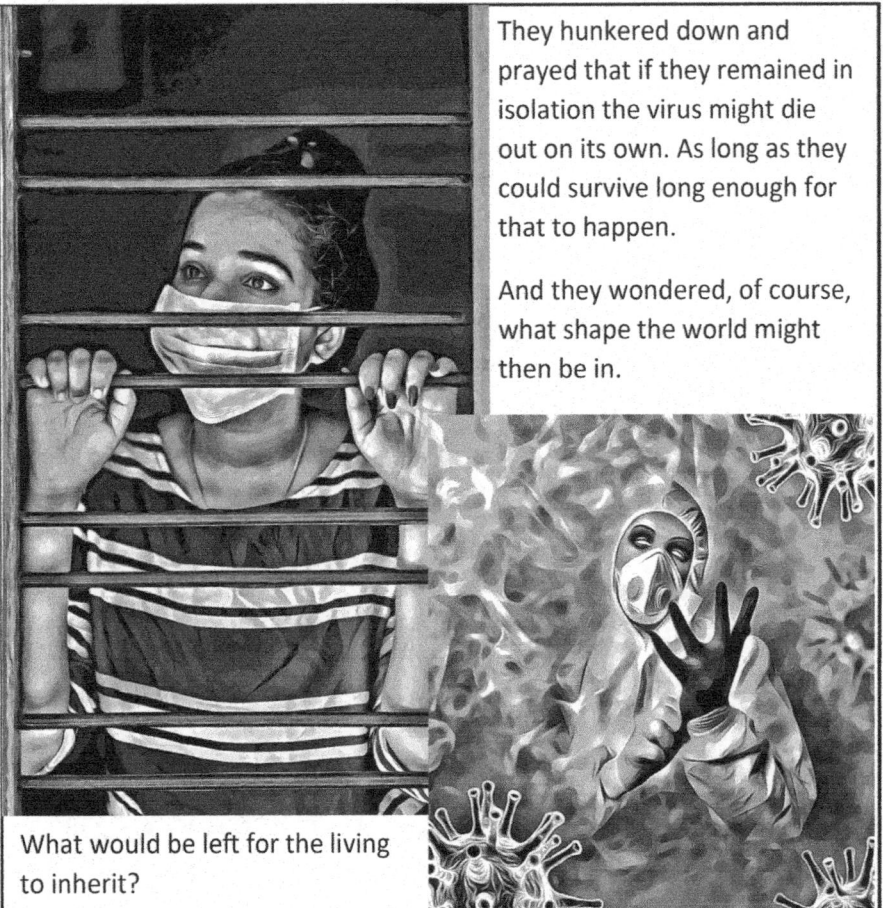

They hunkered down and prayed that if they remained in isolation the virus might die out on its own. As long as they could survive long enough for that to happen.

And they wondered, of course, what shape the world might then be in.

What would be left for the living to inherit?

51

EVIE FOUND HERSELF standing on the grass on the edge of the National Mall in DC, by the Smithsonian Air and Space Museum, trying to figure out what had happened. There was noise all around her, and smoke, and people running and screaming. She turned around slowly and saw a large pall of smoke rising up from the Capitol Building in the distance. She had to blink a few times before she could accept what she was seeing.

A plane had crashed into the Capitol Building. The plane she had just been on, she supposed. The plane she had helped to bring down.

Sirens were now blaring everywhere. Emergency services and civil defense and everything else she could imagine. She wondered if the Houses had been sitting or not. Wondered how many people had been killed. Felt she had to do something. She started jogging towards the crash site, against the tide of fleeing people. So many people. Where had they all come from?

She stopped as a group of six women wearing large medical face masks came towards her. Bracing herself. Just in case. But they passed right by her, fear in their eyes. Just women wearing personal protective equipment. A part of the panic around the zombie virus. Rioting. Panic-buying of food and toilet paper. The collapse of just about everything.

Evie started running again, not even slowing until she noticed the crowds had slowed and were surrounding her. She stopped. Stupid! Stupid! Stupid! She looked at the crowd carefully. There had been a massive protest rally that had been moving on the Capitol Building. Demons, all of them. Some masked and some not. She could see now they had breached the security barriers and had been crowding into the building like ants over a corpse. But they were now fleeing from the crash site.

Evie took a deep breath. Things were falling apart quicker than she had anticipated. And the demons were all now gathering around her, as if they had been waiting for her. Then there was another explosion from near the Capitol Building. The demons didn't flinch. Then gunshots. She needed to get past them. Had to get past them and find out what was happening. Had to try and do something about this. Something.

She held out her hands and two fireballs formed. None of the demons moved. She let them grow a little larger. Still nobody moved. Evie gritted her teeth. They were determined to stop her. She looked for the biggest and ugliest demon of the group—a lanky insect-like guy with fangs for teeth in the body of what looked like a farmer in a red Make America Great Again cap. She zapped him. The demon disappeared and the farmer fell to the ground unconscious.

"Okay," she said. "Let's play serious." Then she began casting flame balls all around her, spinning in a circle. *Zap. Zap. Zap.* Each demon she hit with a flame ball disappeared, and their human host collapsed.

There were more explosions, but she didn't turn to see what was causing them. More sirens. She just kept turning and zapping the demons. Flame balls flying at them. Zapping them all. Then she suddenly stopped. Clenched her fists shut. The last three people she struck didn't have demons in them. A mother, father and daughter. They were just people trying to get past her.

But they were in a trap within a trap. Something struck her from behind and knocked her to the ground. Evie turned to find Damien standing there. "Hello Evie," he said. "What a coincidence meeting you here."

She growled at him and jumped to her feet. He had a small staff in his hand which he had just hit her with. She stared at him, trying to catch him with her eyes, but when she did she immediately felt an attraction for him. A clever power. She broke off her stare. "I never liked your name," she said. "It brings back memories of a kid in kindergarten who kept shitting his pants."

Damien didn't say anything. Just pointed the staff at her.

"It could have been you, now that I think about it," she said. The staff glowed and a beam of light struck her in the chest. It knocked the wind out of her and sent her flying backwards. She flipped over and landed in a crouch. Put a hand to her chest, feeling for any damage. Nothing she could see, but it felt like she'd been kicked by a horse. A really big one.

Without even standing up straight, she held out her palms and sent a fire ball in his direction. A large one, full of fury and anger and outrage. He held up his staff to deflect it. It struck the staff with a crack and she saw him staring in disbelief at the broken halves of the staff.

She climbed to her feet. Felt the pain fading from her chest. She was growing stronger. She adopted a fighting pose and did something she'd once sworn she'd never do: that little palm flick to beckon an opponent to come and attack.

Damien leaped high into the air—higher than any person should be able to jump—and came down on top of her fast, swinging the two halves of the staff like twin fighting sticks. She could move faster though. Stepping back to avoid him, she blocked the rapidly swinging clubs with her hands. She even snatched one out of his grasp, striking back at him with it. The two sticks sparked each time they hit.

She didn't know why, but she was getting faster and stronger. Then she scored a hit on his arm. She heard bone crack. She smiled. Saw the way his left arm dropped and hung by his side. He looked at it and shrugged, like it was of no consequence. He dropped his stick and pushed his other palm at her. A beam of light rushed at her and she held up her own palm to catch it. Sent it back at him. He caught it and sent it back again.

She stepped to the side and let it go past. Heard the sound of it ripping up the ground and breaking concrete. She didn't even look back, just kept her guard up for his next attack. But he just smiled at her. Held his good arm out wide, as if inviting an attack. She walked forward slowly, keeping her eyes from his. Then he swung at her. No light beams. No weird powers. Just swinging at her like a street thug.

She blocked him with one hand and hit him in the solar plexus with the other. He staggered backwards. Tried to come at her again. She hit him in the throat. Good, old-fashioned, hand-to-hand combat. No fancy, demon-zapping shit needed.

She watched him fall to the ground, gasping for breath.

That was far too easy, she thought suddenly, and quickly spun around. She saw about a dozen SWAT officers running towards her with guns raised. She cursed. Of course. Damien had her putting on a performance for the Mall's CCTV for the security forces to identify her as she attacked civilians. Evie Mickelson, the country's number one terrorist and cause of everything bad happening in the land. And now she was out here in the open, being surrounded by security forces. A trap within a trap within a trap!

She watched the men and women in black surround her and stand back at a distance, guns raised at her. She held out her hands and conjured fireballs. She couldn't let them take her. There was too much at stake. Then one of the men lowered his black balaclava and said, "Stand down, Mickelson."

Damnit! It was King. The one guy she trusted. She lowered her hands.

The SWAT team started towards her. Slowly. She knew they would shoot if she made the slightest move. Had no idea if bullets could harm her or not. She looked at King, but he had dark goggles on. They all did. Then she looked down at Damien. He was laughing softly. Then he said, "You want to stop this? Then call *him*."

"No," she said. There had to be a way out of this. Even if she let them capture her and escaped later.

"I have a shot," she heard one of the SWAT team say into his microphone, and she spun to see that the man who had spoken had the lanky-legged stance of a demon in him. She sent a small fire ball at him. Knocked his helmet off and sent him sprawling without killing him.

His red face snarled at her, a large green tongue sticking out between craggy teeth.

"Hold!" ordered King. "Hold until my word!" Then again, "Mickelson. Stand down!"

"I can't do that," she said.

"You're leaving me no choice," he said.

"I've been set up," she said, not taking her eyes off the other SWAT officers.

"Then come in and we can talk about it," said King.

"I can't do that," she said again.

"Why did you bring that plane down?" King asked. "And intelligence says you're behind the virus and the whole Appalachian thing too."

Evie turned towards him. Bit her lip.

"Some of your men have been compromised," she said. "Some of our leaders too. It's a bigger conspiracy than you could imagine. And I'm the only one who can stop it."

"Listen to yourself," he said.

He was right, of course. She sounded like a complete nutcase. She opened her palms again. She'd have to take them all out. King included.

"Last chance," said Damien. "You aren't bullet proof and you don't have enough power to change this. Call him before it's too late."

"Enough power to change this how?" she asked, without taking her eyes off the SWAT officers. But then she heard it. A plane, low in the sky. She looked up. They all looked up. Saw a second passenger plane coming in low over the city, headed towards the White House. Weren't all flights grounded? Or had that reality changed again already? Then she saw the fighter jet screaming behind it, and saw two missiles streak out from under its wings, and arc towards the passenger plane. "No!" she heard King say. "Oh God, no!"

She closed her eyes and concentrated. Thought hard of a different world to this one.

52

The Appalachian Mountains had long been home to dissident communities, but during the period when the United States was crumbling they began to rally together under a charismatic leader, Pol Pot, who espoused a strange mix of Trumpism and Communism.

Sporting an ever-present, red Make America Great Again cap, Pol Pot led a popular insurgency based in the southern mountains that proved impossible for the individual state governments to counter, as the forces stayed on the move between the states of Alabama, Georgia, Tennessee and Kentucky.

Funded by drug money, the insurgency attracted a lot of support from the under-classes, who used it as an excuse to exact vengeance on those they felt had unjustly better situations in life. Land and business owners. Those on government salaries.

Eventually they were strong enough to proclaim an independent People's Republic of Appalachia.

The first thing Pol Pot did was close the borders of his new territory and turn his insurgency fighters into the Red Caps, who would implement his vision of a new rural society. He decreed a Year Zero, and a return to a pre-technology era, resetting the clock of progress.

He ruled there would be no schools, no books, no hospitals, no learning, no music, no money — everything that had once defined society and people's places in it was now outlawed as having led to social decay. And as those institutions disappeared so too did the family unit and sense of community.

Armed with guns and clubs, the Red Caps emptied the cities and towns, forcing people to relocate to labour camps spread across the countryside, and re-introduced slavery of all coloured people.

This disruption was all used as an excuse to kill, steal and rape, and settle petty vendettas or jealousies. Many on-the-spot killings were justified as purging those who disagreed with Pol Pot's ideologies.

In truth, most of the Red Caps did not really understand the ideology behind what they did, but they did understand that they had power for the first time in their lives and a leader who rewarded their loyalty. And in small steps they turned the dream of a better Appalachia into a nightmare.

Children were separated from their parents and indoctrinated into the Red Caps. Families were ripped apart and those with a skilled profession, like doctors, had to pretend they were uneducated. Ethnic minorities and anyone deemed 'not pure American' were particularly targeted, and either executed in killing fields, tortured in special interrogation centers, or forced into slavery.

And far from proving an agricultural success, the camps became grim places where people were forced to work long hours on failed agricultural projects, with malnutrition and preventable diseases rife.

The dead were used to fertilize the fields.

Of course, some people escaped into the surrounding states, bringing with them accounts of atrocities so shocking they were hard to believe.

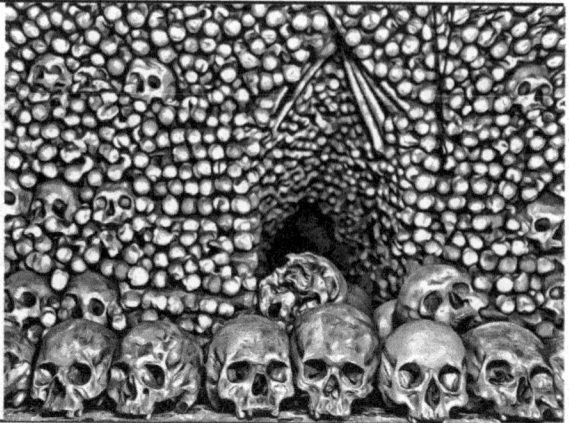

Occasionally, envoys were sent into the People's Republic to discuss border issues or trade—but they rarely returned. And the few that did return seemed changed. Indoctrinated. Ready to spread the ideology—like a malignant virus.

Ready to reset the clock to Year Zero.

53

EVIE WAS AGAIN standing on the lawn of the National Mall near the Capitol Building. But the air around her was red. Damien was standing in front of her, smiling. Marvel Gal was next to him. And Dr Strange. And back there, behind them, a horde of demons, probably everyone she had dispatched, snarling at her and making vaguely threatening gesticulations in her direction.

"Well, thank you very much," Damien said.

Evie let her eyes roll back in her head a little. Wanted to fall to the ground. They'd played her again. Tricked her into creating a dream world—a place where they could all be together once more. And who knew what else could happen here? She turned and looked towards the Capitol Building. It was still there. So there was something positive about this dream version of the world. Or this reality. Or this—what?—who knew exactly what it was?

She opened her arms wide and then paused. That's what they'd expect her to do. Throw more flame balls at them. She had to think differently. She lowered her hands and looked at them. "Stigl, you fat fuck," she said. "I didn't think I'd see you again so soon." Then she pointed at Marvel Gal with her chin. "And Super Bitch there. Must have been hard growing up with a sister who had more balls than you."

Stigl just smiled.

"So what now?" Evie asked.

But none of the three answered her. Instead they joined hands. She watched them carefully, trying to figure out what was going to happen. Then they lifted their clasped hands above their heads. Evie looked up. She felt a chill and shivered. It was the dark cloud, large and menacing and descending upon them. Upon her. Blocking out the buildings and monuments all about them. Like it was engulfing them.

The three demon brats were chanting something, and she suspected they were cocky because they felt they had her now. But she damn sure wasn't going to go down without a fight. She held her arms out as wide as possible—until her muscles hurt—and conjured up the largest fireballs she could. She could even feel the weight of them, like trying to hold medicine balls on her outstretched hands. She threw them at Stigl, the weakest link. The blast knocked him to the ground, unconscious. But Damien and Lucy held his hands still.

Then Damien turned to look at her, trying to do his eye thing on her. She sent a small, hard ball of flame like a golf ball at him, hitting him in the eye. His head jerked back, but he didn't waver in his chanting.

One more blast, she thought. One more big blast and she'd break their grip. She held her arms apart again and then stopped. Something had grabbed one of her arms.

She looked up. A dark cloud had formed behind her and was coalescing, becoming denser. She felt strong fingers wrapping tightly around her forearm, hurting her. Then she felt another hand upon her chest.

She tried to shrug it off. Pushed her free hand at the cloud, sending fireballs into it, trying to dissipate it. The fireballs lit up the inside of the cloud, showing a dark figure in there. *Him!* Feeding on the energy. And the grip on her tightened. She could no longer breathe. *He* was crushing her. Then she heard Damien laughing. Turned to see his face—one eye dead, the other filled with hate and victory. "You're going to die," he said. "Soon *he'll* be strong enough to be free. Can you feel it?"

She felt her ribs coming close to snapping. Felt tears forming in her eyes. This was the end game. Grow her power and use it to free him!

She was suddenly a small girl again. Wishing her father was there to protect her. Her brother. Her mother. Her family. The pressure on her increased. The one whose name could not be spoken was solidifying. *He* was huge and dark, and she could see the muscles forming on *his* arms. *His* face was the embodiment of all demons rolled into one, and *his* mouth was red and filled with a deep glow…and *he* was laughing. A terrible and horrific laugh.

"Fucking patriarchal power games," she said. But she felt afraid, as if *his* presence alone weakened her, filled her with doubt, sapped the strength from her limbs. She did not have the power to withstand *him*, she knew.

He was going to kill her. Absorb her into *him*. Be stronger than ever. Her legs started shaking. It was fear and anger both. And then she called to her father. She raged in fury and grief. "How could you let this happen to me?" Then she closed her eyes. Felt tears filling them. "Where are you?" she whispered.

The dark lord, the demon king, the embodiment of evil in any religion—reached out to touch her. The way random violence touched the innocent in shootings and hijackings and suicide bomb blasts in schools and in public places and airports and in hotels and in bus terminals and shopping malls—wherever the innocent played and loved and learned and lived their lives. She felt those hands on her and shivered. So cold! They lifted her up, pulling her into *him*. She bit her lip, waiting for the end.

Then the grip suddenly loosened.

"I'm here," said a familiar voice. A voice from her childhood. Strong and comforting. Her father reached down and took the final piece of the talisman from her but rather than press it into his own body, he pressed it into hers. His strong hand held against her. There was a momentary burning on her skin and she was filled with light and strength and power. Like being made whole again. Like being born anew.

54

Emergency services were called to an all-girls school in Providence, Rhode Island, when teachers called 911 in distress.

Several of the girls at the school had started screaming in the school assembly and then fallen to the ground in a faint.

Students who witnessed the incident said first one girl just stood up and screamed as if she had been stabbed and then fell to the ground shaking.

Everyone, of course turned to see what had happened; and then a second girl screamed and fell to the floor.

Within five minutes over a dozen girls were screaming and dropping unconscious and the other girls were rushing to get out of the hall, fearing something had infected them.

The last few screaming and fainting fits were captured on mobile phones and quickly shared to social media.

By the time the emergency services crews reached the school, they found dozens of teachers and students stumbling around the playground screaming and trembling.

And more succumbed as they tried to work with those who were on the ground.

What was happening?

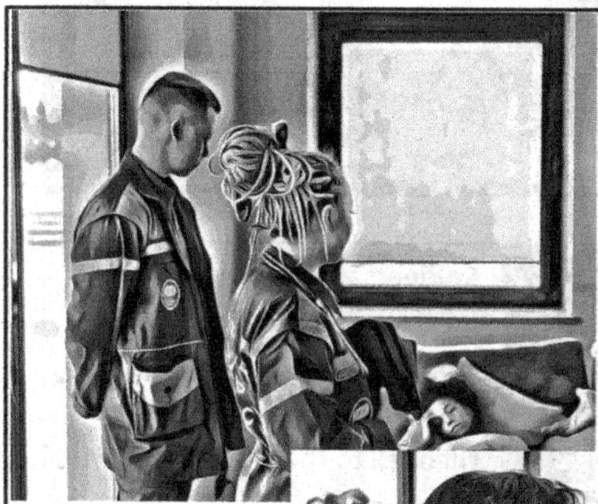

Fearing a nerve agent contamination, they quickly called for backup and isolated those displaying the worst symptoms. By the end of the day 1,100 students and five teachers had been admitted to hospitals in the region.

But strangely, no sign of contaminants could be found in their blood or in tissue samples.

And other schools were now reporting similar attacks of screaming and strange coughing and shivering.

And everyone was asking, "What the hell was happening?"

Public health experts struggled to keep up with the spread of the phenomenon, but were at a loss to understand what they were dealing with.

Eventually one junior health worker, with girls of her own in a private school, noticed that the only schools in the area that had not reported any symptoms were those that had phone-free policies.

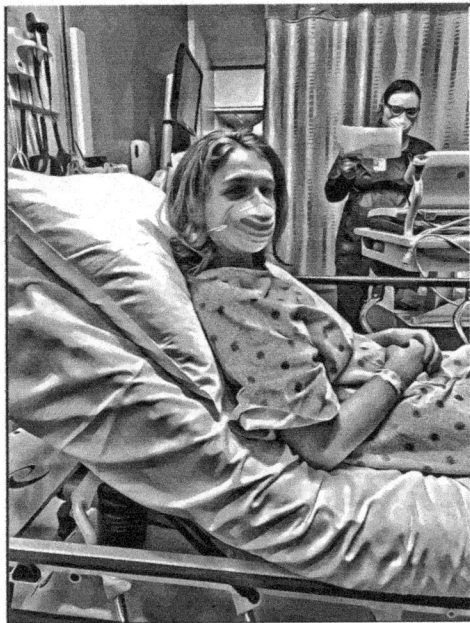

The path of the infection, it was suggested, might be social media, not a pathogen or chemical agent.

And with nearly 1,900 people in hospital, and the numbers only increasing, health workers tried treating those hospitalised for mass hysteria rather than an unknown contaminant.

And strangely enough, the bizarre epidemic subsided.

When the very first girl who had stood up screaming in school assembly, was interviewed and asked what had suddenly triggered her, and thereafter the whole epidemic, she claimed that she had suddenly seen a face of pure evil there in front of her.

Something many of the other girls agreed with.

After they had heard her story.

55

AND EVIE HAS A SUDDEN memory of a dream that she'd had as a young girl. Something the presence of the talisman had kept from her. She was six or seven years old. Her father had come home. Wounded. Still trying to fight evil even though he no longer had the powers he once had. Her mother was distraught. Evie was seeing this from all angles at once. Saw her father lying on the lounge room floor at the same time that she saw him stumble in the door at the same time she saw her mother trying to patch his wounds.

Adam was there too. A young boy. Crying and afraid.

And outside Evie could see demons circling their house. They had come to finish him off. Had followed him here and were trying to get in. Trying to get him. She knew who they were. There were terrorists and there were gangsters and there were murderers and child abductors. All out there trying to get into her house. All trying to get her father and she had to stop them.

She went to the door and threw it open. Or just made it disappear. Or something. Her mother called to her to try and stop her going outside where all the evil was, but Evie knew that she was the one who could save them. Only she could do it. She was Dream Girl now and she had the power to change dreams and change realities.

She stood there in front of them all, and she reached out to them from her mind, somehow, grabbing up each figure there. Turning them from a person and a living embodiment of evil and harm into a flat caricature that could only exist in a comic or on TV as a costumed villain. One by one she grabbed them and cast them out of this world into another one. Into a fantasy world where they could not do any harm to her and her family and where they did not need to be feared.

Hijackers and murderers and Nazis and lynch mobs and racists and sexual predators. All of those who had crept into her dreams and frightened her. She sent them all away. Until she was standing there at the door of her house, the sun rising on an empty street and she knew they were safe. She had protected them.

And the memory of that dream was like the antidote to all fear and anger and terror. And it wasn't scary. It was fantastic!

As the memory faded, Evie looked up saw her father as he really was. Something she had never seen before. Tall and glowing and white and strong and with two huge white wings bearing him aloft. And a large flaming sword in his hand. Michael the Guardian. The role he had abandoned to marry her mother.

He was stupendous. And he faced the dark lord without fear. Evie watched as he flew at the dark figure that towered over him and slashed at him with his sword. The dark lord growled like deep thunder and roared as the flaming sword cut *him*. *He* was still not fully formed yet, but was close. Dark, rippling muscles were hardening across *his* torso.

Evie's father circled back and attacked again. Flying like an arrow, with the sword held out in front of him. Straight at the dark lord's face. He was fast, but the dark lord was faster, and a huge fist knocked him out of the air, sending him tumbling to the ground. But then another Guardian was swooping in to catch him. Rafael, the Guardian of healing.

Then Evie saw the other two. Gabriel the Guardian of connection and Uriel the Guardian of transformation. Saw all four of them come together. The saviors of the world. Like superheroes. The Guardians of the Earth. And they attacked in formation, flying around the dark lord and battling *him* from different sides.

Evie expected to see them now defeat *him*. See their combined strength halt *him*. But instead she saw dozens and dozens of demons rising up from the ground to attack the four Guardians. There were so many of them, like a plague hoard, so thick they obscured her view of her father.

Then she saw Damien and Marvel Gal rise into the air, flying like they had gravity belts on, and start sending light beams at the Guardians. At her father. She saw feathers blasted from his wings. Saw the demons swarming over the Guardians and tearing at them. Watched them fall from the sky.

And the dark lord was so close to being fully formed now, it might only be a matter of moments. But then *he* made a mistake. *He* looked down at Evie and laughed.

And she didn't feel fear of *him* anymore. Didn't even feel anger. She opened her palms to create flame balls. And as she did she felt power coursing through her body. Like she had just ignited something. Knew what she was capable of. Closed her palms and opened her mind. Used her dream powers to change things again.

She seized the demons first. Grabbed them in clusters. Turned them into harmless pictures of monsters with comic deformities. Sent them away in that form. She scanned across the sky quickly, scooping them up. They started to flee from her, but they were too slow. She grabbed them and they were gone. The dark lord's brats stared at her in shock. As though they knew what was coming, but couldn't believe it. They would keep a moment longer. She turned her attention to the dark lord himself.

Evie willed herself as big as *him*. Bigger. Let *him* feel her power. Then she saw *his* look of horror as *his* form began coming apart at the edges. Began turning back into cloud.

He was stumbling, *his* sharp-taloned hands dissipating before *his* eyes. She would turn *him* into a mockery. A red, behorned, long-tailed devil like one of the cartoon Hot Stuff the Little Devil's ridiculous brothers.

And after *him* she'd turn her attention to his children. And after them she'd rid the world of all the violent crazies in it. Islamic State and Boko Harem and Al Qaeda and all the Islamic and Christian nutcases and everyone who used terror to threaten and kill and harm others. Every evil fucker who terrorized little girls and made them fear for their safety and the safety of their families; she'd rid the world of all of them—sending them away so they only existed as characters in fantasies. Fairytale figures and cartoon and comic strip villains. Like the Big Bad Wolf and Blue Beard and Captain Hook, who could only invoke their fear in dreams rather than in real life.

The dark lord tried to shake her off, but she was too strong for *him* now. She bent and reshaped *him* like a plaything. Squashed *him* into a small red blob and then pulled out long thin spindly legs and arms. Shaped a fat stomach and thin chest. Gave *him* an elongated neck and weak chin. A bald horned head and a comical goatee. Then she pulled out a long and awkward tail, with an arrow-point on the end. And she finished it off by wrapping him in a diaper. She had him spin like a buffoon and only had to give *him* the smallest of pushes so he would remain like that forever. A creature of ridicule. Nothing could stop her.

Nothing except a soft hand on her arm. And a firm voice in her ear. "No," her father said. "Evie. You must stop."

She turned and looked at him in confusion. "But I can destroy *him*," she said. "I can save everyone."

"No," he said, with a plaintive look on his face. "I can't allow that to happen."

56

Do beliefs have the power to shape one's reality? Belief in any deity or devil or demon—as a way to explain the inexplicable? Faced with environmental and social catastrophe, many people turn to beliefs that will make some sense of it all for them.

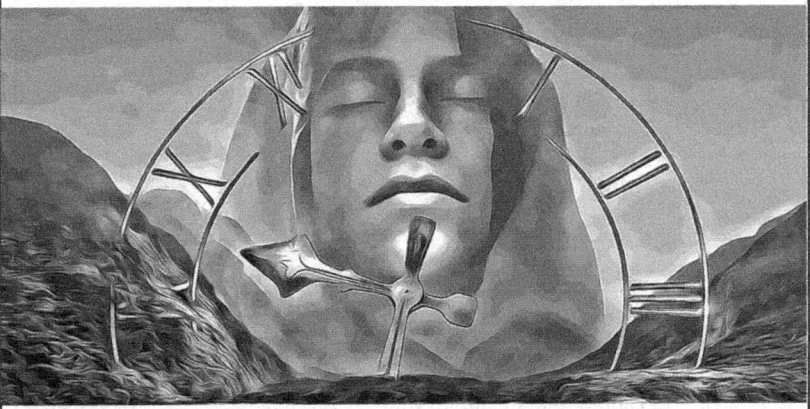

The Order of the Solar Temple was one such group, attracting wealthy professionals to their headquarters in upper New York State.

Members of the Order believed that humanity was reaching the end of their tenure over the planet Earth —and the world was soon to be destroyed in a cataclysm— but the believers would be saved and taken up to live on a planet near the star Sirius.

They were so ardent in this belief that they committed all their money and possessions to the Order, and followed the arcane rituals demanded of them, a mish-mash of religious beliefs based on the Knights Templar.

They even adopted the dress and red cross of the crusaders, swearing allegiance on a sacred sword that was said to have belonged to one of the original knights.

The cult had attracted many members and was so secretive that sometimes even husbands and wives did not know that each other were members.

Cult members' beliefs were tested when one of the two cult leaders claimed that the three-month-old child of one cult member, Tony Dutoit, was the Antichrist and needed to be ritually slain.

The decision was made to kill the baby by repeatedly stabbing it with a wooden stake.

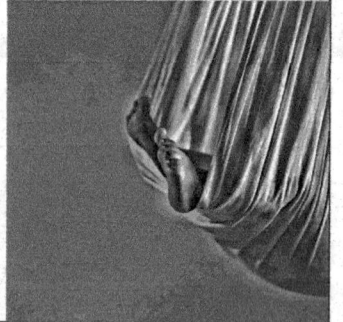

Many members felt unsettled by this, but cult leaders proclaimed the end of days were upon them, summoning all the members to their lodges in New York State, New Hampshire and Maine.

Members were told that the time for the ascension had arrived, and following the necessary rituals they would be taken up to the stars, leaving their earthly bodies behind, which would be consumed in a cleansing fire.

Their arguments were easy to believe. The state of the world's environment was dire, with the number of mass extinctions growing and increased civil unrest in cities across the nation.

Cyber and military conflicts were breaking out globally as nations fought for ever-diminishing resources. Severe food and water shortages, climate extremes and rapidly spreading new diseases were adding to social breakdown.

But the collapse came from within as the Order's lodges, which had claimed to offer a sense of safety and security, were locked from the inside and then burned to the ground. What the authorities found, in the days that followed, was evidence of ritual suicides by the true believers and the murder of the doubters.

In the burned-out ruins of one of the Order's lodges, police found 15 people dead by poisoning, and 30 more having been shot or suffocated. In another lodge, the dead were found in a secret underground chapel where the bodies lay in a circle, bare feet pointing into the middle, each with a plastic bag tied over their head. Most had also been shot in the head.

The two cult leaders, Joseph Di Mambro and Luc Jouret, were among the many dozen dead.

For the cult members who were left after the cataclysm, the choices were difficult.

Should they believe that the Order was a group of crazed, power-mad fanatics, duping people to follow them, as the mass media was portraying it?

Or should they follow the example of the cult leaders and leave the failing Earth to be taken to the planet near Sirius?

As happens with many extreme beliefs, when confronted with evidence that their beliefs may have been mistaken, it simply reinforced their ideology.

Over the next several months there were more ritual suicides, with over a dozen more members in different locations choosing to follow their beliefs—adamant that they would also be taken up to the stars. Their dead never to witness if humanity had the faith and commitment to fight for a different path, for a better future on Earth.

57

THIS IS HOW Evie liked to tell it. The final Revelation. Her father and the other Guardians finally explaining everything to her. They sat in the back yard of the family home in Cleveland, enjoying the late afternoon's sunshine. Even Malikulmaut had come to join them. It was all a bit like one of those closing scenes in a family movie where everyone got together and had an outdoor party.

Evie didn't want to return the dark lord to his own form, didn't want to let *him* go. She'd invested too much in that moment of retribution. But her father had said, "Everything has a purpose. The dark lord has to be left alive. That is a part of the balance of things. It's all about maintaining the equilibrium."

"Fuck the equilibrium," she said now , for the umpteenth time.

Malikulmaut gave her one of his stern looks and opened another beer. "You need to understand how vital it is to maintain a balance," he said. Then, "...if you are to accept the role of being the one to maintain it."

"Accept the role?" she asked. "I was thinking of taking a vacation."

Her father gave her a smile. A sad one. "I'm so sorry, Evie, that we couldn't tell you beforehand," he said.

"Yeah, yeah," she said. "I get it. It was all about getting the circumstances right to trigger my powers. I get it. But it just doesn't seem fair."

Nobody answered her. There was no answer that would sound fair.

"I mean, everything from when I was a small girl. Blocking my memories of my dream powers with the talisman. Having to give up some of your own powers to achieve that. Then sending me on a crazy mission across the country to get the pieces of the talisman back to you all, and battling those crazy offspring of the dark lord and fighting psycho demons—everything was just a part of getting everything just right! But I get it!"

Her father nodded. He was wearing an old pullover with holes in the sleeves. Nothing quite as regal as his angel outfit, but he managed to make it look angelic. At least in Evie's eyes. Though she'd never tell him that.

"Evie," he said. "The temptation to change things for the better is a strong one. And there is no certainty that is a temptation that you will be able to avoid. So Rafael is going to cast a new talisman. Something to control your powers."

"And you'll each have to give up some of your Guardian powers again?" she asked.

"Yes," he said. "We are prepared to do that. I might even leave Cleveland. Find somewhere new to live and something new to do. Maybe go into youth counselling."

"You'd actually be pretty good at that," said Evie. Then looked to the other three Guardians. "And what are you three going to do?"

"I'll be setting up a new angel therapy school in Australia," Gabriel said.

"And I'm going to Hollywood," said Rafael. "I want to see the Avengers walking down the street. See what real heroes look like."

"I'm going to Macau," said Uriel. "The casinos there are pretty good. Even if there are less Elvis impersonators than in Vegas. And the women—well. What can I say that wouldn't offend you?"

Evie gave him a hard admonishing stare. Then she said, "So that just leaves me?"

"I'll be around to lend a hand," said her brother.

"And Lucy and her two dickhead brothers will be against us on the other side of things, yes?"

"You need to know," said her father. "Lucy is you. From another world. One where she has submitted to the dark lord."

Evie's jaw fell open. "Well, that explains my love-hate thing with her," she said.

"There's an image I'll never get rid of," said Adam.

"But if I have a talisman to block my powers, does that mean I am supposed to do all this with just the eyeball power thing?" she asked.

"A little bit more than that," said Malikulmaut. "I think Astaroth would say, you've opened up a whole can of kick-ass powers."

"Whoop-ass!" corrected Evie.

Malikulmaut shrugged. "It might not seem fair that you now have the burden of the four Guardians to carry," he said. "But that is how it is. The struggle between good and evil is eternal, but it is the struggle that keeps the world in balance. It is only when one side gains the upper hand that it destabilizes everything."

"And all those crazies out there, the religious and political ratbags of every persuasion, and the demons who are in disguise all over the world…they just get to play their games and have people kill other people?"

"It must go on," Malikulmaut said. "There can be no end to it. The good and the bad, in eternal conflict, but in eternal balance. You fight the good fight for balance, not for victory."

Evie looked down at the bottle of beer in her hand. She wanted to keep drinking the whole afternoon until this finally made some sort of sense to her. But she doubted it ever really would.

"So do I at least get a superhero outfit?" she asked. "Or a fortress of solitude? I mean, if it is going to be me fighting all those demons and douchebags, you'd think I at least get a neat new outfit."

Nobody answered. But she didn't really expect one.

"Do you know," she said, "I can remember a dream I had some years ago. I was here, sleeping in my own bed, my childhood things on the walls and shelves about me, and the world was at peace. There were no demons out there driving people to violence and craziness. No greed and lust and killing. Just everyone working to make everyone else happy. What do you think of that?"

"I think Astaroth would say that sounds like a pretty boring world," said her brother.

They were all looking at her and she could see the concern in their eyes. The fear that she might refuse the talisman and use her powers to create a world like that. Throw out the balance of things.

"Sometimes a dream is just a dream," Malikulmaut said.

"I know that one," she said. "Bob Dylan, right?"

"Amen," said her father.

Endnote

All the graphic chapters are based on real events from recent history, relocated to the USA. They are:

Chapter 2. Malaysian airlines MH370, 2014

Chapter 4. Paris terror attacks, 2015

Chapter 6. School attack in Trollhattan, Sweden, 2015

Chapter 8. Suicide bombing at wedding in Jordan, 2015

Chapter 10. Charlie Hebdo attack, France, 2015

Chapter 12. Cave of the Patriarchs attack, Hebron, 1994

Chapter 14. Boko Harem kidnaping at Chibok Nigeria, 2014

Chapter 16. Fort Dix Six, New Jersey, 2007

Chapter 18. Truck attacks in Nice, France, 2016

Chapter 20. Attack on Armenian Parliament, 1999

Chapter 22. ISIS mass execution in Libya, 2015

Chapter 24. Mosque attacks in Christchurch New Zealand, 2019

Chapter 26. School attacks in Peshwar, Pakistan, 2014

Chapter 28. Beheading of teacher in France, 2020

Chapter 30. Mall attack in Nairobi, Kenya, 2013

Chapter 32. Gulbarg massacre, India, 2002

Chapter 34. Mumbai attacks, India, 2008

Chapter 36. School attack in Beslan, North Ossetia-Alania, Russia, 2004

Chapter 38. Norwegian terror attacks, 2011

Chapter 40. École Polytechnique massacre, Montreal Canada, 1989

Chapter 42. Srebrenica massacre, Bosnia, 1995

Chapter 44. Union Carbide disaster, Bhopal, India, 1984

Chapter 46. Slaying of the royal family of Nepal, 2001.

Chapter 48. Cochabamba Water Wars, Bolivia, 2000

Chapter 50. Marburg virus, Germany, 1960s and Ebola, West Africa, 2013-16

Chapter 52. Year Zero, Cambodia, 1975

Chapter 54. Mass hysteria, Sri Lanka, 2012, Malaysia, 2019, Nepal 2016-18.

Chapter 56. The Order of the Solar Temple, France, Switzerland and Canada 1994-95.

Note on Graphic images

All images used in this book were obtained from or under creative commons or copyright free image libraries, (including Pexels, Pixabay, Unsplash, Gratisphotography—and I thank the original creators), various government archives, or are original or composite images produced by the author.